Reviving My Heart

Book Three of the Hearts Trilogy

Sabrina Wagner

Copyright © 2016 by Sabrina Wagner
Reviving My Heart
Book Three of the Hearts Trilogy

Cover art by Jill White at Jillzeedesign.com

All rights reserved. This book or any portion thereof may not be reproduced, transmitted, or used in any manner whatsoever without the written permission of the author except for the use of brief quotations in a book review.

This book is a work of fiction. All characters and storylines are the property of the author, and your support and respect are appreciated. Names, characters, businesses, places, and incidents are either the products of the author's imagination or used in a fictitious manner. Any resemblances to actual persons, living or dead, or actual events is purely coincidental. The author acknowledges the trademarked status of various products referenced in this work of fiction, which have been used without permission. The publication/use of these trademarks is not authorized, associated with, or sponsored by the trademark owners.
.
The following story contains mature themes, strong language, and sexual situations. It is intended for adult readers 18+.

Stay Connected!

**Want to be the first to learn book news, updates and more?
Sign up for my Newsletter.**

https://www.subscribepage.com/sabrinawagnernewsletter

**Want to know about my new releases and upcoming sales?
Stay connected on:**

Facebook~Instagram~Twitter~TikTok
Goodreads~BookBub~Amazon

**I'd love to hear from you.
Visit my website to connect with me.**

www.sabrinawagnerauthor.com

Books by Sabrina Wagner

Hearts Trilogy
Hearts on Fire
Shattered Hearts
Reviving my Heart

Wild Hearts Trilogy
Wild Hearts
Secrets of the Heart
Eternal Hearts

Forever Inked Novels
Tattooed Hearts: Tattooed Duet #1
Tattooed Souls: Tattooed Duet #2
Smoke and Mirrors
Regret and Redemption
Sin and Salvation

Vegas Love Series
What Happens in Vegas (Hot Vegas Nights)
Billionaire Bachelor in Vegas

Table of Contents

Prologue
Chapter 1: Tyler
Chapter 2: Kyla
Chapter 3: Tyler
Chapter 4: Kyla
Chapter 5: Tyler
Chapter 6: Kyla
Chapter 7: Tyler
Chapter 8: Kyla
Chapter 9: Tyler
Chapter 10: Kyla
Chapter 11: Tyler
Chapter 12: Kyla
Chapter 13: Tyler
Chapter 14: Kyla
Chapter 15: Tyler
Chapter 16: Kyla
Chapter 17: Tyler
Chapter 18: Kyla
Chapter 19: Tyler
Chapter 20: Kyla
Chapter 21: Tyler

Chapter 22: Kyla
Chapter 23: Tyler
Chapter 24: Kyla
Chapter 25: Tyler
Chapter 26: Kyla
Chapter 27: Tyler
Chapter 28: Kyla
Chapter 29: Tyler
Chapter 30: Kyla
Chapter 31: Tyler
Chapter 32: Kyla
Chapter 33: Tyler
Chapter 34: Kyla
Chapter 35: Tyler
Chapter 36: Kyla
Chapter 37: Tyler
Chapter 38: Kyla
Chapter 39: Tyler
Chapter 40: Kyla
Chapter 41: Tyler
Epilogue

Prologue

Reviving My Heart

I've been through hell.
I've seen the fiery gates and bowed down before them.
When you've lost everything,
What else is there to lose?
My heart has been shattered.
I am not what I was before.
Do I lay down and die or is it time to rise?
Do I fade into the ashes or become the fire?
One thing is for sure~
The day of reckoning is coming.
Only when I've righted the wrongs,
Will I be able to spread my wings and fly.
My chest will be able to breathe…
And my heart will beat.
Only then,
Will I fully be able to love again.

Chapter 1
Tyler

I drove away feeling defeated.

I waited and waited for Kyla to open the door, hoping she heard the words I said. I knew she was there, just behind that door. I poured my heart out to her shamelessly. I was honest when I said I wasn't giving up on her… on us. For all the bullshit I put her through, I would wait for as long as it took. Cody was right when he said she was the best thing that ever happened to me. I was just too blind to see it.

She had to have gotten my gift. I paid extra to have it delivered on Christmas Eve. I didn't care if she didn't acknowledge it. I would not stop trying to convince her to come back to me. I would send her flowers every week for the next year if that's what it took. She couldn't ignore me forever.

I drove the almost three hours back to my parents' house through the snow. It was just starting to get dark when I pulled into the driveway. My mom and dad knew where I went. They didn't blink an eye, even though it was Christmas Day and I missed dinner. I walked in the house and sat down at the table with them.

"Well?" my dad asked. "Was she there?"

"She was there," I said.

"And?" my mom prodded.

"She wouldn't open the door. I sat on her doorstep for a half hour, and she never opened it. I called her, and I could hear her phone ringing, but she wouldn't answer that either. So, I talked to her through the door. I don't even know if she heard me," I answered dejectedly.

"I know this isn't easy, Ty. Just give it time. Sounds like she waited a long time until she gave up on you. You can't change that in a few days... or even weeks," my mom encouraged.

"Keep at it. She'll come around," my dad said.

"She hates me. I don't blame her. I would hate me too."

"She doesn't hate you, honey. She's hurt. You can't blame her for trying to protect herself." My mom was trying to make me feel better, but it wasn't working.

"Maybe."

I got up from the table, went to my room, and lay down on the bed with my arm over my eyes. I needed to figure out what my next step would be. My phone buzzed on the nightstand, so I reached for it and picked it up. I smiled when I saw the text message.

Ky: *I heard every word. Was it true?*

I quickly typed back my answer.

Ty: *Yes! Every word!*

I waited anxiously for her response. I waited for fifteen minutes, before I realized she wasn't going to text back. That was okay. At least she'd heard me and that made me feel a little better. It was the first thing I'd heard from her in months, besides the get-well card she'd sent. It was something.

The next morning, when I woke up, I had another message from Kyla. It was three words.

Ky: *Wait for me.*

Chapter 2
Kyla

It was 7:45 in the morning the day after Christmas. I sat in my car waiting for someone to open the place up. I had on a thick sweatshirt with the hood up, my hair tucked inside, and my sunglasses covering my face. I wouldn't know anyone here, but I didn't want to take any chances that someone might recognize me.

I listened as Halestorm's "I Am the Fire" blasted through the speakers of my car. I was going to be the fire. I was going to rise from the ashes. I wouldn't let Jake break me. That fucker would pay. If I wanted Tyler back, I would have to fight through my own insecurities and fears. I would need to be brave and strong. I was more than what I had become over the last year. A mere shell of myself.

I knew it was deep inside me, waiting to rise to the surface. Only I could make this happen. I was going to take back control.

Finally, a pick-up truck pulled up and an older man got out. He fumbled with his keys in the lock and opened the door. I quickly finished my cigarette and threw the butt out the window. I got out of the car and followed him in.

The man looked like he might be a biker. He had a long, gray beard and a rough face. He had on what I assumed was a motorcycle club cut. He looked up from what he was doing as I walked to the counter. He was sizing me up as much as I was sizing him up.

I stepped to the counter. "I need to buy a gun."

He looked me up and down. "How old are you?" he asked in a raspy voice, probably from years of smoking.

"Old enough," I said. "I'm twenty-one."

He nodded his head suspiciously, like he didn't believe me. "Let me see your I.D."

I reached in my purse and pulled out my driver's license. I handed it to him over the counter. He looked at it carefully, then set it back down. "I need to see your face," he said gruffly.

My jaw tightened. I slowly lowered the hood from my head and removed my sunglasses. He looked at my battered face but showed no reaction. "You report that?"

I kept my face just as emotionless. "Nope. But it won't happen again."

The old guy just looked at me for a few minutes. I reached across the counter to pick up my license when he grabbed my wrist. He pushed up the sleeve and saw the welts around my wrist where the skin was raw and red. "He tie you up too?"

"Handcuffs," I stated, looking him in the eyes.

He ran his hand through his long, gray beard. "Do you even know how to use a gun?" he asked.

"No, but I can learn." I was determined.

He crossed his arms over his chest and looked me up and down some more. "I've lived a rough life," he said. "Done a lot of things I'm not proud of, but I don't believe in hurting women. I got a granddaughter 'bout your age."

I was starting to feel uncomfortable and impatient. "Can you help me or not?"

"I can help you. Tell me about the guy who did this to you."

I didn't want to tell this man my story, but I needed his help. What choice did I have? "I dated him for a couple of months. I tried to break up with him, and he didn't take it well.

Last thing he told me was, *'this isn't over'*. I disagree. He won't touch me again."

"He rape you?"

I cringed. I hated that word. It made me sick. It made me feel dirty. Tears started to fill my eyes, but I blinked them back. I barely nodded my head in response.

He looked up at the ceiling. "Fuck!" He reached his hand over the counter for me to shake. "Name's Sid."

I cautiously took his big hand in my small one. "Kyla."

"What kind of gun are you looking for?" he asked.

Now we were getting somewhere. "Something small, so I can fit it in my purse. I came here one time with the ex-boyfriend. He let me shoot his, but it was too heavy, and I wasn't very good at it."

"Couple of things. One, I need to do a background check for you to buy a gun. It's the law and it takes a few days."

"What if I don't have a few days? What if he comes after me tomorrow?" I wanted that gun today. I didn't have time to wait.

"Let's fill out the paperwork and we'll get you hooked up with something else while we wait for it to clear. Number two, you can't carry a gun in your purse without a CPL."

"What's a CPL?"

"A Concealed Pistol License. We offer a class next month, but I'm thinking you won't want to wait that long."

I shook my head. "I can't."

"I teach the class. I'd be willing to do a private class for you tomorrow."

"Really? You'd do that for me?"

"Yeah, I would. Now, let's find a gun you're comfortable with and I'll teach you how to shoot it." Sid reached into the cabinet under the counter and started pulling out a few different guns. This was getting very real. He had me hold each one, until I found one that felt good in my hand.

"Sid?" He looked at me with kindness in his eyes. "Are you my guardian angel?"

He let out a gruff laugh. "I'm no angel. I'm just a guy who doesn't want to see you get hurt again. Now, let's teach you how to shoot this thing." Sid walked to the front door and locked it. He nodded to the gun on the counter. "Pick it up and follow me."

I reached for the gun on the counter and then hesitated. This all seemed so much easier in theory, but actually holding the gun scared the fuck out of me.

Sid watched me carefully. "Kyla, you can't be afraid of it. Pick it up. Keep your finger off the trigger and point it at the ground." I closed my eyes and took a deep breath. I followed Sid's directions and followed him out to the range.

Sid handed me eye and ear protection and I put it on. "This is a nine-millimeter." Sid showed me how to release the clip and load the bullets. He snapped the clip in and pulled back the slide. "Now there's a bullet in the chamber. See this switch right here?" I nodded. "That's the safety. Once you push it down, it's ready to fire." Sid set the target and sent it out twenty feet. He stood behind me and put his hands over mine, showing me how to hold the gun. "Now aim at the target and pull the trigger. It's going to have some kickback, but not too much.

I closed one eye and aimed at the target. I took a deep breath and pulled the trigger. The kickback wasn't nearly as bad as the gun Jake had me try. I looked at the target. I hit it in the lower right-hand corner.

"Not bad," Sid said. "Do it again."

I aimed again and fired. This time I hit the target on the very outside of the circle.

"Again," Sid said.

I emptied the clip, firing over and over again. My shots were getting better. Closer to the center.

Sid pulled the target back and looked at my progress. "Not bad," he said approvingly. "I think you might be a natural at this. Let's do it again. This time you're going to load it."

I tried to remember what Sid had shown me as I slid the bullets into the clip. I locked it in place and pulled the slide back. Sid sent the target back out. This time I didn't hesitate. I took aim and pulled the trigger. Several of my shots hit dead center.

Sid pulled the target back. "How'd I do?" I asked.

"I think he's going to regret fucking with you," Sid said with a smile.

I turned and stood on my tip toes. I gave Sid a huge hug. "I don't care what you say, Sid. You're my angel. Thank you!"

"Sweetheart, you don't have to thank me. You give that fucker what he deserves if he comes after you and that'll be thanks enough. Let's do it again."

I loaded the gun with confidence. I aimed at the target and emptied clip after clip. When Sid and I were finished for the day, I thanked him again and promised to come back early the next morning. He was going to do a crash course with me for the CPL and do some more target practice. He wanted to make sure I felt comfortable. Before I left, Sid hooked me up with a stun gun I could carry until all my paperwork went through, and a couple canisters of pepper spray. I felt confident that if Jake bothered me again. I would be prepared.

On the way home, I pulled my hood back up and put my sunglasses back on. I stopped at the drug store to buy some hair dye and nail polish. I was going to do a total transformation. I was a new woman with a new purpose. Nobody was going to fuck with me again.

I took my purchases home and laid them out on the bathroom counter. I was starting my internship in less than two weeks. They had no idea what I looked like. What I had bought would make me look edgier, and more creative. My long blond hair was beautiful, but people didn't take me seriously. The dumb blond syndrome. In addition, it would be a temporary disguise from Jake. He would figure it out eventually, but maybe I could hold him off for a little bit.

I opened the box of the hair color and read through the directions. I pulled on the plastic gloves and mixed the color. I held it up to my head, hesitated, then ran the first streak of black through my hair. I colored all of it and massaged it into my strands, then waited the required thirty minutes. I washed away the excess color and combed through my long black locks. I looked like a different person. I let my hair dry, then added the purple streaks. It was different for sure.

When I was finished, I took off my pink nail polish. I painted my fingers and toes black, then added the silver sparkles to it.

I looked in the mirror at what I had done to myself. I scowled at the bruises on my face but focused on my hair and nails. It was a long way from the All-American girl I'd always been.

Tori was going to be so pissed when she got home. This was not what she expected me to look like for her wedding. I didn't care. For a change, I was thinking about me.

I felt a renewed energy inside of me. Yes, I still looked like shit physically, but I actually felt good. I felt like I was taking control of my life for the first time in a long time. I decided to go for a run and get out my excess energy. I hooked my pepper spray to my sweatpants and downloaded Halestorm onto my phone. I hadn't thought about it much before, but I found the music empowering. Lzzy Hale's voice blasted through my earbuds and gave me a sense of purpose as a woman. I would not let anyone take advantage of me again. When the song "The

Reckoning*"* came on, I couldn't help but think of Jake, and what would be waiting for him if he came after me.

I continued to run, and my thoughts turned to Tyler. Even though he hurt me emotionally, I never had to worry about him hurting me physically. He would never do that. I trusted him with my life. He would never let anyone hurt me. I wanted him back as much as he wanted me, but I wasn't in a place to accept it yet. I needed to discover who I was before I would be strong enough to let him back in my life. If he was being honest when he spoke outside my door, he would wait for me. Time would tell. But for now, my focus was me.

Chapter 3
Tyler

The rest of my break flew by in a blur. I waited for more from Kyla, but it never came. I sent her another bouquet of flowers. I was going to be relentless. I didn't care if she had a boyfriend. I wasn't giving up. Her three words, ***Wait for me***, gave me hope. I returned her text with two words: ***I will.*** She didn't text back, but I knew she heard me. I would give her the space and time she needed. Lord knew, she had waited long enough for me to get my shit together.

I drove back to campus on New Year's Eve. There was a party at one of the frat houses. I went and had a good time, but I went home alone. I was done with the one-night stands. If I was serious about getting Kyla back, I needed to change my ways. It was surprisingly easy to say no and go home by myself. I had a bigger prize waiting for me. Kyla was the love of my life and my future wife. I was sure of it, now I just had to convince her.

Chapter 4
Kyla

I was sure that Sid was sent to me. Maybe not an angel, but pretty damn close! He sat with me and made sure I understood the answers for the CPL exam. He also spent countless hours with me at the gun range. I turned from being a scared girl to a confident woman when it came to shooting a gun. My shots were dead on time and time again.

True to his word, Sid pushed through my paperwork for both the gun license and the CPL. He sold me the gun I practiced with and a holster to carry in my purse. I felt empowered.

Since I destroyed the other one with my hairbrush, I bought a new mirror for our bathroom. I found Chris's tools and installed the new mirror before they ever came home. I threw the old one in the dumpster without a second thought. The fewer clues that I left about the destruction that had taken place here, the better. Tori was going to know something was up when she got home. Jake was gone, and I had a new look. I would deny everything. There was no way Chris and Tori could ever know what happened when they were gone.

So far, Jake had stayed away from me. But I didn't trust it. That fucker was sneaky. He was probably watching me. There were very few people I trusted—Chris, Tori, Sid… and Tyler. Everybody else could go to hell for all I cared. Trust had to be earned.

My suspicions were confirmed when I got a text from Jake. It was a picture of me running with my hood on. The caption said: *I see you*. I didn't carry my gun when I ran, but I did have the pepper spray. His text made me understand why I had all the creepy feelings when I'd been running before. He'd been watching me all along.

Tori and Chris came home the day after New Year's. The bruises on my face had faded, but not disappeared. The bruise by my right eye and the cut were still there.

I was sitting on my computer going over my portfolio when Tori walked in. Tori's eyes went big when she saw me.

"Wow! What'd you do to your hair?" She walked over to where I was sitting and stared at me.

"Changed it. You don't like it?"

She walked around me to look at my hair from every direction. "It's different, but actually, I really do like it." She picked up my strands and let them fall through her fingers. "The purple streaks look kick-ass."

"You're not pissed that I did this before your wedding?" I asked.

She waved me off. "Hell, no. It's sexy."

Chris came in a few minutes later carrying their suitcases from the car. He dropped them at his feet when he saw me. "Whoa! What'd you do?"

I just laughed. "You two are so much alike. That's exactly what Tori said." I ran my hand through my hair. "It's the new me. I'm trying something different for my new job next week. I start that internship and I wanted to be a little edgier."

"I think you accomplished that," Chris said. "What does Jake think about it?"

"Who cares? I broke up with him. He wasn't exactly happy about breaking up, but he'll survive." I shrugged my shoulders and played it off.

"What happened to your face? Jake didn't do that to you did he?" Tori questioned. She touched my cheek and ran her finger over the cut.

"God, no! I was hanging Christmas lights in my bedroom. I lost my balance on the chair and smacked my face on the corner of my nightstand. It actually looks a lot better than it did before." It was little truth mixed with a lot of lies. The truth was irrelevant. I was a liar, and I was okay with that.

Tori looked at me skeptically. "You sure?"

"Yeah, it's no biggie. Hey, I was planning on going clothes shopping for my internship tomorrow. Do you want to come?" I needed to change topics so that she would not obsess about my face.

"Sure. I could use some girl time."

"Cool."

The next day Tori and I headed to the mall. Tori kept trying to pick out things for me that were the old Kyla. I was looking for the new Kyla. I chose items that were dark colors: black, blue, or purple. Somewhat professional, but with the edge I was hoping to achieve. No pinks. No baby blues. I was trying to create an image for myself that was in line with my new attitude.

My final stop on our shopping trip was the jewelry store. I wasn't sure what I was looking for, but I would know it when I saw it. We were looking through the earrings and I knew right then what I wanted.

I asked the woman behind the counter. "Can I see those?" I pointed to the earrings in the case.

"They're kind of big, don't you think?" Tori asked.

"No. I think they're perfect."

The lady behind the counter pulled out the earrings I selected, and I tried them on. "I'll take them," I said. The lady wrapped my three-inch silver hoop earrings and put them in a box. I kept looking through the jewelry case. "I'd like to see that too." It was a silver ring shaped like a butterfly. It took up my whole finger to the first knuckle. It was beautiful. I put it on the middle finger of my left hand and admired it. It complemented the butterflies tattooed up my side. If nothing else, it would serve as a reminder of my goal to get my life back.

By the time we left the mall, I had spent way too much money, but for the first time in my life, I didn't care. I had the money. It was time I started to treat myself a little bit.

Chapter 5
Tyler

Shortly after the New Year, I got a text from Chris that made me smile.

Chris: The boyfriend is gone! Your girl kicked him to the curb!

Ty: Cool! Thanks for the info!

I was so happy. One less obstacle and one step closer to getting her back. I sent Kyla another bouquet of flowers. I thought long and hard about what to write on the card, thinking about everything that happened to us over the last year. It'd been the worst year of my life. I wrote: *Let's leave last year in the past. A new year is a new beginning. I Love You~ Ty.* The last year was awful for her. I wanted to try to bring some happiness to her life. Even if it was just flowers.

I had another appointment with Dr. Browning in mid-January. It had been a little over two months since I broke my clavicle and arm. The brace he put on last time, was way better than the cast, but I was anxious to start working out again.

Dr. Browning did several more x-rays of my arm and shoulder. It was kind of weird seeing the metal plates and screws that were now a permanent part of my body. Even though the bones were practically healed, Dr. Browning wanted me to wear the brace for another month. It wasn't what I wanted to hear, but I knew if I ever wanted to play football again, I would have to follow his orders.

He gave me the go ahead to start running again, so that was something. Dr. Browning also wanted me to start physical therapy. The range of motion in my shoulder was limited and the muscles were stiff from being immobilized for so long. He gave me the name and number of a sports injury therapist that was close to MSU. He was supposed to be one of the best and I was thankful for that.

Before heading back to school, I wanted to check out the tattoo shop that Kyla went to. The scars on my arm and shoulder were almost healed. I wanted to get a tattoo that would cover them. I looked up Forever Inked and headed over. I knew the guy who did Kyla's work was named Zack. He'd done an awesome job on her tattoos and if she trusted him, I did too.

I walked in the shop and looked around at all the pictures on the wall. One, in particular, caught my eye. It was a picture of Kyla's shoulder, with the two hearts surrounded by roses. I ran my hand over the picture and imagined I was touching her skin.

"That one's pretty awesome," someone behind me said. I turned and saw a tall guy covered in tattoos and piercings.

"Yeah, it is. You draw this?" I asked. I already knew the answer, but he didn't know that.

"Nah. I did the ink, but the girl in the picture drew it herself. She did another one too, I just haven't put it up yet. I think this is one of the best tattoos I've ever done." He pulled a frame out from under the counter. I recognized the flaming broken heart immediately. What I hadn't expected to see were the butterflies that flew out from it. They were intricately designed with vibrant colors. Each of the four butterflies had its wings a little further opened. They wrapped around her side and ended on her rib cage, right under her breast.

I was mesmerized by it. "Wow! It's really… beautiful," I said. I knew art was important to Kyla, but I never really appreciated it before. I was too focused on myself. I was selfish. "The girl has got talent. Does she work here?"

He took the picture and placed it on the counter. "I wish. I've tried, but she's away at school right now. I'm hoping to get her to do some designs for me when she comes back."

I knew it was sneaky and a long shot, but I did it anyway. "Think she'd be willing to design something for me?" I asked.

He shook his head. "I doubt it. She was pretty adamant about not doing anything until summer."

"Can you call and ask her? I'd be willing to pay her good money for the design."

He crossed his arms over his chest and quirked his eyebrow at me. "How much we talking about?"

I threw out the first thing that came to mind. I needed to make it appealing to her and money wasn't an issue for me. "If she agrees, I'll pay her a thousand bucks just for the design."

His eyes went wide. "A thousand dollars? Just to draw up a design? Why her? I could draw you something for a lot cheaper than that."

I lifted my chin at him. "I'm sure you could, but I want it to be her. I've got an idea of what I want and seeing her work… it's got to be her. A thousand dollars for her to draw it. Five for you to ink it."

"Five grand? What did you have in mind?"

I had his attention now. I pulled off my shirt. I pointed to the scars on my arm and shoulder. "I want these covered." I ran my hand up my bicep. "I want a dragon that starts here with the head coming over my shoulder. I want it to be holding a cross in its claws. It needs to have a Celtic feel to it. Intricate."

He reached his hand over the counter for me to shake. "My name's Zack. I'll call her. The design sounds cool. She might dig it. And for what you're offering to pay her, I don't know how she could it turn it down. But I'm not making any promises. Kyla's kind of stubborn."

"Kyla?" I questioned like I didn't know who he was talking about.

"Yeah. That's the name of the chick. How soon are you looking to have it done?" Zack asked.

"Doc said I should be good in about a month."

"Cool." He nodded. "I want to measure your arm and draw up where the scars are, so she'll know exactly what she's working with. We'll take some pictures too. If she agrees to this, I can tell you it'll be kick-ass when she's done."

Zack took a couple of pictures that I was careful to keep my face out of. He measured my arm and drew it out. He added the scars to the drawing. When he was finished, he took my name and number.

"I'll call her today and let you know what she says. I think the money might persuade her."

"Cool, Zack. One more thing… don't tell her my name, okay." He looked at me kind of weird. "Trust me, I've got my reasons."

"You pay me five grand to do this thing and I don't care what your name is." He laughed.

I left the shop and headed home. Okay, it wasn't the most honorable thing I'd ever done, but it would be so worth it. One day, I wanted Kyla to see her own artwork on my body. I couldn't think of a better way to pay tribute to her.

Chapter 6
Kyla

Saturday night I got a call from Zack. He never called me. I always called him, so I was curious. "Hey, Zack. What's up?"

"Hey, beautiful. I've got a proposition for you," he said.

"I'm not sleeping with you, Zack," I joked with him.

He laughed. "Awww girl, you're breaking my heart. That's not why I called though. I got an opportunity for you to make some serious cash."

"Oh yeah. What's that?"

"Okay, I know this is gonna sound weird, but hear me out. This guy came into the shop today. He was looking at the pictures on the wall, saw the one of the tat on your shoulder, and was super impressed. He wants you, specifically, to design his next tattoo. He's willing to pay big bucks for you to do the design."

I sighed. "Zack, you know how I feel about this. Once I'm done with school…"

"Kyla, he wants to pay you a thousand bucks."

I was shocked. "Excuse me? A grand just to draw a design? What's the catch?" I asked.

"No catch. He's got some scarring he wants covered."

"It's not going on his ass or dick or something weird, is it?" There had to be catch.

Zack laughed. "No, nothing like that. It's going on his arm and up over the shoulder. He was very specific. He wants a dragon holding a cross with a Celtic feel to it. Are you interested?"

"Yeah, I guess. A thousand dollars is damn good money. I'm starting my internship on Monday. When does he need it by?"

"He said about a month. I took some pictures of his arm and drew it up, so you'd know exactly what you'd be working with. I can email it to you with the details."

"Sounds good. I was planning on coming to see you in about three weeks anyway. I've got a couple of little things I want you to do. I can bring it then," I said.

"Cool. I can't wait to see what you come up with. Text me your email address and I'll send it. And, Kyla, thanks. I told you people would like your stuff."

"Yeah, yeah. We'll see if he's still willing to pay when he sees it. I've never done a dragon before, but I'll come up with something."

I hung up with Zack and sent him my email. A thousand dollars for a design? This guy had to have more money than brains. Whatever! I got on my computer and started pulling up pictures of dragons and Celtic artwork so I could get some ideas. By the end of the night, I already had some preliminary designs worked out. They weren't detailed or anything, but it was a start.

Sunday, I got another bouquet of flowers from Tyler. That boy was going to go broke at this rate. I sent him a quick text.

Ky: Thank you!

I kept everything simple. I know he said he wanted me back, but I didn't trust it. And honestly, with what happened with Jake, I was in no place to have a relationship. Even if I wanted it, my head was not right. I was so fucked up from what Jake had done to me, it would be a long time before I ever let a man touch me again. Even Ty.

I got in my car and drove to the gun range. I couldn't let my guard down. I went every week, just to make sure that my skills were sharp. As I pulled in the parking lot, my phone buzzed.

Jake: Your hair looks like shit! Change it back!

Attached was a picture of me getting in my car. I looked at the picture carefully. He must have just taken it because I was wearing the clothes I had on now. Fucking freak! I looked around the parking lot but didn't see his car. Hopefully, he didn't follow me.

I grabbed my gun and went inside to the range. Sid was standing behind the counter and came out to give me a hug when he saw me. Even though he looked menacing, Sid was a big teddy bear. He took me under his wing, and I loved him like a father figure.

"Hi, sweet girl. You ready for practice today?" Sid always went out to the range with me to help me improve my shooting.

"Yeah, but can I show you something first?" I pulled out my phone and showed him the two texts I got from Jake. "What do you think about these?"

Sid pulled his glasses out from under his vest and placed them on his face. He looked at each one carefully. "I think he's not going to just let you go. This is stalking. Even if he hasn't threatened you directly, it's implied. How'd you end up with this guy anyway?"

"He was super sweet when we first started dating, then he just kind of turned crazy."

Sid took his glasses off and put them back in his pocket. "He's obsessed with you. Don't erase those. They show a pattern of behavior. I think you should file for a personal protection order against him. If he does go after you again and you need to defend yourself, the PPO will help justify your actions. I know you don't want anyone to know what happened, but you've got to protect yourself."

I sighed. "You're probably right. I wish I had taken pictures of my face, so I had some proof."

Sid pulled on his long, gray beard and pointed at the camera on the wall above the counter. "I got a picture from the first day you came in here. That camera stores everything for six months. You never know when some crazy is going to come in here to buy a gun and then do something stupid."

"Really?"

"Yep. Let's go in back and take a look."

I followed Sid to the back room, and he sat down in front of the computer. He pulled up the camera, typed in December 26, and set the time for eight a.m. Sure enough a picture of me popped up on the screen. I had my hood up and sunglasses on. Sid pressed play and the footage moved forward. I watched myself pull out my driver's license and put it on the counter. Then I slowly took my hood down and removed my glasses. Sid froze the screen and then enlarged the picture. What I saw sickened me. My face was bruised and battered. The cut on my cheek was visible and the handprint clear. I choked down the bile that was rising in my throat and looked away from the screen.

Sid saw my reaction. "You've come a long way since then," he said. "You've become so much stronger in just a few weeks. I'm proud of you Kyla." Sid printed three copies of the picture and put them in envelopes. "You take one, give one to the police, and I'll keep one here in the safe."

"The police will want to know why I didn't report it," I said.

"You're not pressing charges against him unless you want to tell the whole story. This is just support for why you want the personal protection order. They may or may not take it seriously, but at least it will be on record."

He was right.

After my target practice, I drove to the police department. I asked to speak to someone regarding a personal protection order and was sent to speak with a detective.

"I'm Detective Jones. How can I help you?"

I sat in the chair across from his desk. "I want to file for a personal protection order," I said.

Detective Jones leaned across his desk. "Based on what?" he asked.

I pulled out the picture of what Jake had done to me. "He did this to me. It was on Christmas Eve. Also, he's been sending me text messages."

Detective Jones looked at the picture. "Did you report this when it happened?"

I dropped my head. "No, I was too scared and ashamed, but now he won't leave me alone."

Detective Jones let out a breath. "Do you have any evidence that proves who did this to you?"

"No. I didn't tell anyone. Only one person even knows about this."

"Miss O'Malley, it's hard for us to do our job when you don't report it. This happened almost three weeks ago. Let me see the text messages."

I handed my phone to him. He looked at the pictures and handed it back to me. "While I agree that this... Jake... is watching you, there isn't anything in the messages that qualifies as a threat. At this time, you don't have enough evidence to file a personal protection order."

This was frustrating. "So, what do I do? Just wait for him to come after me again?"

"Did you have a relationship with this man?"

"Yes. He was my friend for a while and then we dated for about three months. When I broke it off, he didn't take it well. I'm afraid he's going to try to hurt me again."

"Miss O'Malley, I believe you. Really, I do. But the law requires certain standards to be met before a personal protection order can be issued. My advice is, be vigilant. Don't put yourself in dangerous situations, like being alone at night or going to secluded areas. If the texts become more threatening, maybe we can help you. What's his full name?"

"Jake Andrew Hening."

Detective Jones typed it into his computer. "His record is clean. There's not much I can do for you."

"Can you at least give me a letter that states that I inquired about a personal protection order and that you wouldn't issue one? Then at least I'll have proof that I believed he was a danger to me. You know, in case something happens."

Detective Jones put his elbows on the desk and rested his chin on his hands. "I can do that, but it won't be a legal document. It probably wouldn't hold up in court."

"I don't care. I just need some sort of documentation that I was here."

"Just give me a few minutes and I'll type something up for you."

"Thank you," I said. I waited patiently while Detective Jones worked on his computer. About ten minutes later he handed me the letter I asked for.

"Kyla, I'm sorry I can't be more help. Keep record of any communication he has with you. If the texts become more threatening, come see me. And if tries to hurt you, report it. I attached my card. Don't hesitate to call me. Stay safe."

I left feeling frustrated, but part of this was my own fault. When Jake had attacked me, I was so embarrassed. I should have reported it. Sid was the only one who truly knew what happened to me, and I wanted it to stay that way. I didn't want to go to court and relive the whole thing. I just wanted to be left alone. I put the letter in the envelope with the picture and hid it in my closet where no one would ever find it.

I started my internship on Monday. I got a text as I pulled into the parking lot.

Ty: Good luck today! Kick some ass!

I just smiled. I figured Chris must have been feeding him information on me. I should have been pissed at Chris, but I wasn't. I knew he was rooting for Tyler and me to get back together. It was actually kind of cute.

I didn't know what the dress code here was, so I had on black slacks, a fitted black blouse, and my tall boots. I wore my hair clipped up and put on my big silver hoop earrings. The necklace Tyler gave me for Christmas hung around my neck. I hadn't taken it off since Christmas Eve.

I met with my mentor, Michael. He was cool, in a nerdy sort of way. He was probably about thirty. He wore his black hair slicked back and wore thick-framed, black glasses. He was definitely the artsy type and I fit in here perfectly.

Michael was one of the top execs and I would be working with him directly. I sat on one side of the desk, while he sat on the other with his leg crossed over his knee. He was thumbing through my portfolio. "You've got the artistic skills. These are really quite good. I want to see if you can transfer this into an advertising capacity. Many of our clients come to us with a vague idea of what they want. It's up to us to create something that fits in-line with their thinking. Usually, we'll make three or four mockups for the client to choose from. From those designs we perfect a product the client uses for the business. Some clients are easy to please and some, not so much. We'll be working together for the most part."

"That sounds great," I said. I was super excited to actually do something productive with my art. "Where will I be working?"

"I've set up a work area right outside my office. We'll provide whatever tools you think you'll need to do your work. Every artist is different, so don't hesitate to take what you need. I want you to feel comfortable here. We use a couple of different software programs. Adobe Illustrator is great, but Autodesk 3ds Max and SketchbookPro are my favorites. Have you used any of those programs before?"

"I've actually used all three in my classes. I'm not a pro at any of them, but I'm a quick learner."

"All right. Let's introduce you to some the other people in the office and then you can set up your workspace. I've got a couple of practice exercises for you to do with the software, so that you can play around with it a little bit. You'll have an hour lunch and after lunch I'll show you some of the accounts I'm currently working on."

"Michael, I think I'm going to like working with you. I love having a plan and you seem like a planner. I have to tell you, I'm really happy and excited to be here. Thank you for this opportunity."

"You're very welcome. Come on. Let's go meet your co-workers." Michael stood up and we walked to the door. My new adventure was starting, and I couldn't have been more excited about it.

Chapter 7
Tyler

A few days later, I got a call from a number I didn't recognize. "Hello"

"Tyler?"

"Yeah, this is him," I said.

"This is Zack from Forever Inked."

"Oh, hey. Did you hear back about my tattoo?" I asked.

"I did. She's onboard. Kyla said she'll have the design done in about three weeks. She's going to bring it in then."

"Cool. I'm glad she agreed."

"I just have to ask. Are you sure about this? What if you hate it?" Zack questioned.

"I won't. I trust her," I said.

"Okay… it's your money and your skin. I'll see you in a month."

"See you then." I hung up and got a Grinchy smile on my face. She was going to do it. At this point I didn't even care what it looked like. I knew I would love whatever she designed.

Physical therapy was a bitch! My therapist's name was Jerome. He was a big guy, definitely an ex-athlete or military. He was intimidating as fuck. I walked in and introduced myself.

"I know who you are." He said gruffly. "I watched you take the hit. It looked rough."

"Yeah, not one of my finer moments. I should have seen it coming," I said shaking my head.

"Well, shit happens. What do you want from me? What do you hope to achieve here?" he asked, crossing his arms over chest.

I could do without the attitude. "What do I want to achieve? I'm playing football again. It's not even a question. I'm going to be ready and a free agent next year. I'm getting my arm back."

Jerome cracked a smile, showing all his pearly whites. He clapped me on the back. "That's what I wanted to hear. I needed to know how serious you were. I can help you get there, but it won't be easy. I'm not going to baby you."

"I don't want to be babied." I gave him a glare. "I'm willing to put in the work. I'm not giving up after all the years I've put into this."

Jerome nodded his head at me. "Good! You've got drive. Tell me what you've got going on in that arm of yours."

I explained to him about the breaks and what they had done to repair them. He had me remove the brace and lift my arm to shoulder height. It was still sore. Then he had me pull my arm back as if I were going to throw the ball. I raised my arm and rotated my shoulder back as far as I could. "Fuck, that hurts!"

"Yeah, I bet it does. First, we're going to work on getting your range of motion back, then we need to rebuild those muscles," Jerome said.

Jerome worked on my shoulder for almost an hour before we called it quits. He told me to go home, soak it for a half hour, and then put muscle relaxer on it. I was coming back to see him in two days.

This process was going to be brutal. I wished I was going home to Kyla, so she could baby me. I imagined her rubbing my shoulder down and laying with her in bed. I didn't even need to have sex with her, I just needed to be with her.

At the end of January, when my birthday rolled around, I was in a funk. This was the second one in a row that I was spending without my girl. I finally got a text from her in the afternoon.

Ky: Happy Birthday, Ty! I miss you! <3

That was the longest text I had received from her since September. Maybe the flowers were working. I quickly typed out my reply.

Ty: Miss you like crazy! I'm waiting for you!

Ky: I wish I could come see you, but I'm not ready. I don't know when I will be.

Ty: I'll wait. I want my heart back. I'm not giving up!

Ky: Still?

Ty: Always!

That was the end of our texting, but it made me smile. It was almost like a real conversation. I knew she didn't trust me yet. I broke her heart too many times.

Chapter 8
Kyla

I finally finished my design for Zack's mystery client. I thought the whole thing was kind of weird. Why would some guy who didn't even know me want to spend a grand just for my design?

It turned out way cooler than I could have ever anticipated. The dragon wound up the bicep with its wings outstretched. The tail curled around with spikes on it and the back feet looked like they clawed into the skin, as if the dragon was climbing up the arm. The head wrapped around the front of the shoulder. It had horns and sharp teeth, with smoke coming from its nose. The front claws reached down over the shoulder to hold a cross that would be placed on the upper right chest. I added the Celtic designs into the cross and into the scales on the dragon. Overall, I thought it was pretty awesome. It would take Zack a long time to ink it because of all the intricate details.

I drove back home to Forever Inked on Saturday. When I walked in, Zack looked up and smiled at me. He came around the corner and picked me up in a big hug. I loved Zack, as a friend.

"Hey, girl. I missed you!"

"I missed you too!"

Zack reached for the envelope in my hand. "I've been dying to see this." He lifted the flap and pulled the design from the envelope. His expression was unreadable as he stared at it.

"Well?" I questioned.

Zack lifted his eyebrows. "It's fuckin' awesome. This guy is going to love it!"

"Really?"

"Yeah, really!" He laid the design on the counter and kept looking at it. "This is going to take me forever to ink, but it's going to be so cool when it's done." Zack looked me up and down. He hadn't seen me since before Christmas. "You look good. The new hair is cool."

"Thanks. I'm trying something new for this internship. I thought the blond was too… I don't know… good girlish."

"Kyla, the blond was beautiful, but this looks good, too. I totally get what you were going for." He waved me to follow him to the back. "You said you wanted to get some work done. What are we doing?"

I sat down on the table like I had done so many times before. I was never nervous with Zack, but today I was. "Please don't ask questions, okay?"

Zack looked at me with confusion. "Okaaaay…"

I pulled down the top of my shirt and bared the top of my right breast where the scars from the teeth marks were.

Zack's eyes went wide. "Are those bite marks?"

My eyes filled with tears, and I nodded. "I need them covered. I don't want to see them anymore."

Zack leaned in and hugged me, rubbing my back. "It's okay, baby girl. We'll cover them."

I released Zack and wiped at my eyes. "I'm sorry. I just… I can't look at them anymore."

Zack's face showed nothing but compassion. "Want to talk about it?"

"Not really. I just want to forget about it," I said. Putting words to what had happened to me… I couldn't do it.

"What do you want me to do?" he asked.

"I was thinking a skewed heart." I traced the spot with my finger. "It should have a long tail to cover everything. I want it in purple," I said.

"Okay. Anything else?"

"Yes. On my left hip, I want scripted the words, *I am Strong!* I want it to curve over my hip bone."

Zack nodded his head. "You really went through some shit, didn't you?"

I didn't answer him. I just nodded my head almost imperceptibly.

"When did this happen?" he questioned.

"Over Christmas. The day after I last saw you." I started to break down. Tears ran down my face. "I trusted him. I fucking trusted him, and this is what he did to me. I don't know how to get past it, except to cover it up."

"We'll cover it." Zack said, his face filled with sadness for me. If I were in a better place and I wasn't so in love with Tyler, I could see myself with Zack. He was kind and sweet and cute. Zack quickly drew up a heart and placed it over my chest. He seemed satisfied with the drawing and made a transfer. He put it on my skin and let me look in the mirror.

"It's perfect," I said. "Thank you."

"No problem. Let's get this bitch covered." Zack snapped on his gloves and the tattoo gun buzzed to life. It didn't take long. I then pulled my pants down over my hip and let him script the words I had requested. Zack bandaged me, and we walked to the front counter.

"How much do I owe you for today?" I asked.

"Nothing. Consider it a gift."

"Zack, I have to pay you," I insisted.

"Pay me by coming to see me when school is finished. I still want you to work for me." Zack came around the counter and embraced me. It felt true.

"I don't know how to thank you," I said. "Thanks for being you. I couldn't ask for better." I blew him a kiss and walked out of the shop.

I drove home with tears in my eyes. Every time I thought about what had happened to me, I burst into tears. Why couldn't I just get over it?

I pulled into the parking lot of our apartment and shut off my car. My phone immediately buzzed.

Jake: Where the fuck have you been? I've been waiting for you!

I looked around the parking lot and saw his car in the far corner. He was standing there staring at me. Then he got back in his car and squealed out onto the main road.

It was time I had a talk with Chris and Tori.

I walked into the apartment and set my purse on the table in the hallway. I pulled out my phone, so I could show them the texts. Tori was on her back on the couch laughing and Chris was leaned over her. Whatever was going on was lighthearted for sure. I was about to end that.

"I don't mean to interrupt, but can I talk to you two for a minute."

Tori sat up on the couch laughing. "Sure. What's up?"

I sat on the edge of the coffee table and faced them. I turned to Chris. "I know you've been telling Tyler stuff about me." His face dropped. "And I don't care. But what I'm about to tell you stays between us. Ty can't know."

"What is it? What's the big secret?" Chris laughed like it was a joke, but it wasn't.

I got up from the table and started walking towards my room. "Forget it," I said. I went in my room and slammed my door. This wasn't a joke to me. The tears filled my eyes again. I laid on my bed and let them fall. I felt so alone. It was my own fault for not telling them in the first place.

I got up from my bed and headed back out toward the front door with tears in my eyes. "Kyla?" Tori called. I held my hand up and grabbed my purse. I walked out and got in my car. I needed to go to the range. Sid probably wouldn't be there, but I didn't care. I needed to work out my frustrations. Today was very emotional for me and I needed a release.

I got to the range and bought the target shaped like an actual person instead of a bullseye. It was ridiculous really. It was a cartoon character dressed up like a burglar, mask and all. I sent it out twenty feet, loaded my gun, and pulled back the slide.

I was going to kill that fucker someday. Looking at the target, all I saw was Jake. Rage consumed me. I emptied the first clip into his head and reloaded. I emptied the second clip into his chest. And the third? Let's just say he wouldn't be having children anytime soon.

I felt a hand on my shoulder. "You okay?"

I turned and looked at Sid with tears in my eyes. "Not really."

Sid took the gun from my hand and placed it on the counter. He walked me out of the range and into his office. "What's going on?" he asked.

I took several deep breaths. "I can't let it go," I said. I pulled down the top of my shirt. "I had this done today, to cover the bite marks he left on me. I got home, and he texted me again. He won't leave me the fuck alone! I can't take it anymore! All I feel is hate and rage! That's not me." I was crumbling before this man who was fortress.

Sid held out his arms. "Come here." He wrapped me in his big arms, and I cried on his shoulder. "Let it out," he said. And I did.

"I'm never going to be right again, am I?"

"You will," he assured me. "When you forgive yourself."

I wiped at my eyes. "What do you mean?"

"I mean that you blame yourself. You think that somehow you deserved it. You didn't. No means no."

"I should have never gotten involved with him in the first place. I was so stupid. I trusted him."

"That's because you're a good person. You see the best in everyone. It's your biggest downfall and that's not a bad thing."

"I'm weak," I said. There were so many things I let happen to me over the past year.

"You're not weak. You've told me your whole story and you're a remarkable woman. You should be proud to be you. Your parents would be proud."

"I don't think so," I said. "They'd be disappointed."

"They'd be proud of the woman you've become. You're getting stronger every day. Have faith in yourself." Sid pulled me in for another hug.

I stayed with Sid for a while, and then I made my way back to the apartment. I walked into the dark and left the lights off. It was after midnight. I grabbed the bottle of vodka and headed out to the patio, taking a big sip right from the bottle. Then I lit a cigarette and inhaled deeply. Forgive myself? I didn't know how. I let Jake into my life. I'd had sex with him voluntarily. Maybe I didn't deserve what I got, but I'm the one who let him in. The tears poured down my cheeks. I'd cried more today, than I had in the last month. I was one big fucking mess!

I couldn't go to bed. I got in my car and drove the three hours back home again. It was the middle of the night when I got to the cemetery. I drove through the gates and around to where my parents were buried. I hadn't been back here since I laid them to rest. It was so fucking cold, so I grabbed the blanket from my backseat and got out of the car.

I walked through the dark to their grave and laid the blanket down on the frozen ground. Sitting cross-legged on it, I poured my heart out to my parents.

"Hi Mom and Dad. I know this is a weird time of day to talk to you, but I hope you can hear me. I have so much to tell you." I took a deep breath. "I lied to you." I stopped to gather my thoughts, then told them my story. "When Ty and I broke up, I wasn't okay. I had gotten pregnant. I know you would have been disappointed, but I was really happy. I wanted our baby so bad. I was afraid to tell Ty, so I didn't. And then I miscarried. I lost our baby on the bathroom floor and I was heartbroken. I never had an ovarian cyst like I told you. I was a liar." I took another deep breath. "I lied to Ty and I lied to you. Tyler couldn't forgive me and that's why we broke up. I wanted him back so bad, but he didn't want me. I tried to move on, but I couldn't."

I laid back on the blanket and looked up at the stars that poked through the clouds on that cold night in February. "And then you guys left me. Were my sins so bad? Was that my punishment for being a liar? I always tried to be a good daughter. I know I made mistakes, but why did you leave me all alone? Can you ever forgive me?" The snowflakes began to fall from the sky. They landed on my lips and eyelashes. I brushed them away and continued.

"Send me a sign. Tell me that you forgive me." The snow came down harder now. It started to cover the blanket I sat on and my parents' gravestone. I turned my head to the sky and let the snow cover my face. Running my hands over my hair, I smoothed down the wet locks.

"After I lost my baby, and Tyler left me, and you left me, I tried to start again. I found a guy who was really sweet, or at least it started that way. I made another mistake by trusting him. He... he raped me. Now, he won't leave me alone, and I don't know if I'll ever be the same. I don't know how to trust again."

I was covered in snow by now, soaking wet from both my tears and the snow that fell down on me. But I wasn't finished. "Tyler says he wants me back. I always thought he was my soul mate, but now I'm not so sure. How do I find happiness? How can I let him touch me when all I can think about is being violated? I'm so mad. I'm fucking pissed that I let this happen to me. I don't know how to move forward. Please help me. Sid says I need to forgive myself, but I don't know how. Help me find my way again. Tell me what to do."

Just then my phone rang, and Tyler's face showed up on the screen. "Really, Mom? This is your solution?" I laughed to myself. My mom was a hopeless romantic, just like me.

I answered his call for the first time in forever. "Hello."

"Ky? Where are you?" His voice was filled with concern.

"Home," I said over the lump in my throat.

"Home? Tori called looking for you. She said you left in the middle of the night and weren't back yet. She's worried."

"I'm not at the apartment. I came back home."

"Like, Shelby home?" he asked. "I don't understand. Why did you drive all the way back there in the middle of the night?"

My words caught in my throat. "I needed to talk to my parents. I needed to tell them the truth. About everything."

"You're at the cemetery?"

"Yes."

"Kyla, it's like thirty degrees out and you're sitting in a dark cemetery by yourself at four in the morning?"

"Yes."

I heard Tyler blow out a breath. "How can I help you? Tell me what to do."

The tears ran down my face. "You can't help me. No one can. I'm the only one who can help me, and I don't know how."

"You're scaring me, Ky," he said.

"I'm sorry. You don't need to worry. I'm going to figure this out."

"Let me help you, baby."

I closed my eyes and shook my head. "I know you think you want me back, but trust me, you don't. I'm not worth it."

"You are worth it. I'm not giving up on you."

"You should. I'm a fucking mess and I don't know when I'll be right again."

"I'm sorry I hurt you."

"This isn't about you, Ty. I forgave you a long time ago. It's about me. Forgiving myself." I reached under my shirt and held onto the necklace Tyler gave me at Christmas.

"I don't know what that means. Kyla, listen to me, baby. Whatever it is that has you upset, you're not going to find the answers in a cemetery."

I turned my face up to the snow falling all around me.

"The snow," I said to myself.

How could I have been so blind? It was a sign from my mom and dad. I was sure of it now. They were listening. They forgave me. Maybe now I could forgive myself. I wiped the tears from my eyes.

My voice became lighter as the pieces started to come together. "Actually, I think I just did." I started to talk really fast. I didn't want him to give up like I had told him. "Forget what I said. Wait for me, Ty. If you truly want me back, if you truly believe in us… wait for me."

"I will. I love you, Ky. I'm not going anywhere. I'll always be here. I just wish I could help you."

"You did, more than you know. Thank you! I love you, Tyler," I said without thinking.

I hung up the phone and stood up. I threw my arms out and spun around in circles in the snow. Then I shouted at the top of my lungs, "Thank you, Mom! Thank you, Dad! Thank you! I love you, I love you, I love you!"

When I got back to the apartment, the sun was finally coming up. It was a new day. It gave me hope that I could forgive myself, and that started by not being ashamed about what had happened to me. It wouldn't take away the hate I felt towards Jake, but it might help wash away the guilt I felt. It wasn't my fault. It was Jake's.

I walked into the apartment and Tori ran up to hug me. She squeezed me so tight I thought my ribs were going to crack. "I'm so sorry," she said. "I'm sorry we blew you off last night."

I unwrapped her arms from around me. "It's okay," I told her.

Chris came around the corner. "No, it's not," he said. "We're supposed to be your friends and we weren't last night."

"I'm sorry I called Tyler, but you wouldn't answer your phone. I didn't know who else to call. I thought maybe you went there," Tori apologized.

I walked into the kitchen and sat down. "It's fine. That was the first time I've talked to him since September. I'm glad I talked to him."

Chris and Tori followed me into the kitchen and sat across from me. "He said you went home. You went to the cemetery?" Chris questioned. "Want to talk about it?"

I blew out a breath. "No and yes. No, I don't want to talk about it, but I need to."

"What is it?" Tori asked.

"Wait here just a minute." I went to my room and pulled the envelope from my closet. I sat back down and looked at both of them. "Before I tell you anything, you have to promise not to tell Ty. I don't know if and when I'll tell him, but I have to be the one to do it. No one else. I mean it. You have to promise me that first."

"You know he still cares about you, right?" Chris asked.

"I know," I said. "And this would destroy him if he found out from anyone but me."

Chris and Tori exchanged a look and nodded at each other. "We promise. What is it?" Tori asked.

"This is so hard," I said. "Remember when I broke up with Jake?" They both nodded. "He didn't take it very well. I mean, at first, I thought he did, and everything was good. But then he came back the next day and he was so mad. No, not mad… furious. He went crazy."

"Did that fucker hurt you?" I could see the anger rising in Chris.

I bit my lip. "Yeah, he did." Chris's jaw tensed up as he waited for the details. I opened the envelope and pulled out the picture. I looked at it and closed my eyes in disgust. Then I slid it across the table. "This is part of what he did to me."

Tori's hand went up to cover her mouth. "Oh, my God!"

Chris was calm. Too calm. He ground his teeth and his eyes bored into me. "You said part of what he did. What else?"

I couldn't answer. My eyes filled with tears.

He pounded his fist on the table. "What else?" he yelled.

I flinched back in fear as flashbacks of Jake swam in my head. I started taking short, rapid breaths.

Tori put her hand on Chris's arm. "Chris, stop! You're scaring her."

Chris took a deep breath to calm himself and reached across the table for my hand, and I tentatively took it. He spoke softly, "What else, Kyla?"

"He... he handcuffed me to the bed. And he bit me... here." I pulled down the top of my shirt. "I made Zack tattoo over the teeth marks, so I wouldn't have to look at them anymore."

Chris looked at me with pleading eyes. "Please tell me he didn't rape you."

I burst into tears and covered my face. My secret was out, and I was so ashamed. Chris stood up abruptly and his chair fell to the ground as he started pacing back and forth in the kitchen. Tori came around the table and wrapped me in her arms "I'm so sorry! Why didn't you say something before?"

"Because I was embarrassed and ashamed that I let him do that to me." I snuffed my tears back. "I thought it was my fault."

Chris turned to me. "How in the fuck was this your fault?"

I started yelling back, "I'm the one who dated him! I let him in my life! I had sex with him! I should have fought back harder!"

"Kyla, he's twice your size. I don't care what you let him do before. It doesn't excuse what he did to you!"

"I know!" I screamed. "But I was still embarrassed, that's why I couldn't tell you. I couldn't tell anyone!"

Tori sat in the chair next to me and took my hands in hers. "When did this happen?"

"Christmas Eve."

Chris stopped pacing and looked at me like he just had a revelation. "That's why you wouldn't open the door for Tyler on Christmas Day."

"I couldn't let him see me like that. He can't know about this. It would destroy him."

Chris picked up the chair from the floor and leaned on the back of it. "That... I'll agree with. He loves you so much. This would annihilate him."

"I want to be with Ty again. I love him so much it hurts, but I need to finish this first. I have to get my head right." I decided it was time to drop the second bomb. "Jake's not going to let me go."

"What the hell does that mean?" Chris asked.

"He told me that this is not over. He's been following me. Sending me pictures of myself." I pulled out my phone and showed them the texts. "He was here last night. Watching me. But this will never happen again. I can promise you that."

"Oh yeah," Chris let out a frustrated laugh. "How are you going to stop him?"

I went to the front hall and picked up my purse. I reached inside, pulled out my gun, and set it on the table. "Cuz I'm going to kill that fucker if he comes near me again." My tears were gone now. They were replaced with the rage inside me.

Tori's eyes went wide. "Where did you get that?"

Chris piped in, "Do you even know how to use it?"

I picked it up and dropped the clip out of it. Then I released the bullet from the chamber. "I bought it, and yes, I know how to use it. And, actually, I'm damn good at it. I've been going to the range every week. Sid taught me everything I need to know."

Chris looked at me in astonishment. "Who the hell is Sid?"

"He owns the gun range. I went the day after Christmas to buy this. I was all battered looking and he figured out what happened to me. He's helped me a lot. I have my Concealed Pistol License thanks to him. He taught me everything.

Tori looked at me with wide eyes. "If you shoot him, you'll go to jail."

I looked at her and shook my head. "No, I won't. I have a plan. I'm not going to be a victim anymore. The police already have my request for a personal protection order. They wouldn't grant it, but it's on record. When he comes for me, I'll be ready."

Tori tried to be sensible. "Why not just file rape charges against him? Send him to jail?"

"Because I never reported it, and I washed away all the evidence. It would be his word against mine. I'm not going to sit in court and listen to him justify that it was consensual. I'm not going to relive my nightmare and watch him get off."

"This is crazy!" Chris said. "I can't even believe we're having this conversation."

"We're not," I said with conviction. "You two don't know anything about this. It's called plausible deniability. When this happens, it's going to be on me and me alone. It might be tomorrow, or it might be three months from now, but it's going to happen. Jake's not going to let this go."

"How can you sit there and be so calm about all of this?" Tori asked.

"Because I've had a lot of time to think about it. I blamed myself for a long time. Sid said I needed to forgive myself, and I'm trying. I can't blame myself anymore. I'm pissed. And Jake will pay."

Chris tried to take control of the situation. "I don't want you taking any unnecessary risks. If you want to go out at night, take Tori or me with you. When you go running…"

"I have my pepper spray. I want him to feel like I'm vulnerable. It's the only way he'll make his move. He won't do it unless he thinks he won't get caught. He knew you two were away last time. He wants to be a cop. He's not going to do anything that he thinks will jeopardize that."

"This is all so… surreal," Tori said.

"No," I said. "It's real." I put the clip back in and racked a bullet into the chamber. "And you two aren't going to say a word to Tyler about it. I'm going to handle it. And then maybe, we can have our happily ever after."

Chapter 9
Tyler

When I got that call from Tori, I panicked. To be honest, I was relieved, but shocked, that Kyla even answered the phone when I called. She'd been shutting me out for months. Sometimes I felt like giving up, but then I remembered what we had. What it felt like to have her by my side. To watch her laugh and see the smile that would light up her face. To make love to her and have her fall apart beneath me. She was my forever. I would not give up on her.

I couldn't figure out why she would leave her apartment in the middle of night and drive back home. I could picture her sitting in a cold cemetery in the dark. It freaked me the fuck out. Some of the things she said didn't even make sense. No one could help her? She wasn't worth it? She had to forgive herself? She sounded fucking suicidal. But then, it was like a switch flipped and she was telling me to wait for her.

I would.

I made my appointment with Dr. Browning for the next Saturday morning. He removed the brace from my arm for good. The x-rays showed that the bones were completely healed, and the muscles were healing nicely too. He was impressed with how much I had improved my ability to rotate my shoulder. I had to give Jerome all the credit for that. He'd been kicking my ass for the last month.

After my appointment, I headed over to Forever Inked. I was surprised Zack recognized me from my previous visit, but then again, he knew I was coming.

"Hey, man, I think you're going to really like what she came up with."

"Yeah? Let's see it," I said.

Zack pulled an envelope from under the counter. He slid the drawing out and pushed it across the counter. I just stared at it in amazement. I really had not given Kyla the credit she deserved. I ran my fingers over the intricate designs she drew along the back of the dragon and through the cross. "It's awesome." I stared at it a little longer and then turned to Zack. "Let's do this!"

Zack led me around to the back of the shop where I sat on the table. He quickly made the transfer and applied it to my arm. "This is going to be so fucking cool! It's gonna cover those scars real good. What are they from anyway? You have some kinda surgery?"

"I broke my arm and shoulder playing football. I got blindsided and that was it. I ended up getting metal plates put in," I answered.

"You should have gotten one of those terminator tattoos." I looked at him in confusion. "You know where it looks like the skin is torn back and you see all the gears and shit underneath."

I nodded. "I've seen those before. They're cool, but this is so much better."

"You know this is going to take a while, right?" Zack asked.

"I know, but it's totally worth it."

"I just got to ask you a question, man. Why were you willing to pay that much money for a design, when you didn't even know what it would look like? I just can't figure it out."

I looked at Zack and assessed the situation. "I'll tell you the truth, but you can't tell Kyla."

"Man, she's my girl, and I respect her. I can't lie to her."

"I'm not asking you to lie. Just not to tell her the whole truth."

Zack nodded. "I'm down with that. So, what's the story?" He slipped on his gloves and started the tattoo gun.

I sat there in the chair, while Zack began the outline of my tattoo. "I knew all along it was Kyla designing it." Zack quirked his eyebrow at me. "She and I used to date. We started back in high school. She was my everything, but I fucked up and things went south a year ago. Anyways, I knew she got her tats here. I admired the fact that Ky drew her own designs. I never realized how talented she was, until I saw the hearts on her shoulder. They're beautiful, just like her. I thought the best way to pay tribute to her, was to have her draw up my next tattoo, but I figured she wouldn't do it if she knew it was for me. So... I'm hoping that one day she'll see this and know that I truly love her."

Zack stopped his tattooing. "Are you serious? I know your fucking story. She told me all about it when I was doing her ink. That's some serious Romeo and Juliet bullshit. You know that ink she has is all about you, right?"

"It's about us. I broke her heart. I want her back, but I have to earn it. She and I went through some serious stuff. I'm just not the same without her."

Zack paused in his work. "When's the last time you saw her?"

I blew out a breath. "She wanted more from the relationship, and I wouldn't give it to her. She finally reached her limit last September. I haven't seen her since. She's texted a few times, but they're short. I've only talked to her once and that was last weekend, but it was a really weird conversation."

Zack's eyebrows narrowed. "Weird how?"

"She was crying and saying stuff I didn't really understand. Stuff that didn't make sense to me. She was obviously upset about something, but I don't know what it was."

Zack shook his head. "Fuck! I knew she was upset when she left here. I should have never let her drive home like that."

"She was here? Last Saturday?"

"Yeah, she came in to drop off your design. I did a little work on her, too," Zack said, not volunteering anything else.

"What was she upset about?" I probed.

"You know I can't tell you that. Hell, I don't even know all the details. Just… it was bad shit."

Fuck! I wished I knew what was going on with her. I had to respect Zack for keeping her privacy though. He was obviously a good friend to her. I was a little jealous though that she would tell Zack her secrets, but not me.

Zack and I continued to talk, but he didn't give anything away about Kyla. After five hours, I was ready to be done. The tat on my back had taken a while, but I had it done in two sessions, so it wasn't that bad. I was anxious as fuck to see Kyla's design on my skin. Zack finally wiped the last of the blood and ink from my chest. "You ready to see it, man?" he asked.

I was beyond ready. I got up and walked to the mirror. Running my fingers over the intricate work, I could barely see my scars through the ink. Kyla did an amazing job. "It's better than I could have ever imagined."

"It looks amazing. I gotta get that girl to work for me this summer. She's the real deal."

"Yeah, she is," I sighed as I looked in the mirror. Zack bandaged me up and I paid him cash for both his work and Kyla's. "Thanks. And remember, what you and I talked about stays between us."

Zack tapped on the pile of money on the counter. "My lips are sealed. Good luck getting her back. I hope this works out for you."

"Me, too."

I stayed the night at my parents' house and Chris came home on Sunday. He wanted to get our tuxes reserved for the wedding and needed help picking them out. He and Tori were getting married in June, and it was going to be here before we knew it.

We looked around the store at all the different tuxes. "Tori wants vests. What do you think?" Chris asked.

"I think you should make your woman happy. Besides, I hate those cummerbund things. Just the name is fuckin' stupid. Vests are cool. What colors is she going with?"

"Classic black and white. You know Tori. She's not frilly. She wants it classy."

"Well, that's another bonus for us. No pink or blue ties," I said.

"Thank God. Pink is really not my color." Chris laughed.

"Sooo… does Kyla know I'm the best man?" I asked tentatively.

"Yeah. She's cool with it."

"Really? I thought she was going to hate it." I was surprised because she'd shut me out so much.

Chris looked me in the eye. "Dude, that girl loves you. She's just working through some shit right now."

"So, I gathered. I wish she'd let me in. What was going on with her last weekend? She was all crying and shit on the phone. She got me worried."

Chris turned his back to look at another tux, but I got the feeling he was trying to avoid eye contact. "Just some stuff with the ex-boyfriend," he said vaguely.

Now I was starting to get pissed. "What kind of stuff? Is he harassing her?"

Chris rubbed his hand over his face. "Look. You two are both my friends. I can't betray her trust. Don't put me in that situation. She's got a handle on it. I can't say more than that."

That answer didn't satisfy me all. "Fine. I don't like it, but I get it."

"I'm sorry, man. It's just the way it's got to be." Chris pulled out a fitted tux with a vest. "What do you think about this one?"

I got the message. The conversation about Ky was over. "That's cool."

Chapter 10
Kyla

Sid was right. Once I started to forgive myself, I felt lighter. It also helped that I finally told Chris and Tori what happened. I didn't feel so alone anymore. I didn't feel like I was keeping a big secret from them, and the guilt started to wash away.

I kept getting texts from Jake. Same type of bullshit. He'd even resorted to putting notes in my car. I picked them up with tweezers and put them in plastic bags. I wanted his fingerprints all over them. I put the bags in the envelope with the picture and the letter about the personal protection order. I was collecting all the evidence I would need to take him down.

I knew he was watching me, but I was watching him too. I saw him sitting in the parking lot at the apartment. I saw him watching me while I was running. I started staking out his apartment too. I started making notes about his comings and goings, figuring out his routine. I felt like I was finally taking control of the situation. He hadn't realized yet that he had fucked with the wrong person.

My internship was going well. Michael was totally cool. He didn't treat me like some dumb college kid. He treated me with respect and listened to my ideas. I had a knack for understanding what the client wanted and delivering a product in line with their thinking. So far, I was loving it.

"Kyla, I need to see you in my office," Mr. Tolliver, Michael's boss, called to me.

I set aside what I was working on and made my way to his office. I walked in and shut the door behind me. "Have a seat, Kyla."

I didn't know what I could have possibly done wrong, but I was here to learn, and I would take any criticism with grace. Mr. Tolliver was a hard-ass and notoriously difficult to work for. I took a seat across from him and waited for the criticism I was sure was coming. "You've been working on the Infinity Jewelry Collection for Inspiration Jewelers." He stated.

I nodded my head, "Yes, sir. Is there a problem with my work?" I asked.

"No. Just the opposite. They've been very impressed with your work. A happy customer makes me a happy man," he said, although he looked anything but happy.

"That's a good thing, right?" I questioned.

"Yes. Very good. I know you've only been here a few months, but I'd like to offer you a full-time position. When you finish your internship, we'd like you to come work for us. I'm going to move you up to work under Mr. Thomas. He's our head of Internet Sales. It takes a special kind of talent to understand what a client wants without actually meeting them. I think you're ready for the challenge. I'd like to see how you do in that department."

"Wow! Thank you, Mr. Tolliver." I hadn't expected to get a job offer so soon. "I appreciate the opportunity." I stood up to leave and then turned back to face Mr. Tolliver. It was a long shot, but if I didn't ask, I wouldn't know. "Mr. Tolliver? I know this company has another office close to my hometown by

Detroit. Is there a chance I could move to that office at the end of my internship?"

Mr. Tolliver put his hand under his chin and tapped is finger against his lip. "Let's see how you do with the Internet Sales and then we can discuss that possibility. If you do a good job, it won't matter what office you work out of."

I smiled at him. "Thank you. I'll do my best."

Mr. Tolliver nodded and went back to his work. I was dismissed. I couldn't help the smile that was spreading across my face. I desperately wanted to go back home for good. I wanted to be close to my parents and do work for Zack. And I needed to get the fuck away from Jake.

I got back to the apartment after work to find Tori and Chris waiting for me.

"Happy birthday, girlfriend!" Tori hugged me. It was my first birthday without my parents, and I was sad about it. I was used to them calling me first thing in the morning on my birthday. When that call didn't come, I missed them tremendously.

Chris picked me up and spun me around. "Happy birthday, baby girl! We're taking you out tonight. Ready to do some drinking and dancing?"

Chris put me back on my feet. "Thanks guys, but really you don't have to do that. I'm fine just staying home."

Tori sidled up next to me and threw her arms around my shoulder. "Nonsense. It's Friday night and you spend way too many of those stuck in this apartment. We're leaving in two hours, so go get yourself prettied up. We're going to have some fun tonight." She backed away moving towards her bedroom. "No arguing about it. Oh, and by the way… there are two deliveries for you on the kitchen table."

I knew better than to argue with Tori. If they wanted to take me out tonight, I was going. I smiled at the thought. It would be good for me to get out. I hadn't gotten out to have fun in a long time… and it was my birthday.

I moved to the kitchen and saw two floral boxes sitting on the table. Two? One I'm sure had to be from Tyler. He'd been sending me flowers for weeks. I was surprised he hadn't texted me today, but at least he sent me flowers.

I clipped the straps on the first box and pulled off the top. It was a beautiful arrangement of wildflowers. The colors were vibrant, and the scent filled my senses. I pulled out the card and read it. *Happy Birthday, Ky! Love Always~ Tyler.* I knew he wouldn't have forgotten.

I clipped the straps on the second box and pulled the top off. My breath caught in my throat. A white lily sat inside the box. I hated lilies. They reminded me of funerals, in particular, my parents' funeral. Only a few people knew that about me, and I was pretty sure I knew who would send this to me. With shaky fingers, I opened the card. *Happy Birthday, Pretty Girl. I'll be seeing you soon. It's not over. ~J.* I dropped the card like it burned me. I specifically remembered telling Jake about my aversion to lilies. Was this a threat? And what did *I'll be seeing you soon* mean? Was he getting ready to make his move?

I quickly picked up the lily and threw it in the garbage, along with the card. I would have to be extra vigilant. That fucker was a dead man.

I dressed in black jeans and a black fitted T-shirt that covered the tattoo on my chest. I had just touched up the color on my hair a few days before and the purple highlights were super bright. I wasn't so sure I liked it when I first colored my hair, but

I loved it now. I threw it into a messy updo and clipped in my silver hoop earrings. I finished applying my dark eyeliner and several coats of mascara. I looked in the mirror and my bright green eyes popped with the dark makeup. I looked so different than I had a few months ago.

I checked my purse before leaving, making sure both my pepper spray and gun were tucked inside. I knew it was illegal to have a gun while drinking, but at this point I didn't care. I had to be ready no matter what.

We got to the bar and grabbed a table. Tori and I ordered our drinks and Chris ordered two beers. I didn't think much about it until the waitress brought our drinks. Chris slid one of the beers in front of the empty chair next to me. "Expecting company?" I questioned.

"Yeah. One of my friends is going to meet us up here," he answered.

I nodded my head and took a sip of my drink. I hoped this wasn't going to be an attempt to set me up with someone, because honestly, I wasn't interested. I needed to focus on my job and the other issues with Jake. I just wanted to have fun tonight and not be sucked into idle conversation. Plus, my heart still belonged to Tyler. His gift from Christmas hung around my neck as a reminder of what I wanted most.

"As a matter of fact, he just walked in," Chris announced. I turned my head in the direction Chris was looking. What I saw took my breath away.

"You didn't?" I exclaimed.

Chris got a smirk on his face. "What? He's my friend and I invited him."

He strolled toward the table with his dimples on full display. He looked so good in that tight black T-shirt that pulled across the muscles of his chest and those jeans that fit his ass perfectly. I laid my arms on the table and set my head down, shaking it back and forth. I lifted my head and looked at Tori. "You guys suck."

"I'm sorry, but you two need a little push. You both love each other. Stop fighting it."

I gave her the evil eye and downed the rest of my drink. I motioned to the waitress, and she came over to our table. "I'll have another, and I think we're going to need some shots. Four, tequila."

The waitress left, and Tyler sat down in the empty chair. He hadn't seen me since I colored my hair and he looked at me, appraising my new look. He ran his fingers through the strands coming out of the clip on top of my head. I squinted at him with my darkly lined eyes. "Happy Birthday, Ky. You look beautiful. Different, but beautiful." I saw his eyes drop to my chest where his necklace sat.

"Thank you," I said breathlessly. I looked away and squeezed my eyes shut as my insides fluttered to life. Damn him for having this effect on me. I couldn't fall back into him. Not this fast. I needed to put some space between us. "Will you excuse me for a minute?" I got up from the table and rushed to the bathroom. I felt his eyes on me as I hurried away.

I got to the bathroom and leaned on the counter trying to pull it together. Looking in the mirror, my cheeks and neck were flushed. Why would Chris and Tori do this to me? I worked so hard to chase him from my mind until I was ready. One minute in his presence and I was already a mess. My eyes began to water, and I took deep calming breaths.

Tori came in and stood next to me. "You alright?"

I nodded my head. "A little warning would have been nice. I wasn't ready for that."

"I know it's been a long time, but you need him. And he needs you. That boy is so in love with you. And you know you love him too."

"I do, but this shit with Jake..." I started.

"May never happen. Just try and be happy."

"I'm trying, but this shit with Jake is not done." I looked at Tori. "That second flower box was from Jake. He sent me a lily. A fucking lily. A fucking funeral flower. Does that sound like he's done?"

Tori's eyes went wide. "No... I'm sorry. But please just try to enjoy tonight."

"I will, but... fuck!" I wiped under my eyes and pulled myself together. "Let's go."

When we got back to the table Chris and Ty were laughing and having a good time. Our drinks had arrived, and I passed the shots around the table. I raised my glass and made a toast. "To good friends." Everyone clinked glasses and Ty watched me as I downed the tequila and sucked the lime into my mouth. I was going to need a few more of those. I signaled to the waitress to bring another round.

I couldn't breathe with his eyes on me. I was suffocating. I wanted to be with him so bad, but at the same time I was afraid to let him touch me. My heart knew I was safe with Ty. My mind was a different matter. What if I freaked out when he touched me? I couldn't let that happen.

I looked at Tori. "I'm going to step out front to have a smoke."

Chris looked at me and I saw the tension in his jaw. He lifted his chin. "Tori, go with her." Ty just looked confused as to what was going on.

I rolled my eyes and got up from the table taking my purse with me. Tori followed me out front, and I leaned against the wall. Lighting my cigarette, I inhaled deeply. Instantly, the calm washed over me. I looked at Tor. "Call your guard dog off. Tyler's totally going to know something's going on."

"Then you calm down! You're acting erratic. Pull your shit together! It's fucking Ty for God's sake. How are you going to handle the wedding if you can't handle this?"

I inhaled again and blew the smoke out through my nose. "I'm trying, but you two threw me into this." I looked out into the parking lot, staring at nothing, when bright lights shined in my eyes. I put my hand up to shield them but couldn't see anything. I stubbed out my cigarette and headed back in. "I'll handle it." I opened the door and popped a mint in my mouth.

I sat back down and saw our shots had arrived. I picked mine up and threw it back, sucking on the lime. I turned to Tyler. "How's your shoulder doing?"

"It's pretty much all healed. I've been in physical therapy, so that helps. I should be back throwing the ball in a few months."

"What about the draft?" I asked, downing the shot he had left on the table.

"I'm going to miss it. No one would draft me in this condition."

I frowned. "So now what? You've worked too hard for this to just let it go." My heart hurt for him. I hadn't thought about the implications of his injury on his dreams. I'd been too self-consumed to think about anyone but myself.

"I'm going to finish my business management degree and get a personal trainer. I'm hoping to be ready as a free agent next year. I'm not giving up." Then his blue eyes pierced mine. "I'm never giving up on what I love."

I swallowed the lump in my throat as I caught his meaning.

"How's your internship going?" Ty asked.

"Really good!" I explained to him what I was doing there and that they had already offered me a job when I graduated. I told him about my hopes to move back home. Tyler hung on every word. He was genuinely interested in what I was saying. Everything started to feel so... normal again. I relaxed back into that special place that Ty and I always shared. It was a comfort I never felt with anyone else.

Ty excused himself and walked over to the DJ. When he came back to the table, he held out his hand. "Dance with me?"

I nodded my head and let him lead me out to the dance floor. Immediately, "Far Away" started playing. I put my hand over my mouth and tears filled my eyes. "How did you know?" I asked, barely getting the words out.

"I know you," he whispered in my ear. I put one hand on his shoulder as he clasped my other hand and pulled it to his chest. His arm circled around my waist pulling me in close. I inhaled his cologne and I felt like I was home. We swayed to the music and I snuggled into his warmth.

Tyler kissed the top of my head and looked down at my face. Our eyes were pinned to each other. His blue to my green and everything else melted away. I felt a tear run down my face. "I love you, Kyla. I'm sorry for everything I've ever done to you. Give me a chance to make it right. It's only ever been you."

"I love you too. I've never stopped, but I need to go slow."

"Just like the first time, I'll wait for you. I'll wait as long as it takes." Tyler bent down and pressed his lips to mine. It was slow and sensual. I opened my mouth and let his tongue in to tangle with mine. I didn't care that we were in the middle of the dance floor. It was as if the rest of the world disappeared, and it was just the two of us.

When the song ended, I made my way to the bathroom. I finished up and washed my hands, then fixed my makeup. I was so in love with Tyler. My heart began to swell and for the first time in so long, I felt hope growing inside me. Hope that we could be happy again.

I opened the bathroom door and turned to walk back to the table when a hand grabbed my arm, and I was dragged back into the dark hallway. I was pushed against the wall with such force that it knocked the wind out of me. My eyes began to focus in the darkness, and I saw Jake towering above me. Fear began to creep in, and I realized I had left my purse at the table. I never thought he would come after me in a crowded bar. I misjudged him.

Jake pinned my shoulders to the wall, and he leaned down close to my face. "What the fuck do you think you're doing? I thought you and the football star were done. Did you forget you belong to me?" His breath reeked of alcohol and his eyes were black as coal. "Do I need to remind you? Do I need to fuck that pussy again? Take what's mine?"

His words fueled me, and my fear was replaced with rage. I smiled at him and spoke sweetly, "You don't need to remind me of anything. I'll give you exactly what you deserve." Then I reared my knee up and hit him square in the balls. "Go to hell, motherfucker!" His grip on my shoulders released and I slipped away, leaving him in the hallway holding his dick in his hands.

As I hurried away, I heard him say, "You're dead, bitch!"

I rushed back toward the table and caught Tori on her way to the bathroom. I grabbed her arm and pulled her to the side. "Jake's here. He just cornered me in the hallway and threatened me. I wanna go home."

"Shit! Shit! Shit! Okay I'll text Chris and tell him we need to go." Tori pulled out her phone and typed out a quick text to Chris.

We walked back to the table and Chris shot us a look of concern. "You alright?"

Tori put her hand on her head. "Yeah, I'm just getting a massive headache. Do you guys mind if we move this back to the apartment?"

"No that's fine." I had to give them credit. They we're playing this off perfect. Chris turned to Tyler, "You still staying the night?"

What? He was staying the night? In our apartment?

Tyler looked at me questioningly. "If that's still alright? I really don't want to drive back tonight."

I'm sure the shock on my face was evident. "Of course. It's no biggie."

"Do you want to drive with me?" he asked.

"Sure." I looked over my shoulder to the hallway I had just come from. Jake was standing there staring daggers at us. Tyler reached for my hand. I willingly took it, and he led me out to the parking lot. He opened the door for me, and I got in the car.

I loved Tyler's black Challenger. It held so many memories for me. Our first kiss. All the times we made out in the back seat. The first time he made me come. Our trip Up North that first summer. Just the smell of this car took me down memory lane.

Tyler hopped into the driver's seat and started the engine. It rumbled to life, and we headed back to my apartment. He reached over the console and took my hand. "Are you okay?"

"Yeah... I was just thinking about all the action the backseat of this car has seen. We did a lot of fooling around back there."

"Yeah, we did." He picked up my hand and kissed the back of it. "Are you sure you're okay with me staying the night? I'll sleep on the couch."

"It'll be fine. You know... it's not that I don't want to be with you. I do. It's all I've ever wanted. It's just that I can't jump feet first into what we had before. I need to know it's real. Cutting you off was one of the hardest things I've ever done, but I had to do it for me. No matter how much it hurt."

"I know. I was an asshole. I don't blame you. I want to start again to build your trust in me."

"I want that too."

Later that night, Tyler was set up on the couch to sleep. I laid in my bed. Alone. I couldn't sleep knowing he was out there sleeping in the other room. Even the Xanax wasn't helping. Every time I closed my eyes I thought about our dance and the kiss we shared. I hadn't felt that loved and complete in such a long time. I ached for it.

After an hour, I couldn't take it anymore. I threw back the covers and tiptoed out to the front room. I peeked over the couch and looked at Ty, sleeping there in his T-shirt and shorts. He opened his eyes. "Why aren't you sleeping?" he asked.

"I couldn't. How did you know I was here? I tried to be quiet," I whispered.

"I could smell you. I've missed that coconut shit you always use. Besides, I couldn't sleep either."

I walked around the couch and sat down by his feet. "What are you thinking about?"

"Us. How much I miss you. What I should have done different. How I wish I was in your bed instead of being on this couch."

I dropped my head and my hair fell over my face. "I can't have sex with you." I wanted to, but I didn't trust myself.

Tyler sat up and pushed my hair out of my face and over my shoulder. "I don't want to have sex with you. I mean… I do, but that's not what I meant. I just want to hold you in my arms, feel you next to me."

I looked up at him from under my long lashes and reached out my hand to him. "Come on."

Tyler took my hand, and I led him back to my room.

Chapter 11
Tyler

I slipped between the sheets on Kyla's bed and patted the space next to me. She crawled up next to me and nestled into my chest. I wrapped my arms around her tightly because I didn't want to let go.

We laid there in the dark snuggled together. I still couldn't sleep, and I knew she couldn't either. I felt like there was so much we didn't know about each other. She was right, we needed to start over. I spoke into the darkness. "Can I ask you some questions?"

"Depends. What do you want to know?" she asked.

"I saw your pill bottle last summer when I was at your house. What's the Xanax for?"

She sighed. "I had a really hard time after I lost our baby. It keeps the nightmares away."

"Do you still have nightmares?" I asked.

"Yes, but not about that."

"What are they about?"

"Pass. Next question."

"Fair enough. Tell me about your hair. Why did you change it?"

"You don't like it?" she asked in return.

"I didn't say that. Your blond was beautiful, but no matter what color it is, you'll always be beautiful to me."

Kyla squeezed her arms tighter around me. "It won't make sense to you." I gave her a squeeze back and encouraged her to continue. "The blond made me vulnerable. People saw me as weak. The black makes me feel stronger. In control of something."

She was right. It didn't make sense to me. "You're right. I don't get it."

"That's okay because it makes sense to me."

I played with ends of her long hair. "Who are the flowers in the trash from?"

"Pass. My turn. I gave you everything. Why wasn't I enough for you? Why all the other girls?"

"Jeez. Talk about going for the balls." I let out a nervous laugh. "Ky, you were always enough. I was trying to forget you, but it never worked. It was always you I wanted underneath me. Your eyes I wanted to look into."

"Then why did you keep pushing me away?"

"Because I was a stupid guy. It took you shutting me out to realize what I lost. I haven't been with anyone since that day. And when I broke my shoulder... I realized you were the only one I wanted by my side. Ever."

She trembled in my arms. I slipped my hand under her shirt and rubbed small circles on her back. "Why did you buy me this necklace?"

"Because my love for you is infinite. Our two hearts will be connected forever. I wanted you to know how I felt about you." I placed her hand over the tattoo on my chest. "We loved with a love that was more than love."

"We did," she said.

"And we can again. Why are you wearing it tonight?"

"I always wear it."

"Always?" I asked.

"Always," she said.

"I want to kiss you again."

Kyla raised her head from my chest and looked at me. "So, kiss me," she said breathlessly.

I pulled her up to me and pressed my lips to hers. They were soft and sweet, just like the rest of my girl. I rolled Kyla to her back, so I hovered over her. Her hands went to my hair as I stared into her eyes. She pulled me in and parted her lips. I ran my tongue along the seam of her lips and then slipped it inside her mouth. Our kiss was gentle at first and then became feverish. We couldn't get enough of each other.

Kyla's hands slipped under my shirt, and she ran her long, black nails up and down my back. I rolled her to the side and slipped my hands under her shirt. I ran them over her stomach, up the sides of her body, and up her back. The fire was burning inside me, and I fought to keep my hands PG. My dick hardened from the thought of being inside her again. "Baby, I really want you. I want to make love to you."

I heard a soft gasp come from her throat. "I want that too, but… I just can't. This is all I can give you right now."

"It's enough," I whispered and kissed her forehead. I pulled her back up against me. She snuggled into my chest and sighed.

"I need more time."

"I'll give you whatever you need. I love you, Kyla. Sweet dreams, baby." I closed my eyes with her wrapped tightly in my arms. I didn't know what she was afraid of. Why she was holding back. I just knew that having her in my arms again was the best feeling in the world. I wanted to spend the rest of my life holding her and keeping her safe.

I woke to the sun shining through the blinds. Kyla was snuggled into me, and I had to remind myself this wasn't a dream. We were really together, and I couldn't have been happier.

I felt her stretching out next to me. She lifted her head and put her chin on my chest. "Good morning," she said in a raspy voice. It was sexy as hell. Her hair was a mess, and her face was clean of makeup. She was beautiful. "When are you leaving?" she asked.

I smiled down at her. "Are you trying to kick me out?"

Kyla flopped her head back down on my chest. "God, no. I was just wondering how long I had you for."

"As long as you want. I don't have anywhere I need to be, except right here."

"Mmmm. That sounds nice. What do you want to do today?"

"I don't know. Want to go for a run and we can stop at that place you like to get your fancy-ass coffee," I asked.

She giggled. "Hey, I like that fancy-ass coffee."

I kissed the top of her head. "Yeah, I know. Come on, let's get up."

We crawled out from under the sheets, and I helped her make the bed. She stopped and stared at me. I followed her eyes to my tented shorts. I shrugged, "Sorry. You can't expect me to lay in bed with you all night and not be affected."

She held a pillow in her hands and bit her lip. "I'm sorry. I didn't mean to… do that to you."

I walked over and pulled her lip from under her teeth. "Then you can't bite your lip like that. You know it drives me crazy." I rubbed her arms up and down. "I spent the first seven months we were together like this. I can handle it."

I looked closely at her face. I hadn't noticed it last night in the dark, but in the light of day, with no makeup, I saw it. I ran my finger over a fine-lined scar on her right cheek. "How'd you get this?"

Her fingers went up to touch her cheek and she turned her head away. "It's nothing."

She was hiding something. "It's not nothing. Kyla, how'd you get a fucking scar on your face?"

Her voice was quiet, almost a whisper, "I said it was nothing."

Now I was getting pissed. What the fuck was going on? I grabbed her by the shoulders and turned her to face me. "What the fuck happened?" I roared. "Did someone fucking hit you?"

Then I saw it. The fear in her eyes. She started hitting at my hands and pushing me away, like I was going to hurt her. "Stop! Just stop!" she screamed.

I let go of her. She ran to the bathroom and locked herself in. I followed her to the bathroom and put my ear to the door. I could hear her breathing hard and crying. *What the hell just happened?*

I stalked across the hall to Chris and Tori's room and banged on the door. I didn't wait for an answer. I just barged in. Chris was on top of Tori going at it, but at least the sheets covered them. I turned my back, but I wasn't leaving.

"Fuck, dude! Seriously?" Chris scrambled around pulling his boxers on. He picked up a shirt from the floor and tossed it to Tori. "Get dressed, baby."

I waited a minute then turned to face my best friend. "What the fuck happened to her?"

Chris's face fell, and Tori's eyes got big. "What do you mean?" he asked.

"I mean she's got a scar on her face that she won't tell me about! Did someone fucking hit her? I pressed her to tell me, and she freaked the fuck out on me. Hitting me and telling me to stop. She's locked herself in the bathroom."

"Oh shit!" Tori scrambled from the bed and ran across the hall to Kyla.

Chris rubbed his hand over his face. "Have a seat." He pointed to the chair in the corner.

Having a seat was the last thing I wanted to do, but I needed answers. I sat down and leaned my arms on my legs. "What the fuck happened to her?"

"What'd she tell you?"

"Nothing. She just freaked out. I saw it. The fear in her eyes. Like I was going to hurt her."

"Did you touch her? Raise your voice to her?"

"I grabbed her by the shoulders and yeah, I was pissed that she wouldn't tell me. What is going on? How'd she get the scar? Did someone hit her?"

Chris took a deep breath. "Yeah, someone hit her."

I felt the rage boiling up inside me. "Who?"

"Remember I told you there was something I didn't like about the ex-boyfriend. When she broke up with him, he beat her up. Bad. It happened over Christmas. Tori and I were back home planning the wedding and we didn't know. We just found out not that long ago."

"Why the fuck didn't you tell me?" I couldn't believe he would keep this a secret from me.

"She made us promise not to. She didn't want you to know. She was embarrassed and ashamed. She said she was going to tell you in her own time. I had to respect that. She's been handling it on her own."

I motioned to Kyla's bedroom, "That's handling it?"

"That's the first time she's freaked out that I know of. You should go talk to her."

"Yeah, I should." I started to walk away, then turned back to Chris. "Sorry about barging in here."

"It's all right. It's not like you've never seen my ass before."

"Yeah, but I was trying to forget about it. It's all hairy and shit." I laughed.

Chris picked up a shirt and threw it at me. "Get the fuck outta here."

I went to the kitchen, where Tori was making coffee. "Where is she?" I asked. Tori motioned to the back slider. I opened the door and sat next to my girl.

She had her bare feet pulled up on the chair and her chin rested on her knees. Her eyes were red from crying, as she stared off. She inhaled on her cigarette like it was the air she needed to breathe. "I'm not good for you. I'm not good for anyone. Thank you for coming for my birthday, but you should leave. You don't need this."

"I'm not leaving. You can't push me away anymore. I won't let you."

She took another drag and turned to me. "Are you fucking insane? You saw what just happened. I'm not right. I can't even trust myself. How could you trust me?"

"I trust you. There's no one I trust more. I'm sorry I scared you back there. You know I'd never hurt you, right?"

"I know it in here," she said pointing at her heart. "It's up here," she pointed to her head, "that's having the problem."

"Tell me about the guy who hit you," I said calmly.

"Why? What did Chris tell you?" she asked.

"Not much. Chris said when you broke up with him that he beat you up pretty bad. Is that true?" I needed to hear it from her.

She dropped her head and looked at her bare feet. "Yeah. His name is Jake. At first, I thought he took it really good, but I was wrong. He came back the next day, Christmas Eve, and did this to me." She touched the scar on her cheek. "I wasn't expecting it. He was sweet to me when we started dating. I trusted him. I should have never trusted him," she said shaking her head.

That was where her shame came from. The fact that she was trusting. "Is that why you wouldn't open the door for me at Christmas?"

Kyla nodded her head. "I couldn't let you see me like that. I wanted to open the door so bad, but I couldn't. I didn't want you to know."

"You could have told me."

"We weren't together. It was my problem. My failure. My embarrassment."

"You shouldn't be embarrassed. You were a victim," I said.

Something inside of her flipped. "Don't use that word with me. I've been working on myself for months now. I'm not a victim and I won't be a victim again." She took another hit off her smoke.

"Okay, Ky. Talk to me. It's over with him. I would never, ever hurt you like that."

"I know you wouldn't. You never have. But something in me just snapped and it was like I was back there again. I can't believe I did that you. I'm sorry." Kyla reached over and took my hand. "Are you sure you want to deal with this? I can't promise it won't happen again. I'm giving you an out. I would totally understand."

I pulled her over to me and sat her on my lap. I pushed her hair back and ran my finger down the side of her face, over the scar on her cheek. "I'm a big boy. I can handle it. I've let you deal with too many things on your own. It's not happening anymore. You're the most important person in my life. I'm not letting you go over something like this."

She rested her head on my shoulder. "Do you think we can really do it? Go back to being us?"

I rubbed my hand up and down her back. "Yeah, I do." I cupped her face with my hands and kissed her deeply and tenderly. "Let's get out of here. You still want to go running?"

"Yes. I need it. Let me go change. I'll be ready in five."

Kyla got off my lap and I tapped her on the ass. I followed her inside and went to the kitchen. "How is she?" Tori asked.

"She's good. I want to come back here for the next couple of weekends. Would you and Chris be cool with that?"

"Yeah, as long as you don't walk in on us having sex again." She smiled at me over her coffee cup. "I really want this to work for you guys. She won't admit it, but she needs you."

"I need her too." I grabbed my duffle bag off the floor. "And... sorry about this morning." I headed to the bathroom to change. I pulled off my shirt and looked in the mirror at the tattoo crawling up my arm. I didn't know when I was going to tell her about it. It seemed that we both had secrets from each other. I still hadn't told her about my Harley or my trust fund. And I was pretty sure there was more to the story about the ex-boyfriend. I would bet the flowers in the trash were from him.

I brushed my teeth, put on a clean shirt and shorts, and made my way to the front room. Kyla was sitting on the couch tying her shoes. Her hair was slicked back in a ponytail, and she looked reenergized. "Do you need ear buds, or do you have a set?" she asked.

I pulled some out of my bag and plugged them into my phone. "I'm all set. Am I going to be able to keep up with you? I've only been running again for a couple of months and it's usually on the treadmill," I teased.

Ky stood up and bumped me with her shoulder. "I'm sure it won't be a problem. I always used to slow you down. I've got short legs, remember?" She kicked her leg out and held it up.

I reached down, picked her up underneath those legs and held her in my arms. "I love those short, little legs. They're adorable." I kissed her and placed her back on her feet. "You lead the way since this is your town."

We did a few stretches and then she started down the sidewalk. By the time we made it to the first corner, Kyla had picked up the pace considerably. I could see her lips moving as she sang the words to whatever song was playing on her phone. She ran like the devil himself were chasing her. I could see the determination on her face as she pushed herself harder. I had been only kidding about being able to keep up with her, but she was faster than I remembered.

About five miles later, we slowed to a stop in front of the coffee shop. Kyla shook out her legs and walked back and forth with her hands crossed on top of her head. We were both breathing hard and trying to catch our breath. "Damn girl. I'm impressed. I haven't run with you in forever. Those little legs are fast."

"Well, I run almost every day now. It's a great stress reliever."

"I'm surprised your lungs can take it since you started smoking." I hadn't said much about her smoking. It bothered me less than I thought it would. She wasn't one of those girls that reeked of cigarettes. In fact, I barely smelled it on her at all.

She put her hands on her hips. "I wondered when you were going to say something about that. It's not what you think. I only smoke when I'm feeling stressed or sad or mad. If a cigarette once in a while makes me feel calmer, then so be it. It's no different than you having a beer."

I held up my hands in surrender. "I'm not criticizing. It really doesn't bother me."

She quirked her eyebrow at me. "Really? I expected a big fight about it."

"Nope. We started dating when we were seventeen. It makes sense that some things were going to change. We're not the same people we were then. I mean... I'm not crazy about it, but I can live with it."

"Okay. Well, maybe when I get my life pulled back together, I'll quit." She pulled the front of her shirt up to wipe the sweat from her face. I saw the butterflies peeking out from under it.

She started to drop her shirt back down. "Wait!" I touched her stomach. "Can I see?" She pulled her shirt back up. I ran my hand on her back, along her side, and up onto her ribs. "It's beautiful, Ky. You drew this, right?" She nodded her head. "It's like they're flying right off your skin. It's so detailed." I wanted to run kisses up and down her skin, but then she pulled her shirt down.

"Thank you. I kind of love it," she said. "Coffee?"

I ordered my black coffee and her Carmel Frappuccino. We took them to sit at a table out in front of the café. It was a warm spring day and both of us wanted to be outside to enjoy it.

"I can't believe we're going to graduate in a month," Kyla said with a sigh.

"I know. What are your plans after that?" I asked.

"Well, I want to move back home. I'm actually really anxious to get out of here. I want to rent a condo on the water, so I can look out at the lake every day."

I took her hand across the table. "Ky... I want to move back home with you. We've spent too much time apart. I want to live together."

Kyla's eyes went big with shock. "Do you think we're ready for that? I mean we're just getting back on track. That's a big step. I feel like we hardly know each other anymore. Don't you think we should ease back into this a little bit? What if I freak out on you again and you decide it's not what you want?"

"I already know this is what I want. I want you in my life. Forever. Nothing is going to change that. I tried to live without you, and I was miserable." Kyla's eyes started to get teary as I proclaimed my love for her. "If you're not ready to live together, I get that. But I don't want to be so far away from you anymore. What if I found us condos in the same complex? That way we could see each other every day and work on our relationship, but still have our own space."

A tear rolled down her cheek and I brushed it away with my thumb. "That sounds perfect," she said. "Are you sure this is what you want?" She bit her lip again and I pulled it out.

"I'm sure. I told you I'd wait for you. I'll do whatever it takes to get you back. I want to stay with you on the weekends until we graduate. I want to get to know each other again. Get us back to where we were before everything fell apart. I'm going to take care of you."

"I love you, Ty. Yes! Yes, to all of it."

"When we get back to the apartment we can start looking online for condos."

"What are you going to do when we move back home? I mean for a job?"

"You know my Uncle Lou, that had the landscaping company?" She nodded her head. "He's kind of an entrepreneur. He's opening a nightclub and wants me to work with him on the start-up. He already bought a building, but I would be in charge of reconstruction, hiring a staff, and getting it up and running. Of course, he'd have the final say on everything, but I think it'd be kind of cool. It's a big undertaking, but I think I could do it. Besides, you know I can't sit in an office all day. This would give me the flexibility to work with my trainer too. I am going to be ready next year. I've got to give pro football one more try."

"The nightclub thing sounds cool, but if you make it to the pros, where will that leave us?" she questioned.

"What do you mean?"

"I mean we'll be apart again. I don't think I can handle that."

"We're never going to be apart again. I want you to come with me. You said yourself that if this internet thing works out for your graphic design you could work from anywhere. Hell, you could start your own company."

"It all sounds so overwhelming." Kyla looked nervous and I knew her mind was going a mile a minute. She was a planner, and this plan wasn't all neat and organized the way she liked things.

I took both her hands in mine and kissed them. "Yeah, it does. But it's a year away, Ky. We both know how much things can change in a year. Take a chance with me. Baby steps. Let's start by finding a place to live."

She nodded her head. "Okay."

Chapter 12
Kyla

Ty and I ran back toward the apartment. My head was spinning. Everything was happening so fast, even though I had promised myself I was going to take it slow. I wanted to be back with Tyler more than anything. He was where I felt safe and loved.

But at the same time, I could never feel safe until I knew this thing with Jake was over. Him cornering me last night at the bar unnerved me. His words *Do I need to remind you? Do I need to fuck that pussy again? Take what's mine?* made my skin crawl and my blood boil. He was never going to leave me alone until I ended him. It had been three months and he was still stalking me.

Last night I wanted to make love to Tyler. I wanted to feel what I knew only he could provide. If he stayed tonight, maybe I could give a little more. I desperately wanted more, but I was afraid that when he touched me, I would freak out on him again. I couldn't believe that I had done that to him today. I acted like a crazy person. And still, he stayed.

Not only did he stay, but he still wanted me. Wanted more. He wanted to live together. When I first got pregnant, I wanted that more than anything. To start our life together. But now, I was afraid. Afraid that this thing with Jake would never end. Afraid that things wouldn't work out. Afraid that I wouldn't be able to give myself to Tyler completely. Afraid he would leave me again.

Financially, it would make sense for us to move into together. We would probably spend most of our time together anyway, but it was just too much, too fast. Maybe after six months, we could move in together, if everything went well.

I was so in my own head, that I didn't even realize we were back to the apartment. As we rounded the corner to the parking lot, I saw a familiar car in the corner. *Fuck!* I must have really pissed him off last night. It didn't take long for my phone to buzz. I looked down and read the text:

Jake: Did you fuck him last night?

For the first time, I replied. I quickly tapped out:

Kyla: Maybe! He fucks better than you!

I looked up and saw his car squealing out of the parking lot. I felt a sense of satisfaction in my reply.

"You okay?" Tyler questioned, while watching the car pull away.

"Yeah. Why?" I asked.

"Because you have a pissed off look on your face," he said.

"Just something I don't feel like dealing with," I said, honestly. We finished stretching and moved inside. "I really need to shower. How about I go first and then I'll make us some lunch?"

"That sounds good," he said. "Can I use your computer? I want to start looking at what's available for condos back home."

"Yeah. It's on my desk. Help yourself. I'm just going to grab some clothes and then you can shower after me." Ty followed me to my room, and I started to gather my things. Before going to the shower, I asked, "Are you staying here tonight?"

"Do you want me to?"

"Yes, if you can."

"Then, I'm staying."

I walked over to him and placed a gentle kiss on his lips. "Good." I went to take a shower and left Tyler in my room. I stripped out of my clothes and stepped into the hot water. I couldn't help but think about the last time we showered together and how Tyler took care of me. The heat began to pool between my legs and desire consumed me. When I finished washing myself, I removed the showerhead from the wall to rinse. My hands went down to my clit, and I got lost in the feeling, imagining Tyler's hands on me. Before I knew it, the pressure was building inside of me, taking me higher. I gave into the feeling and let myself fall over the edge in ecstasy. God, I needed him so bad. If I could just get my head to cooperate with my heart.

I quickly dried off and got dressed. I opened the bathroom door and went to my room, where Ty was busy on my computer. I tried to calm myself so that he wouldn't know what I had just done. "Your turn," I announced.

"Ky, I saw this short cut on your computer. I hope you don't mind, but I looked at your portfolio. This stuff is really good. I'm totally impressed."

I waved him off. "That's mostly things I had to do for my classes. It's nothing really."

"No, it is something. I was thinking, how would you like to do the promotional stuff for the club? You know, design the logo and all that."

"Ty, I'm not a professional. I'm just getting started. I'm sure your uncle would prefer someone with some experience."

"Well, think about it. I think this stuff is good enough and I get to call the shots. Remember?"

"I'll think about it. Your turn for the shower. Pull out anything you want washed and throw it outside the door."

"Kyla, you don't have to do my laundry. I can do it when I get home."

"I'm going to do laundry anyway, so it's no big deal. I'll just throw your stuff in with mine. There's really no reason for you to take home a bunch of dirty clothes."

"Okay." He got up and moved to the bathroom, taking his duffle bag with him.

I gathered my clothes from the hamper and threw them in the laundry basket. I suddenly remembered that I hadn't given Ty a clean towel for his shower. I grabbed one from the linen closet, made my way back to the bathroom, and opened the door. "Hey, I forgot to give you…" I froze as I saw Ty's naked body standing there. I quickly looked away. "Oh my God, I'm so sorry."

He grabbed my arm and pulled me inside, shutting the door behind me. "It's not like you've never seen me before," he said.

I covered my eyes. "Yeah, but I should have knocked." I held the towel out so that it covered him from my sight. I felt the blush creeping up my cheeks.

"I don't care if you see me," he said. I uncovered my eyes and focused on his chest as he took the towel from my hands.

I looked at the tattoo on his chest and then let my eyes wander over the rest of his body. What was on his shoulder, floored me. I reached out and touched his arm. "It was you?" I didn't know whether to be pissed or flattered. I ran my fingers over the dragon that crawled up his arm and over his shoulder.

"Looks pretty cool, huh?"

"Yeah, it's better than I ever imagined. Zack did a great job." I admired the work, then narrowed my eyebrows at him. "You paid me a thousand dollars for that. I can't take your money."

"Kyla, it's my money. I can spend it on whatever I want. It was important to me to have you design it."

"You could have just asked me. I would have done it for free. How can you even afford that?" I knew Ty's family had money, but a grand for a tattoo design was excessive.

"Are you mad?"

"I'm not mad. It's flattering, actually. I love seeing it on you. It's kind of sexy knowing I designed something that will be on your body forever, but I don't understand."

"I'll explain everything after I shower," he promised.

"I can't wait to hear it." I bent down to pick up his dirty clothes from the floor and then realized I was right in front of his hard cock. I quickly grabbed his clothes and hurried out of the bathroom. I leaned back against the door and tried to calm myself. What was wrong with me? I had seen Ty a million times, but today I was blushing like a virgin. The heat pooled between my legs again. I really needed to rein it in.

I made my way to the laundry room and started our wash. Then, I went to the fridge and gathered what I needed to make chicken salad. I started boiling the eggs and chopping the chicken. By the time I finished putting everything together, Ty came into the kitchen freshly showered and changed. He came up behind me and wrapped his arms around my waist, pressing soft kisses along my neck. "I love you," he said.

I turned in his arms. "I'm giving you your money back. I can't take it."

"Yes, you can. If we're going to be together, then it's our money."

"But..." Ty put his fingers to my lips to silence me.

"You're keeping it. End of story. I have plenty."

"Do your parents know this is what you're spending money on?" I protested.

"It's not my parents' money. It's mine."

Now I was really confused. As far as I knew, Ty never had a job while we were away at college. "I don't understand."

He led me to the couch and sat me down. "Kyla, last year, I found out I had a trust fund that my grandfather left me. It became mine when I turned twenty-one."

A trust fund? That explained it a little bit, but still. "I can't take your money. Your grandfather left that for you. You shouldn't waste it on something like this." I pointed to his arm.

"Baby, it was a lot of money and I'll spend it how I want. Like I said, it's our money."

"But a thousand dollars? That's ridiculous. It was fine when I thought I was taking it from a stranger, but I can't take it from you."

Tyler took my face in his hands and placed a kiss on my lips. "The trust fund was two million. I can take care of you."

I pulled away. "Dollars? Oh my, God!" I tried to process how much money that was. I shook my head. "This doesn't change anything. I have my own money. I mean, it's not even close to that, but I can pay my own way."

"I know you can but let me spoil you a little bit."

I didn't know what to say. I thought about it and made my decision. "Fine, I'll take the money for the design, but no more."

"That's fine, but eventually it will be yours. I want you to be happy."

"Ty, you're all I need to make me happy."

Later that night, we got ready for bed. Tyler sleeping on the couch wasn't even an option. I needed him in my bed with me. I brushed my teeth and took my Xanax. Now that I knew about his tattoo, Ty didn't wear a shirt to bed. He was sexy as could be. I couldn't wait to snuggle into his warm chest and feel his skin against mine.

I crawled into bed next to him and turned out the light. "I love you," I whispered into the dark. I wrapped my arms around his wide chest and laid my head on it. I felt the steady rise and fall of his breathing and a sense of calm washed over me as I imagined what it would be like to spend the rest of my life like this.

I raised my head from his chest and moved up to place a soft kiss on his lips. His arm went around me and pulled me in close. We deepened the kiss as I ran my hands up and down his body. I loved this man more than anything.

Tyler's hand went up under my tank to rub along the skin of my back. I needed to feel him skin on skin. I hesitantly reached for the hem of my tank and lifted it up over my head. I laid my breasts against his warm skin and sighed.

"You okay, baby?" he questioned, as he continued to rub my back.

"Yes. This feels nice." I was content. "I really enjoyed spending the day with you today."

"Me, too," he said as he kissed the top of my head. "Ky?"

"Hmmm?"

"Can you tell me about your tattoos now? You promised you'd tell me someday. They're beautiful and I want to know what they mean to you."

I sat up and switched the bedside light on. I kept my back facing him. I crossed my left arm over my breasts and touched the design on my left shoulder with the other hand. "The two hearts represent how love connects two people. It's for the love my parents shared, the love I had with you, and the love I had for our baby. The roses that surround the hearts represent the beauty that love brings and the thorns..." I turned my head over my shoulder to look at him, "...the pain. The thorns piercing the hearts are for each time my heart bled because of love."

Tyler ran his fingers over the design. "One for your parents, one for our baby, and one because of me."

I nodded my head. "I was so lost when everyone left me." I blinked away the tears in my eyes.

He placed soft kisses along my shoulder. "I'm sorry. I'm sorry I wasn't there for you. I'm here for you now, and I want to take away the pain and the sadness. I want to stop the bleeding."

"You already are," I whispered. I turned over my right wrist with the purple infinity symbol. "This is because my love for you is infinite."

Ty kissed the inside of my wrist, then placed his hand on the lower right side of my back over the heart. "And this one?"

"What do you think it means?" I asked quietly.

I heard him take a deep breath. "I think the flaming heart is us. The way we burned for each other." I nodded, and he continued. "It's cracked wide open, because I broke your heart." I nodded again.

He ran his fingers up my side and under the arm that was covering my breasts. "The butterflies are my rebirth, my journey. The first one's wings are closed because I was so weak, I couldn't fly yet. Each one has its wings a little further open, to show how I got stronger." I turned to face him, so he could see the last butterfly. I pointed to it and explained. "This one is my goal. Its wings are fully stretched out and it's ready to take flight. Ready to soar and live free." I smiled at him. "I'm not there yet, but I will be."

"I want you to fly, baby. I want your dreams to come true." Ty placed his hand on my arm and gently pulled it away from my body. "Don't hide from me."

I sat there in just my shorts, with my breasts bared to him. His finger ran over the long, skewed purple heart that sat on my right breast. I knew he could feel the bumps that sat under the ink. The teeth marks that were a permanent reminder of what Jake had done to me. "Did Zack do this for you, too?" he asked with tears in his eyes.

"Yes. He helped me cover the pain and the shame."

Ty shook his head and a tear fell from his eye. "I don't know what happened to you and I'm not going to ask you to tell me. But nobody is ever going to hurt you again. I'm going to protect you and keep you safe." He pulled me to him and crushed my body against his.

Then his lips met mine and I got lost in the feeling. It was deep and passionate, our tongues tangled and twisted together in a slow dance. I let out a moan and bent my head back to give him access to my neck. Tyler placed gentle kisses down my throat, nipping the skin along the way. I closed my eyes and breathed in the smell of his cologne. It took me back to a time when everything was perfect between us. When we only needed each other to breathe.

Ty ran his tongue along my collar bone, and I thought I was going to combust from the heat building inside of me. Then he kissed along the top of my chest and down to the swell of my breasts. He paused when he came to the tattoo on my chest, almost like he knew it might be a trigger for me. I feared the same. I wasn't sure how I would react to having his mouth in the same place where Jake had bit me so viciously. But then I felt soft kisses butterfly across my tattoo, and I knew everything would be okay. Tyler would never hurt me. He would only worship my body. And he did. The emotions built inside of me, and I couldn't contain the tears that ran from my eyes. He was healing me with his gentle touch. With every kiss, I felt the fear melt away.

"More," I gasped out breathlessly. I needed this. I needed him. Ty's tongue circled my nipple, and he ran the tip over my hard peak. He placed a soft kiss on my hardened nipple then gently sucked it into his mouth. Then he ran his tongue through the valley of my breasts and did the same to my other nipple. His touch was exquisite. This was love. "Touch me," I whispered.

Tyler laid me down on the bed and his fingers ghosted around the outside edges of my breasts. His fingers traced the butterflies that moved up my side and under my breast. He followed the path again with his lips, placing soft kisses on my skin. He took both hands and slid them under my breasts, palming them gently. I arched up into his touch and let out a soft moan. He massaged me and ran his tongue along my flesh. He lightly squeezed one breast, bringing my nipple to his mouth, sucking the hard peak inside, and swirling his tongue around it. The wetness between my legs drenched my panties. I wanted to go further, but I couldn't.

One step at a time. For today, this would have to be enough. I had crossed one barrier, but the next was even scarier to me. I remembered the pain. The intrusion. The feeling of being violated. My head was stubborn, but I knew in my heart that Ty would take it all away for me, just like he was doing right now.

When he finished his sweet torture, Ty kissed back up my chest to my neck and ended at my lips. "Thank you," I gasped. "Thank you for always knowing what I need." I ran my hand along his hardened length. "I feel like I should repay the favor."

Tyler shook his head. "No, were going to do this together. We're going to get you through this. And when you feel safe and you're ready, then we'll move forward. Together. Always together."

I wrapped my arms around his shoulders and pulled him to me. "I love you, Ty," I said through the lump that was caught in my throat. I swallowed it down. "I love you so much."

He ran his hand through my hair and held me tight. "Shhh, baby. I told you I'm going to take care of you and I am." He rolled to his back, taking me with him. I was wrapped tight in arms, feeling safe and secure. I rested my head on his chest and fell into a peaceful sleep.

Chapter 13
Tyler

Leaving Kyla's apartment to go home on Sunday was torture. I didn't want to leave her alone, but I knew Chris and Tori would watch over her. I was such a mess of twisted emotions.

When I went there on Friday for her birthday, I just wanted to get her back. I wanted to hold her and remind her what it was like to be together again. I had hoped for the best. I knew she was going to be surprised to see me, so I wasn't shocked by her reaction. But what I learned over the course of the weekend didn't just shock me; it angered me until my blood boiled and saddened me until my heart broke.

Kyla told me she needed to go slow, and I thought it was because she didn't trust me to not break her heart again. I thought it was all about me. I was so wrong.

I never realized the hell she was going through. I knew something was wrong when I saw the scar on her face, but then she freaked out on me, and she was so scared. It had to have taken something huge to instill that kind of fear in her. Chris told me that shitbag ex-boyfriend hit her, but I didn't know the extent of it. Then, when I saw the tattoo on her chest, I knew there was more. When I ran my fingers over it, I could feel the scarring underneath. What the fuck did he do to her? I couldn't ask her. It obviously was bad. Really bad. I couldn't make her relive it. And honestly, I didn't know if I could listen to it. The thought of anyone hurting her ripped me apart on the inside. Destroyed me. I just prayed that he didn't… I could barely think the word. It was such an ugly, nasty word. All I could picture was someone holding down her small body while they forced themselves on her. Thrusting into her while she cried and screamed for someone to help her. I prayed it wasn't true, but something deep inside told me it was.

Everything was starting to make sense. The pieces were clicking into place. Now I knew why she wouldn't open the door for me when I went there. He had attacked her, and she didn't want me to know. She wasn't just protecting herself, but me as well. She knew I wouldn't be able to handle it and so she carried the weight of what happened on her own. She didn't even tell Tori, her best friend since third grade. She was so selfless. Now I knew why she was making me wait. She was trying to heal herself first.

She said the Xanax kept the nightmares away. I couldn't even imagine what she saw in her nightmares. She drugged herself every night just so she could sleep. I hoped that in time, she would feel safe enough with me that she could sleep without it.

The black hair and nail polish, the dark eyeliner, it was all a way for her to escape. Change what she saw in the mirror. She said that she felt like her blond hair made her vulnerable. I thought it made her beautiful, but she was trying so hard to change what she thought of as a weakness.

I understood the night she went to the cemetery and the strange things she said. She thought she was damaged goods. She didn't think she was worthy of love because someone had shown her that she wasn't. But she was so wrong.

If I had just given her what she wanted all those months ago, this would have never happened. She would have never been with him. She had never asked for much. Her wants were simple. All she ever wanted was me, and I pushed her away. Kept pushing her away until she gave up. I pushed her into being with someone else. And he hurt her. Destroyed her. I destroyed her.

My girl was a mess, but she was a beautiful mess. And she was mine. She was my beautiful mess.

My mom said to find out what she needed and to be that for her. I didn't know what that was at the time, but I did now. I would be her strength. I would be her protector. I would be her safe haven. I would give her the love she so desperately deserved and needed. I would give her the happily ever after she always wanted.

When I got back to the apartment, Cody was sitting on the couch watching some shit on *ESPN*. I went to the fridge and grabbed us each a beer, then flopped down next to him letting out an exasperated breath. I was emotionally exhausted. My mind wouldn't shut the fuck down.

Cody clicked off the TV and took the beer from me. "How'd it go? I figured when you didn't come home yesterday that things were going well, but you don't look like it did."

"I fucked up." It was the only thing I could say.

"Again? Now what'd you fuckin' do?" he asked, rolling his eyes.

I shook my head. "Not again. I mean before. Why couldn't I have just taken her back like she wanted?"

"Because you're a stubborn jackass. You already know this." Cody tipped his bottle back and took a long draw off it. "Is Kyla going to take you back or not?"

I picked at the label on my bottle. "Yeah. She loves me. Always has."

"So, what's the problem, dude? That's what you wanted, isn't it?"

"She's fucked up. Like really fucked up."

Cody looked at me with confusion. "What do you mean she's fucked up? She's one of the sweetest girls I know. She get into drugs or something?"

"No, but she drinks more than she ever did before. Smokes too. She colored her hair black. Wears thick black eyeliner. But she's still beautiful." I downed half my beer in one gulp. "She found someone else when I wouldn't let her in. The fucker hit her. I don't know the details, but he fucked her up good. I think he did more than hit her. I think he…" I blew out a breath because I still couldn't say it. "I can barely touch her without her freaking out. She's trying, but she's struggling. There's shit she's not telling me. And you wanna know the really fucked up part? I'm not sure I want her to tell me."

Cody looked at me with sympathy and disbelief. "You think he raped her?"

And there it was. The word I didn't want to acknowledge. "Yeah… I think he did."

"So, what are you going to do?"

"The only thing I can do… love her. I'm not letting her go ever again. I'm gonna help her get through this." Then I let the anger seep into my soul. "And if I ever see that douchebag motherfucker, I'm probably going to kill him with my bare hands. Then I'm going to chop his body into little pieces and bury them where no one will ever find him. I'm not going to let him get away with doing this to her. He's going to regret ever touching her."

"I know you'll do right by her." Then he clapped me on the shoulder. "I'm sorry, man." There was nothing else to say.

Getting through the week was tough. I didn't want to be in Lansing. I wanted to be back in Kalamazoo with my girl. After sleeping with her in my arms for two nights in a row, my bed felt empty and cold. I had classes to attend and finals coming up. Three weeks. I just had to get through three more weeks of studying, and then I'd be able to spend every day with my girl.

I also had my physical therapy with Jerome. Monday after class, I headed over to the gym we'd been working out of. I was in a shitty mood for sure. I walked in with a bad attitude and Jerome recognized it immediately.

He crossed his bulky arms over his chest and eyed me up and down. "Someone piss in your cornflakes this morning?"

I tossed my shit on the floor. "Something like that." I had a lot of pent up energy and needed a release. I rolled my shoulders and cracked my neck. "We gonna do this or what?" I snapped. I was taking my mood out on Jerome, but I didn't really care.

He nodded his head at me. "You're pissed. That's good." I glared at him and the attitude he was giving back. "You're gonna need that fire today. We're getting you back on the weights and it's gonna hurt like a bitch. But you're gonna have to push through the pain."

"I'm not worried about the fucking pain."

I should have been worried about the pain. Jerome worked my muscles relentlessly. It'd been five months since I lifted, and I was so out of shape. My arms still had definition, but the muscle had diminished.

When I finished my work out with Jerome, I moved onto the leg machines. At least I had been able to keep that up. After about twenty minutes of working on my legs, I moved to the treadmill. I put in my earbuds and cranked up my music. I needed angry, punishing music… Disturbed, Drowning Pool, Godsmack. I blasted it in my ears and all I could think about was the fucker that hurt my girl. I lost it when "Just For" came on. I didn't even know who he was or what he looked like. All I had was a name... Jake. I wanted to go after him, but I knew it wouldn't solve the problem. All I could hope for was that he would be stupid enough to show his face when I was around. And then I would fucking take him out. Fucking coward beat up on a girl who was five-foot tall and a hundred ten pounds soaking wet. Let him mess with someone his own size. He was going to regret meeting me at six-foot-two and two hundred pounds of muscle. I was looking forward to the day.

I ran harder and faster, 'til my muscles ached, and my lungs burned. I ran through it, pushing myself. All I could picture in my head was what Kyla must have gone through. I pictured her struggling. I pictured her crying. I pictured her screaming. And I pictured some faceless asshole pushing into her. "Fuck!" I yelled out. I pulled the earbuds from my ears and stopped the machine. I was a sweating, dripping mess and my anger hadn't gone away at all.

Jerome knocked me on the back. I wanted to turn around and hit him, but I'd have to be a fool to mess with him. He was fucking huge. "You all right, man? You're pushing yourself pretty hard today."

I put my hands on my hips and stared at him. "Yeah... no, not really. Just got a bunch of shit on my mind." I rolled my neck and stretched out my shoulder. "Jerome, you know I'm done here in a month. I'm moving back home with my girl. You think I'm gonna be ready by then?"

"You'll be ready. I'll give you a list of stuff to keep working on. Where's home?"

"About a half hour north of Detroit. I gotta find a personal trainer too if I'm going to be ready next year. You don't happen to know anybody in that area, do you?"

Jerome tapped his finger on his lip. "I know a guy who might be interested."

"Cool. Think you could give me his name and number so I can check him out?" I asked.

"Oh, I can guarantee you'll like him. He's a little bit of a hard ass though," he said.

"More than you?" I laughed. "Does he have your charming personality too?"

Jerome smiled his big white grin at me. "As a matter of fact, he does."

"Great." I rolled my eyes.

"What? You don't like me?" he asked lightheartedly.

"Jerome, you've been kicking my ass for the last couple months. I wouldn't be where I am without you. I like you a lot. In fact, I might even love you."

"You're all right too, kid. You've worked hard. Listen… about this trainer. What would you think of me working with you?"

"That'd be great, except like I said, I'm moving back home."

"Yeah, I heard that part, but I got family in that area. I'm out there a couple times a week as it is. I think I could squeeze in some workout time with you." He winked.

I was shocked. Working with Jerome would be perfect. "Are you serious? Why would you do that for me?"

"You've got potential kid. I saw you playing for MSU. I really think you can do this and with the right training, you'll be a shoo-in. I played pro, until I got hurt. I fucked my knee up pretty good. I can't play anymore, but I know what it takes."

"That would be awesome. What team did you play for?" I asked.

"Played for the Raiders for two years."

I nodded my head. "What was it like? Playing pro?"

"Best years of my life. I miss it like crazy. But then, once in a while a kid like you comes along, and I feel like I'm making a difference in somebody's life."

I reached out and shook his hand. "Jerome, you just made my day."

Chapter 14
Kyla

When Tori and Chris took me out for my birthday, I never expected the weekend to turn out the way it did. I certainly didn't expect to be spending it with Tyler. I was a little pissed when I got blindsided by my friends, but it ended up being a good thing. A really good thing.

I felt like we were starting to get to know each other again. We were falling in love with each other again, although I never fell out of love with him. God knows I tried, but I never did. And for all the whoring around Ty did, I don't think he ever fell out of love with me either. We couldn't. We were destined for each other from the start.

I shared, albeit involuntarily due to my freak out, some of what happened to me. I expected him to be pissed like he was at first. What I didn't expect was his patience in dealing with me. But he still didn't know the worst of it, and I was going to try to keep it that way for as long as possible.

What I had to figure out, was how to deal with Jake. He was a big problem. He was standing in the way of our chance to be truly happy. As awful as it sounded, I didn't think I could get past everything until I knew I had had my revenge.

Revenge was a feeling that consumed me. Every time I got a text or saw his car, the rage burned inside of me. He wouldn't let me forget and move on. He had to be a constant reminder of the torture I endured at his hands. I also knew he planned on moving back to the same area I was going to when we graduated. He would never let me go.

Monday morning, I got another text from Jake.

Jake: Have a good weekend? You're a dead bitch. If I can't have you, nobody can!

Attached to it was a picture of Tyler and me. He was getting careless, which meant he was starting to lose it. I could feel it in my bones, he was getting ready to make his move on me.

I called Detective Jones and made an appointment to see him after I got off work. I brought my phone with all the text messages and the notes he had left in my car.

He stood up when I walked into his office. "Miss O'Malley, nice to see you again." He shook my hand, and I sat in the chair across from his desk. "I'm assuming you're here because things haven't gotten any better."

"No. They're not. In my opinion, it's getting worse. I think he's escalating." I took out the numerous notes, all in individual plastic bags, and placed them on the desk.

"Kyla, why are these in bags?"

"Fingerprints. I watch a lot of those true crime shows. I haven't touched the notes. I used tweezers to put them in the baggies. I don't want there to be any doubt about who left these in my car."

His eyebrows went up in surprise and he let out a little laugh. "You're smart, I'll give you that. These were in your car?"

I nodded.

"Was your car locked?"

I nodded again.

He started reading the notes through the bags. "What else have you got?"

He was kidding right? I handed over my phone with Jake's most recent text message.

Detective Jones tapped on the glass of my phone. "Now we've got something," he said. "This is enough."

I breathed a sigh of relief. "Finally."

He opened his file cabinet and pulled out some forms. "I'm going to need to you write out your statement. Include everything, from the first time he assaulted you. I have the picture you gave me the first time you came in and I'm going to put these notes in your file too. If you can, include the dates of all the times he's contacted you. It'll show a pattern of behavior."

"Okay." I started writing out my statement. I was glad I dated all the notes and kept all the text messages on my phone. I would have to go see Sid and thank him for his advice. Forty-five minutes later I finished writing my statement. I handed it to Detective Jones, and he read it over. He smiled and stamped it.

"I'll make a copy of this for you. The judge should sign it tomorrow and he'll be served in the next couple of days. You'll receive your official copy of the personal protection order in the mail."

"Thank you, detective." I stood and shook his hand again. "Unfortunately, I think this is only going to make him madder. What do I do if he violates the order?"

"He's not allowed to come near you or contact you. If he does either, call the police."

"Okay." I turned to leave but thought of one more question. "I'm planning to move in the next month. Will this still be in effect if I move?"

"It's good anywhere in Michigan. Try to move on and hopefully he'll leave you alone. You've got my number if you need anything."

I nodded and left. The paper in my hand was going to do one of two things. One, he could decide I wasn't worth it and move on or two, it could piss him off more. I would have to be even more vigilant until I knew which way this was going to go.

I drove directly over to the gun range to see Sid. He was behind the counter ringing up an order. I stood back and waited for him to be finished. When Sid saw me, he held out his arms for me. I was all smiles as I ran into his arms and gave him a huge hug. "What's going on, sweet girl?"

I stepped back and waved the paper in front of me. "I got it."

Sid pulled his glasses out of his pocket and started reading the protection order. "This is good," he said. He put his glasses back in his pocket but didn't smile. "Kyla, you know this is just a piece of paper, right?"

I let out a big sigh. "I know."

"Come on." He led me to his office and locked the door.

"This is just going to piss him off more, isn't it?" I asked as I sat down. This was why I came to Sid. He knew about this stuff and would be honest with me.

"I've seen it go both ways. In your case, I would say yes."

"So, I've got to be prepared. Make him come to me. What if I lure him in? Make him think I'm vulnerable?"

Sid crossed him arms. "You do realize you're talking about murder?"

"Self-defense," I corrected. "I've got the evidence now that he's been stalking me and the picture. I've established that he's a threat. If he comes into my apartment with intent to harm, isn't it self-defense?" I had done my research. I knew I was right.

"Yes," Sid said. "How do you think you're going to get him to do that?"

"I'll make it attractive for him. He won't be able to resist," I said. I'd been thinking about this for a long time. It was the only way.

"I don't like it. You'll be purposely putting yourself in danger. Shooting a real person is a lot different than shooting a paper target. Trust me on that."

"Sid, this is never going to end if I don't do something. Tyler and I are getting back together. We were together for three years. I love him more than anything and I want to marry him someday, but I can't move forward with this hanging over my head. I've got to get myself right again."

"Tyler know what happened to you?" Sid asked.

I dropped my head and shook it. "Some. Not everything. I can't tell him. It would destroy him."

"He love you as much as you love him?" I nodded. "Then he'll handle it. Secrets are a bad thing, Kyla. He wouldn't like this plan of yours."

"Yeah, I know that. I'll tell him. Just not yet."

Sid raised his eyebrow. "You're going to do this with or without my help, aren't you?"

I shrugged my shoulders. "I have to."

Sid let out a sigh, but I knew he was going to help me anyway. "Let's go into the range." Before we left his office, he grabbed a couple of special targets from the shelf behind his desk. We put on our eye and ear protection and made our way to a lane. Sid fastened a target to the bracket and only sent it out ten feet. The target was not a drawing like I usually used, it was a photograph of a real person. It was unsettling to say the least. "These targets are reactive. When you shoot at it, a red splotch will appear, showing exactly where you hit. It's designed to simulate blood, but it's nothing like the real thing."

I pulled my gun from my purse and checked to make sure there was a bullet in the chamber. I flipped the safety off and aimed. Shooting at this distance was a piece of cake compared to the twenty feet I was used to shooting at. I fired off the first round and it struck right between the eyes. A big red splotch appeared on the target.

"Aim for the chest. Trust me, you don't want to see brain matter splattered across your walls."

Okay, that was just a gross thought. I swallowed down the bile that rose in my throat and aimed again. I fired at the chest and big red spots covered the target. Sid reeled the target in and switched it out for another. "This time I want you to clip the holster to the back of your jeans. You need to learn how to draw it out. Drop the clip. We're not using bullets for this."

I pulled the holster out of my purse and clipped it to the back of my jeans. I dropped the clip from my 9mm and checked the chamber, then reached behind my back and dropped it into the holster. Sid showed me how to grab the gun and hold it while drawing it out. I paid close attention and took in everything he was showing me. After a few attempts, my actions were less jerky, and I was getting the hang of it. I practiced with Sid for an hour without and with the clip in. My aim wasn't so great doing it this way, but it was real. And that's what I needed, real practice.

I went back every day through Thursday to continue practicing. I didn't plan on going over the weekend. Ty would be here, and he didn't need to know about my gun or my plan. I knew I was lying by omission, but I was doing this for us. So we could move on.

Chapter 15
Tyler

I got to Kyla's around six on Friday night. When she opened the door, she was still dressed in her work clothes and looked damn sexy. She always looked good in her jeans or sweats, but this was exquisite. I looked her up and down, taking her in. She wore a black, tight-fitting skirt that hit her above the knee and a black button-up blouse. Her toned legs looked longer with the three-inch heels on her small feet. Her long, black hair flowed down her back in loose waves, and she wore big hoop earrings with the necklace I bought her.

"Damn, baby. You look... wow!" I stepped through the door, wrapped her in my arms, and gave her a passionate kiss. After not seeing her for five days, I just wanted to take her to bed, but I knew that wasn't going to be happening anytime soon, so I pushed the feelings down.

She pulled away so I could come inside. "Thanks," she said sweetly. "Come on. You can put your stuff in my room. I've got to change my clothes too." I followed her back to her room and shut the door. She leaned on the dresser and slipped her heels off. "That feels so much better," she said rubbing her toes.

I dropped my stuff on her bed and picked up the mail that was sitting there. "Did you get a traffic ticket?" I asked.

She furrowed her eyebrows at me in confusion. "No. Why do you ask?" she asked as she started to unbutton her blouse.

I held up the envelope that was on top of the pile. "Because you have a letter here from the Kalamazoo Police Department."

She took the letter from my hand and slipped it in the top drawer of her nightstand. "No, it's not a traffic ticket."

"So, what is it?"

Kyla let out a big sigh. "You're not going to like it." She pulled the envelope out and held it out to me. "I didn't really want you to know about this, but I guess you should." I reached for the letter, and she pulled it back. "You have to promise not to freak out."

I took the envelope from her hands. "You know I can't promise you that." I opened the envelope and unfolded the paper. I started reading. "You filed for a PPO?" She nodded, and I kept reading. "This guy has been harassing you for months. Why did you wait so long to file for this?"

Kyla sat on the bed. "I didn't," she said. "I tried to get one months ago, but I never filed a police report, and they told me that his texts weren't really threatening. But the last message I received was enough to finally get the PPO."

I looked down to the last thing she had written in her complaint and read it. *Have a good weekend? You're a dead bitch. If I can't have you, nobody can!* It was dated from this past Monday. "This is serious, Kyla."

"Don't be condescending. I know it's serious. I'm the one who's been living it. Don't act like I'm a stupid blond who can't comprehend what's going on. In case you haven't noticed, I'm not a blond anymore."

She was getting defensive, and I didn't want to fight with her. I sat down on the bed and twined my fingers with her tiny ones. "I didn't mean to be condescending. I know you're not stupid. I worry about you, that's all. I want to help you."

Her eyes softened, and she squeezed my hand. "You are helping, just by being here. I feel safe with you. But you can't be here all the time. Even if we were living together, you wouldn't be around all the time. I've been careful. I always carry pepper spray. I just want it to be over. That's why I got the personal protection order. It should help."

I understood what she was telling me. And she was right. I couldn't always be there to protect her, but the fact that this guy had been harassing her for months had me worried. "What if he violates the order?"

"He could, but I don't think he will. He wants to be a cop. He won't do something to jeopardize that. And if he does, I'll call the police." She was very calm talking about all of this, but I guess she'd had months to come to terms with everything.

Me, on the other hand, I was far from calm. I reread her complaint. The first item on her list was the day he hit her. Next to it read- *Picture on file.* I tapped on the letter. "I want to see the picture."

Kyla huffed and shook her head. "No, you don't. I don't think you could handle it."

I quirked my eyebrow up at her. "Really?"

"Really. It's not good. I don't need you to have that picture in your head."

"Kyla, it's in your head every day. I can't help you if I don't know what happened."

"Ty, I can't tell you everything. Baby steps, remember?"

I nodded my head. "I know." I struggled with myself all week over this. I wanted to know, but at the same time, I didn't want to know. "Just the picture for now."

She stood from the bed, her blouse still unbuttoned, and went to the closet. She stepped on a crate and stretched up on her tiptoes to reach the top shelf. Her fingers grazed an envelope. She was so damn adorable. I went up behind her and put one hand on her waist, to steady her. I pulled the envelope down from under a purple box and handed it to Kyla. "You could have asked for help." I smiled down on her.

"It's not my strong suit," she said as she stepped off the crate.

"Don't I know it."

She held the envelope to her chest. "You need to prepare yourself. I wasn't exaggerating. It's bad."

"Let me see." She pulled out the picture and looked at it, then handed it to me. I wasn't prepared for what I saw. I closed my eyes, took a deep breath, and looked again. Her right eye was swollen and bruised black. In the middle of the bruise was a dark red gash on her cheek. The left side of her face had a very distinct handprint across it and her lip was cut open. I whispered to myself, "Motherfucker." I couldn't believe anyone would do this to my beautiful girl.

I glanced down at Kyla, who was staring up at me with glassy eyes. "I told you," she said.

I reached my arm out and crushed her to my chest. "I'm so sorry, baby. I'm so sorry this happened to you." I just held her in my arms. "Nobody's ever going to hurt you again."

She pulled away. "Need a drink?"

"Yeah." I sighed.

"Let me change first," she said as she took the picture from my hand and put it back in the envelope. I lay back on the bed processing what I'd seen. I couldn't help but think about what else might have happened to her. The word Cody said kept creeping into my mind. I failed her. I sat back up, trying not to think about it. Kyla was standing in front of her closet in her black bra and thong.

"Come here, baby." She came and stood before me and put her hands on my shoulders. I ran my hands up and down her curves. Then I saw the words inked over her hipbone, *I am Strong!* I ran my fingers over the scripted words, then kissed her hip and looked up at her. "I love you, Ky."

She ran her hands through my hair. "I know, baby." She kissed me on the top of my head and turned back to her closet. She finished getting dressed and we made our way to the back patio, drinks in hand.

She lit a cigarette. "I'm sorry you saw that picture. I didn't want you to see me that way. I'm past it, but I know it was a shock for you."

"Kyla don't worry about protecting me. I'm supposed to protect you."

"We protect each other. And I'll do whatever I have to do. Together, remember?"

"Always," I said. I reached for her hand over the table and held it tight. My mind was still focused on that picture. "Ky, where did that happen? Was it in this apartment?"

She nodded.

I took a deep breath. "In your bedroom?"

She nodded again and bit her lip.

"On your bed?"

She closed her eyes and her lip trembled. Finally, she nodded one last time.

Anger boiled up inside of me. I went to the slider and called for Chris.

He came around the corner from his bedroom. "What's up, man?"

"Do you have any tools around here?" I asked.

"Yeah, they're in the laundry room. Why? What do you need?"

"Grab some screwdrivers and wrenches. I need you to help me take Kyla's bed apart. We're getting rid of it."

Kyla stepped up behind me, eyes wide. "What? What are you doing?"

I grabbed her face in my hands. "Baby, I'm not letting you sleep in that bed for one more night. I'm not making love to you on a bed you were tortured in."

Tori came around the corner. "What's going on?"

Kyla looked at her with shock on her face. "Apparently, we're getting rid of my bed. Help me strip the sheets?"

Tori and Kyla scurried off to the bedroom while Chris got his tools. With his tool bag in hand, he asked, "Ty, you all right, man?"

"Not really, but I'm trying. She showed me the picture of what that fucker did to her. I can't let her sleep in that bed. Can we use your truck later? I want to go get her a new bed tonight."

"Of course. Let's go get this done." Chris was the best friend a guy could ask for.

Kyla and Tori had just finished stripping everything from the bed when we came in. Chris and I got busy loosening the screws and pulling the bed apart. They stood in the doorway watching us work.

Tori had her arm around Kyla's shoulder. Ky just shook her head. "What are you going to do with it?"

I stopped what I was doing and looked up at her. "It's going in the dumpster. We're going out and getting you a new one tonight." I didn't leave any room for arguing. This is the way it needed to be.

Chris and I finished taking the bed apart and then carried the pieces out to the dumpster—mattress and all. When we hauled the last part out and tossed it in, Chris threw me his truck keys. Kyla and I jumped into the truck and headed to the furniture store. She put up a fight about the cost of the bed, but in the end, I won. Once the new bed was loaded into the truck, we drove back to the apartment where Chris and I assembled it. Tori had washed the sheets while we were gone, and they remade the bed.

I don't know how Kyla had slept on that bed all those months, but I would not allow it for one more day. Just knowing I slept on it last weekend, sickened me. A new bed was a fresh start for her. For us.

By the time everything was finished, it was late. Kyla and I crawled into her new bed and snuggled together. "Thank you for today," she said. "I'm so used to doing everything by myself, it was nice to have someone else take charge for a change."

"You don't have to do anything by yourself anymore. I'm here and I'm not going anywhere." I pulled her up to me and kissed her with everything I had. This girl was my life and I promised myself that I would do everything I could to make her happy.

"Ty?" she whispered in the dark.

"What, baby?"

"I've been thinking," she said. "I don't want us to live in the same condo complex."

That surprised me. I thought things had been going really well. "Why not, Ky? I want us to be close together."

She lifted her head from my chest and stared at me. "Because I want to live in the same condo. I want us to live together."

I squeezed her a little tighter and pulled her up so that she was laying on top of me. "You don't know how happy that makes me. I want to spend every night with you in my arms."

She took a deep breath and closed her eyes, then refocused on me. "And I want to try to go a little further tonight, but I'm scared. I'm scared I won't be able to do it."

I brushed her hair behind her ear. "I know you're scared. We'll only go as far as you want."

Kyla tapped her fingers on my chest. "That's the problem. I want to make love to you, but I don't think I can."

"There's no pressure. I told you I'd wait, and I meant it. Let's just see where it goes." It killed me to know she was afraid and hurting inside. There was a time when we couldn't get our clothes off fast enough. We used to fuck like rabbits, we never held back. Now it was like starting from square one. We'd have to get through all her barriers again. Start over.

Kyla sat up so she was straddling my waist. I reached for the hem for her tank and slowly pulled it up over her head. Her tits were so beautiful. She looked at me shyly and bit her lip. "Don't bite your lip, baby." I rested my hands on her hips, gently digging my fingers into the skin as I just looked at her and took her in. I slid my hands up over her stomach and up to her tits, palming them and running my thumbs over her hard nipples. She closed her eyes, dropped her head back, and let out a long sigh.

I sat up and she pulled my head to her chest. She arched her back and pushed her tits out. "Suck my tits, Ty," she gasped. It was the first time I had seen a glimpse of my little sex kitten that I knew was hiding inside of her. I had to hold myself back and remember to be gentle with her, because when she talked like that it drove me crazy and I wanted to devour every inch of her. I placed kisses along the tattoo that covered her scars. Then I ran my tongue around her hard nipple and gently sucked it into my mouth. I sucked and sucked while my hands softly squeezed her fullness. She was so perfect.

I wrapped my arms around her waist and flipped Kyla onto her back so that I was straddling her. She reached up and ran her fingers up my arm and over my shoulder, tracing the tattoo she had designed. "I can't believe you did this for me."

"I wanted to show you how much I love you." I laced my fingers with hers and kissed the tops of her small hands. I put our hands next to her head and leaned over the top of her, placing gentle kisses on her lips. She opened for me and let my tongue tangle with hers. We laid there devouring each other. Lips and tongues and teeth crashed together as our desire consumed us. I wanted her so bad. I wanted to sink my dick deep in her pussy and make love to my girl. I pulled back from the kiss and stretched our arms above her head as I stared into her eyes.

I clasped her wrists together in one hand and she gasped. Her eyes went wide as she tried to pull her hands from my grasp. I released her, and she pulled her hands to her chest rubbing her wrists. Quick shallow breaths came from her chest. "I'm sorry. I felt trapped," she rasped out.

What the fuck! What did he do to her? Had she been tied up? It would explain her reaction to something I had done to her dozens of times. She never had a problem with it before. ... having me be in control usually turned her on.

Kyla turned her head into the pillow. "I'm sorry," she said. "I'm fucked up." She started crying. "It's not fair to you." She was breaking my heart. "You should go. I can't love you like you deserve."

"Ky? Baby? Look at me." She hesitantly turned her face to look up at me. Her green eyes were full of tears that rolled down her cheeks. "I told you, I'm not going anywhere. We'll get through this together. I didn't know. I'm sorry."

She was taking deep breaths to try to get her breathing under control. "You deserve better than this. Better than me."

I wiped her tears away. "No. I deserve exactly you. You're my heart. I'm not losing my heart again."

"But..." I put my finger to her lips.

"But nothing." I crawled off her and leaned back against her new headboard. I pulled her up on my lap and cradled her in my arms. "I'm not letting go."

I woke to Kyla wrapped in my arms, her tits pressed against my chest. Yeah… not much was better than this. I looked down at her sleeping peacefully in my arms and sighed. My fucked-up, beautiful mess of a girl.

Chapter 16
Kyla

When I opened my eyes, Tyler was already awake. "Good morning. How long have you been awake?"

"A while."

I smiled up at him. "Why didn't you... wait, I already know. You like watching me sleep."

"Yeah, I do. You looked so peaceful." He reached down and placed a soft kiss on my lips. "You wanna go running today?"

I got a little smile on my face. "Yes, and then would you go somewhere with me?"

"We can do whatever you want. Where do you want to go?" he asked.

I was excited. I jumped up and straddled his lap. "I want to go look at buying a new car."

His face broke out in a huge grin. "It's about fucking time." He pulled my face to his and gave me a big kiss. "That car you've been driving is so old, I'm surprised it hasn't broken down on you yet."

I swatted at his chest. "It's not that bad."

"Kyla, it has a tape deck in it. It's old." He twirled my hair around his finger. "What do you think you want?"

"I don't know. It's going to be my graduation gift to myself. I've got the money from selling my parents' cars, plus whatever they'll give me for my car..."

"Which is nothing," Ty interrupted.

"Stop. Anyway, I've got a decent down payment, so hopefully whatever I choose won't be too much in monthly payments."

"You're not having monthly payments. Do you know how much interest they charge on those things?"

I didn't like where this was going. "You're not paying for my car. I have money. It just makes me nervous spending it. I mean…what if I need it later?"

Ty sat up and placed me next to him. "I don't mean to get personal, but how much money did your parents leave you?"

I bit the side of my thumb and thought about it. "After paying off the funeral, house payments, and rent for this apartment. There's probably about eight-fifty left, not including the money I got from selling the cars."

Tyler's eyebrows narrowed in confusion. "Eight hundred and fifty dollars?"

I shook my head, "No. Eight hundred-fifty thousand."

He ran both hands over his face. "Oh my God, baby. You refuse to spend a dime on yourself, and you've been sitting on that kind of money?"

"It's not all cash. Some of it's in investments," I clarified.

Tyler rolled his eyes at me. "You do realize that between the two of us we have almost three million dollars."

"No, no, no… your money is your money. I'm not touching that."

I could tell he was getting frustrated with me. "Okay, listen. You get paid at your internship, right?" I nodded. "And you're going to have a job when we get home?" I nodded again. "And you talked about working for Zack. Ky, just pay for the car outright. It doesn't make sense to do monthly payments. You have enough."

"You really think so?" I asked.

"Oh my God, Ky! For being so smart, I don't know why you're having such a hard time accepting this.

I looked down at my hands. "I think... I think it's because it was my parents' money. I don't really think of it as mine."

Tyler brushed my hair out of my face. "I get that, but they left it for you, and they would want you to drive a safe car. Don't you think?"

"Yeah, I guess."

"I know your mom and dad would want you in a safe car and they're probably thanking me right now for talking you into this," he said.

"Probably. They always had faith in you. My mom already sent you to me once." Ty cocked his head to the side with a look of confusion. I sighed. "Remember when I was sitting at the cemetery? Well, I asked them to help me find my way. To tell me what to do. And not even two seconds later my phone rang, and it was you." My eyes got glassy and surprisingly his were too. Tyler pulled me in and held me to him, his hand on the back of my head.

We got dressed and went for a long run. My heart was pumping hard, and my lungs burned. I'd been pushing myself harder and harder lately. I needed to get past my head, so that Tyler and I could be together the way we deserved. Just when I thought I could go a little further, something would knock me down. It was the classic one step forward, two steps back.

But as we finished our early morning run, I got an idea I thought might help. When we got back to the apartment, I told

Tyler to go ahead and jump in the shower first. I waited a few minutes, then quietly slipped into the bathroom. I could see him standing behind the foggy glass rinsing his hair. I quickly stripped out of my clothes and entered the shower with him.

He opened his eyes and I stood before him, baring everything for him to see. "Hi, baby." He cupped my face and kissed me. I stood on my tiptoes and reached my arms around his neck, so our bodies were pressed together. I could feel his length harden against my stomach.

He'd been so patient and sweet with me that I wanted to treat him right. I reached between us and ran my hand up and down his dick. I wrapped my fingers around him and applied just enough pressure to make him groan. "Ky, that feels so good."

"It's just the beginning. I want to make you come," I whispered. Dropping to my knees, I licked the tip of his dick and swirled my tongue around the head. Ty's hands went to my hair, rubbing the top of my head. I opened my mouth and sank down over him, taking him all the way to the back of my throat. I pulled up and sank down on him over and over again. One hand held his leg while the other massaged his balls. I gently rolled them in my hand, using just the lightest pressure. I opened my throat and forced him in deeper, swallowing and swallowing so that my throat would grip him just right. Pulling back, I ran my tongue up and down his long, hard cock, my hand rubbing him from root to tip. "I'm gonna come, Ky. I can't hold back." His words encouraged me to take him to the back of my throat again. I opened up and let him in, taking as much as I could. He hardened even more, and his body tensed. I felt his hot cum slide down my throat as I continued to stroke him with both my hand and my mouth. When I had pumped out the last of his orgasm I stood, wrapped my arms around his waist, and laid my head on his chest.

Ty rubbed my back up and down. "You didn't have to do that," he said.

"I wanted to. I want to treat you right." And I did. I wanted to give him more than a great blow job, but it was all I could offer right now.

"You do. I don't need sex for you to treat me right. I know you love me." Ty turned me in his arms, so my back rested against his chest. "I wanna try something. If you tell me to stop, I'll stop."

I took a deep breath. "Okay."

Ty held me against him with his arm across my rib cage. His other hand gently massaged my breasts. I leaned back into him and let the feelings of pleasure overtake me. He always made sure I was taken care of. His hand rubbed down my stomach towards the place I was afraid of him touching, but I tried to relax back into him. I wanted him to touch me. His fingers went through my folds and down to the wetness that was between my legs. I stiffened when he touched my opening, but he quickly slid his fingers back up to my clit. He spread the wetness over my clit and rubbed gentle circles on my sensitive nub. My God, he was so good at this. I felt the pressure begin to build deep inside of me. A high I hadn't felt in so long. "Oh…it's so good, Ty. Keep going…please," I rasped out.

I clenched my muscles, as he continued to rub my clit faster and faster. I let the feeling build 'til I thought I would explode. My hips moved into his hand trying to increase the pressure. I was so close. My breathing became erratic, and my legs weak. Finally, when I thought I could take no more, the pleasure burst through my body and white lights flashed behind my eyes. I felt wave after wave course through me from the top of my head to the tips of my toes. I couldn't hold myself up any longer, and Ty's arm slipped around my waist to catch my weight. "I got you, baby. You did so good," he whispered in my ear.

When my senses returned, relief washed over me. I wasn't a total lost cause. I turned in Tyler's arms and we wrapped ourselves around each other. We just held on, knowing what just happened was a huge boundary I had crossed.

After going for lunch. We started a search for my car. I really wanted a sports car, but Tyler was against it. Not because he didn't want me to have a sports car, but because they don't handle well in the snow. He wanted me to get something with four-wheel drive. I understood his point, and he promised to let me drive his car when I wanted something sportier.

I was difficult to shop with and I accepted that. I had a list of things I wanted and didn't want. I didn't want anything that looked like a "mom" car. I definitely wanted a sunroof. I would have preferred a convertible, but a sunroof was more practical in Michigan. And being short was a big problem. I just didn't fit right in some of the cars. I needed to be able to see well and sometimes I felt like I could barely see over the dashboard. We concluded that I needed an SUV, and that narrowed it down some. I didn't need all the bells and whistles, but I didn't want it stripped down either.

I finally decided on a black Jeep Grand Cherokee. Ty breathed a sigh of relief when I made that decision. We had been to five different dealerships and spent countless hours talking to salespeople and doing test drives. "Ky, no offense, but that was exhausting. When I got my Challenger, I knew exactly what I wanted. You just walked in and didn't have a clue. I felt like we were on a damn scavenger hunt."

"Awww...I'm sorry, baby. Maybe I should have just kept my old car," I teased him.

"No. Definitely not. I thought shopping for a bed for you was hard. That was a piece of cake compared this."

"Cheer up. This won't seem so bad when we're looking for our first house together."

Tyler groaned. "Just something to look forward to."

We filled out all the paperwork at the dealership. I still had to get insurance and a certified check, but I'd be able to pick-up my Jeep the following Friday. I was so excited that in one week, I would be driving my first new car.

Chapter 17
Tyler

By the time we found Kyla a car… which was torturous… and went to get something to eat, I was exhausted. We were getting ready for bed and were about to crawl in when Kyla spotted the envelope with the picture on her nightstand. She picked it up and handed it to me.

"Ty, would you put that back in my closet for me. And bring me the purple box that was sitting on top of it. I want to show you something."

I took the envelope and slipped it back on the shelf and brought her the box. "What's in here?" I asked. I crawled up on the bed and sat next to her.

"You'll see." She took the box from my hands and put it on the bed in front of us. She placed her hands on top of the box. "This box holds all the things that have been the most important me."

I didn't have a clue about what might be in the box. Maybe things from her childhood, old report cards, or pictures of her parents. When she lifted the top of the box, I couldn't have been more surprised. Sitting in the top of the box was our prom picture that had hung in the hallway at her parents' house. I lifted it out of the box and ran my fingers over it. "Look how young we were," I said.

Kyla wrapped her arms around my shoulders. "I know. So much has happened to us since that picture was taken. Did you think back then that we would be together now?"

"Ky, I always thought we'd be together. You were the best thing in my life. You still are." I kissed the side of her head and set the picture aside. I reached into the box and took out another smaller box. It was marked *Homecoming*. I opened the box and in it sat the first corsage I ever bought her. It was dry and discolored, but there was no mistaking it. "You kept this?" I asked. I was overcome with emotion that she kept this simple flower for over four years.

"I kept everything," she said. "Every moment with you has held a special place in my heart." She pulled out another box marked *Prom*. In it sat her corsage from that night.

"This was the best night of my life," I told her. "There is no one I would have rather lost my virginity to."

"We were so nervous and didn't know what we were doing," she sighed.

"But we were still good at it. I could have fucked you all night."

"I think you did." She was blushing, and it was so damn cute.

I pulled out a heart shaped bottle of sand. "Is this...?"

"Yep. It's the sand we made love on at the lake house that summer."

I remembered putting it in a water bottle that night, but I'd had no idea she kept it. I pulled item after item from the box. There were pictures, movie ticket stubs, love letters, cards from flower arrangements, stuff from my football games. She'd kept it all. Just when I didn't think I could love her anymore, my chest swelled.

At that moment, I felt so elated that we had this second chance, but I also knew that we wouldn't have needed a second chance if I'd never left. I pushed her away time and time again. Now that she had taken me back, I would never push her away again. She was it for me.

When I got to the bottom of the box, my breath hitched. "Are these...?"

"Yeah," she answered.

The first picture wasn't very clear, and I didn't know what I was supposed to be looking at, but the second picture was. There in black and white I could see a head and body with tiny arms and legs. Tears welled up in my eyes as I ran my finger over the image. I pulled Kyla to sit between my legs and I rested my head on her shoulder. If she had felt one-tenth of what I was feeling, I now understood why she had been so devastated. I ran my hand over her stomach where our baby used to sit.

"You wanna see something really cool?" she asked.

I simply nodded as I tried to keep the tears out of my eyes. Kyla reached over to her nightstand and picked up her phone. She pulled up the video app and pressed play. It was a video of her ultrasound, and I could hear a soft whooshing sound in the background. "That's the heartbeat," she said. The video played for a full minute and when it was over, I played it again.

Last year when I found out Kyla was pregnant and the lost the baby, I was so mad at her. I was mad that she had gotten pregnant. I was mad at her for keeping it a secret from me. I was mad that she was so devastated when I never knew about it at all. I even questioned whether or not it was mine.

At the time, the idea of a baby was so abstract. I was focused on the end result, and how I would have handled a crying baby when I had school and football. If I was being honest with myself, I was kind of relieved when I knew it wasn't going to happen. I never really thought about the process of the baby growing, except that Kyla's belly would get big and round. I didn't understand how she could have become so attached to something that wasn't even real to me. And I walked out on her.

But looking at the ultrasound pictures and video, I finally understood. I understood her devastation when this little, tiny person, who had a heartbeat and was growing inside her, had died. I had just thought of it in terms of a miscarriage, not a death. And finally, the loss of what we made, hit me. And it hit me hard.

I set the phone on the bed and just held her from behind, with my hand on her stomach. "I'm so sorry, baby. I'm sorry I didn't understand. And I'm sorry I left you all alone that night." The tears were running down my face, not just because of what we lost, but because of the way I treated her. I cut her off and tried to erase her from my life.

"I would have been okay if I had gotten to keep one of you that night, but I lost you both. I didn't know how to cope."

I rocked her in my arms. I couldn't let go. I pointed to her phone. "I want that with you. I want to have a baby with you. And this time were going to do it right. I want to be there from the time you pee on a stick until you push it out. I want to be there for everything. Together. I want a do over. Good or bad, I'm never leaving you again."

"I want that too. Someday," she said with a sigh.

We sat there, just holding each other for a long time. We were both lost in our own thoughts. We finally broke apart and gathered everything that was on the bed. There was one last thing in the corner of the box. I reached in and pulled out the deep purple, heart-shaped ring I gave her that first summer. Taking her right hand, I slipped the ring on her finger. "You have my heart. You always have. This belongs on your hand, not in a box buried in your closet." I brought her hand to my mouth and kissed it. "I want you to make love to me. I want to make you come and then I want you to ride me."

Panic set in on her face, "Ty, I…"

"You'll be in control. You hold all the power, baby. Let's just try."

"I'm scared. What if I can't," she whispered.

"Then we stop, but I think you can." We'd broken through one barrier this morning. I needed her to take control back. To erase the bad with good. I wouldn't push her if it was too much, but we needed this. She needed this.

"Okay, I'll try."

I knew she was nervous, but she was strong. I knew she could do this. She stripped off her tank and shorts and laid back on the bed in her bra and panties. I stripped down to my boxer briefs, dimmed the lights, and lay down next to her. "You know I love you. I would never ever hurt you, baby."

"I know." She straddled me and pressed her lips to mine. Our tongues tangled together in a slow dance. I reached behind her back and unclasped her bra. It fell down her arms to my chest. She tossed it to the side and moved up higher, so her tits were in front of my face. Taking her tits in my hands, I rubbed her and brought one luscious nipple to my mouth. She smelled so good, just like the beach. I breathed her in as I sucked and rubbed her tits until she was moaning.

I turned her in my arms and gently lay her on her back. "I'm gonna make you come. I'm gonna eat your pussy out, baby." She placed her hands on my shoulders and pushed me down towards her heat. I kissed her down those beautiful butterflies, starting with the one under her breast and working down toward her hip. Kissing across her stomach, I swirled my tongue around her belly button ring and worked my way down her other hip. She slipped her fingers into the sides of her panties, and I worked them down over her slender legs. They fell on the floor next to rest of our discarded clothes. She put her feet up on the bed and spread her legs apart, inviting me in.

So far, so good. I crawled up between her legs, put one her leg over my shoulder and then the other. Her perfect bare pussy was right in front of my face. I looked up over her body. "You okay, baby?"

She nodded. "Just tongue, okay?"

I nodded my agreement. She loved when I finger fucked her, but she wasn't ready for that, so I lowered my head into her. Her essence filled my senses and covered my tongue. I stuck it inside her and ran it all along her slick opening. She was wet and that was a good thing. She wanted this; she was just so damn afraid. I ran my tongue up through her folds until I found her clit. I spread her wetness over it with short flicks of my tongue. She started to moan, and her hips raised off the bed to meet my mouth. I sucked her clit, and her hands went to the back of my head, pushing me into her sweet pussy. I needed to make her come. I didn't want her to be afraid of sex with me. Her pleasure was my only concern. I continued to work her clit, alternating between licking and sucking. It took longer than usual, but finally her thigh muscles started to tense around my head, and I knew she was close. Her breathing turned to short quick gasps of air as the pressure began to build inside of her. She was almost there. "Oh... oh... I'm gonna... oh my God." I sucked her clit through her orgasm and then came up for air.

I stripped off my boxer briefs and crawled up next to her. She grabbed my head and stuck her tongue in my mouth, kissing me like there was no tomorrow. "I love you, Ty. I've missed you so much. I forgot what it felt like for you to love me like that."

"Were not done, baby. I want you to take me. Take all of me." I held Kyla's hand as she straddled my waist. "You can do this. I know you can." She closed her eyes and raised up on her knees. I grabbed my dick and placed it at her opening. "You're in control," I reminded her. "It's all about you right now."

She held her breath as she slipped her pussy over the head of my dick. She stopped, took another deep breath, and sank a little lower. Then a little more and a little more, until she was seated flush against me, and I filled her completely. She let out the breath she was holding, and I saw the relief wash across her face. With her hands on my abs, she tentatively rolled her hips forward and back. It was so slow that I felt every bit of her warm pussy slide up and down my dick. It was sweet torture. I laced my hands with hers and let her use them for leverage.

I watched her face as she moved on top of me. She closed her eyes and started to enjoy the pleasure it was bringing, as my dick slipped in and out of her. "Move with me," she whispered. She was letting go of the control. I lifted my hips to meet Kyla's and soon we found the perfect rhythm. We were so good at this, she just needed reminding about how good it could be.

I'd been with lots of girls, but I'd never made love to any of them but Kyla. She was my heart. When we made love, my chest nearly burst from my love for her. It was like a fire that engulfed my soul and consumed me. It burned me from the inside out in the best way. She was the only one who could do this to me.

Her walls started to tighten around my dick, and she picked up the pace, pushing me to the brink of my control. She dropped her head back and let out a strangled moan, "Oh God!" Her pussy clamped down on my dick and pulsated around me, squeezing out my orgasm. I released her hands and grabbed her hips, pushing up into her over and over again. My orgasm ripped from my balls and up through my dick. It shot hot sparks down my spine and my mind went blank of anything but her.

With me still inside of her, Kyla collapsed on my chest. I wrapped my arms around her back and held her. We laid together soaking up the post-sex bliss. Her voice was so soft I barely heard it. "Thank you. Thank you for loving me." Her body relaxed, and her breathing evened out. I could feel the steady rise and fall of her chest. She fell asleep in my arms while we were still connected as one.

Chapter 18
Kyla

Last night was amazing. I didn't think I could do it, but Tyler forced me out of my comfort zone in the best way. I was so scared that having him inside of me would bring flashbacks of Jake. But Tyler, as always, knew exactly what I needed. I needed the sense of control. He wasn't doing anything to me, I was doing it to him. Once I got him inside of me, I was able to relax. Nothing was being forced upon me. I held the power.

I knew I wasn't fixed. I was far from being okay, but it was a step in the right direction. I wouldn't let him stick his fingers in me, or his dick for that matter. I was afraid I would feel violated. I knew we had a long way to go. I never told Tyler that I was raped, but I suspected he knew. Neither one of us wanted to say the words, to acknowledge what had happened. I knew, and I would never forget the hell Jake put me through, but I loved Tyler too much to say the words. I didn't want that in his head. So, we continued to dance around the truth, even though we both knew what it was.

We were graduating in two weeks. Tyler and I spent Sunday researching places for us to live back home. He knew I wanted to live on Lake St. Clair. It was a small lake compared to Lake Michigan or Lake Huron, but it was big enough, and close to home. I wanted Ty close to his parents, and I needed to be close to mine. We came up with a list of possible places to live. Tyler promised that he would contact them and make appointments for us to check them out the next weekend.

I didn't need much. All I needed was Tyler by my side. I couldn't believe that within two weekends I had become so dependent upon him again. But he was my heart, my partner, my soulmate. We were destined from the start. If this didn't work out, I would be destroyed beyond repair. I couldn't let myself go there. Tyler was healing me, one little step at a time. I needed to believe that he was in this for the long haul.

I regretted ever letting Jake in, but what was I to do? I knew Tyler had been with other girls, but I tried not to think about it. It was a year of mistakes that I wanted to leave in the past. We had a wonderful three years together. I just wanted to move on and forget the last year even existed. I felt like we were back to being us. Nothing else mattered. We'd both made mistakes.

After Tyler left to go home, I wandered into Tori's bedroom. Tori looked up from her computer. "I was just looking at flowers for the wedding," she said. She quickly exited out of her browser and focused on me. "So… how are things going?"

I plopped into the chair next to her. "Really good. I was mad you and Chris set me up on my birthday, but it turned out to be a really good thing."

"I'm glad," she said. "I was afraid you wouldn't forgive us."

"Let me tell you… I was this close," I said holding up my fingers to show her. "But we've totally reconnected. All those times you told me to move on… you were wrong. He and I were meant to be together." I looked up at her for approval. "He and I are moving in together after graduation."

Tori clapped her hands together. "I'm so happy for you… and me. Things won't be totally awkward at the wedding."

"So, you admit it was all a plan to get us back together for the wedding."

"Sort of, but it all worked out for the best, right?"

"Yeah," I admitted.

"So, have you told him everything?"

I shook my head. "No, but I think he knows without me telling him. He's been really sweet."

"Have you two had sex yet?" she asked.

"Yes and no." Tori looked at me in confusion. "I haven't let him have sex with me, but I've had sex with him."

"Come again. That doesn't even make sense."

"It's complicated, but right now I have to be in control. I need to be on top. I don't know how I'll feel with him on top of me. I'm afraid it will trigger something bad in me."

Tori wrapped her arms around my shoulders. "I'm glad you have him to help you through this. When you told me everything, I didn't know how to help you. I'm just happy for you."

"Well, I haven't conquered all my fears, but I'm trying. I don't know if I'll ever be quite right, but I know I'll feel better when Jake is out of the picture," I confessed.

"What does that mean?"

"It means that Tyler and I are going to have a chance to be happy. Plausible deniability, remember? Don't ask too many questions."

"And Tyler?"

"Same goes for him. I'll do what I have to, to ensure our happiness. He doesn't know about Sid, my gun, or anything else, and I want to keep it that way. He would just try to stop me, and I can't risk that," I said with determination. "These past couple of weekends have just reinforced what needs to be done." I turned and walked away from my stunned best friend. I faced her one last time before exiting her room, "He'll get what he deserves. If he comes after me, there will be a reckoning. I'm not going to live in fear."

I continued my practice at the gun range after Tyler left. I didn't care about anything else but ending Jake, especially after his last text.

Jake: *A PPO really? You can run...*

It wasn't said, but it was implied ...*but you can't hide.* I took it as the threat it was meant to be. I didn't call the police, although he had technically violated the order. I wanted him to feel like he was getting away with something.

After my target practice, I went to Sid's office for a little visit. I knocked on the door frame.

"Hey, sweet girl. Come in." I walked in and sat in my usual chair. "I saw you out there tonight. You're looking good."

"Thanks. Sid, I need to ask you a question. You've helped me so much and I never want to put you in an awkward situation," I hemmed and hawed.

Sid always got right to the point. "So, what's your question?"

I loved Sid. He had been my savior since everything happened to me. He was the first to know the truth and he was the one who helped me gain my confidence back. "If I go to jail...?

Sid cut me off. "I'll testify to what happened to you, but nothing else. I don't know shit. Your decisions are your own."

I stood. "That's all I wanted to know. It's enough." I embraced his big, burly body. "I love you, Sid. You've been everything to me." I gave him a kiss on the cheek.

Sid got choked up at my affection. "I love you too, sweet girl."

"I'm moving in a couple of weeks. I just wanted you to know how much you mean to me. Thank you for everything." I started to leave, then turned to face him one last time. "This is going to end." And with that I walked away.

Midweek, when I was out for one of my runs, I got that tingly feel that ran up and down my spine. I looked around and didn't see anything suspicious. My headphones blasted in my ears as I ran through the downtown area. I turned down the volume, so that I could hear everything around me. Just in case.

I looped around the track on campus and headed back. I put the uneasy feelings out of my head and chalked them up to nerves, turning the volume back up and singing to the music that pumped through my ears. As I was passing a little diner, a hand reached out and grabbed me, pulling me between the two buildings. I was pushed up against the wall and a hand went over my mouth. I gasped from the shock of the impact. I should have listened to my instincts and cursed at myself for not being smarter.

I stared into the eyes of the devil and didn't even blink. I should have been scared to death, but I wasn't. It was still light outside, and we were in a semi-public area. He couldn't hurt me here.

It was the first time Jake and I had been face to face since he'd assaulted me in the bar, and I'd gotten the upper hand in that confrontation. "You're being a little bitch, you know that?" I just stared at him. He dropped his hand from my mouth, and I looked at him with malice in my eyes. It was hard to believe that I had liked and trusted him just a few months ago.

This was not a violent confrontation. It was meant to scare me and deep inside it did, but I wouldn't give him the satisfaction of knowing that. "What do you want, Jake?"

"You know what I want. I want you back. We had something good going. I loved you and you threw it away. You told me all about your problems with Mr. Football and now you're just going to run back to him?"

"Is that what you do to people you love? You rape them?" I spewed the venom from my tongue.

"Now, now, that's such a nasty word. We were together. I fucked you, just like I had the times before. You like it rough, what can I say?"

I nodded my head. "Is that the way you're going to play this? Lucky for you, I didn't file charges."

He scoffed at the suggestion, "Like anyone would have believed that. We were in a relationship, remember?

"I remember every detail perfectly," I said in defiance. "If I were you, I'd stick to the PPO." I pulled out of his grasp and started to walk away.

Just as I was about to emerge from between the two building, Jake had to open his mouth one more time. "I will have you again. That's a promise."

I turned and faced him, hands on my hips. "Over. My. Dead. Body." I meant it too. He would have to kill me before I let him put his hands on me or dick in me again. It was a chance I was willing to take, but I was almost sure, it wouldn't be my dead body.

That was the second time he'd surprised me. I vowed to myself that it wouldn't happen again. The next time, he would be the one surprised.

Friday, Mr. Tolliver called me into his office again. The man was more bark than bite, but it still made me nervous. "Have a seat," he instructed.

I did as I was told. "Is there a problem?" I asked.

"I've talked with Mr. Thomas about your work in the Internet Sales Department. Seems that you're better than we were told by your counselor at Western. Mr. Thomas has approved for you to move to our Detroit location. So, if you still want a job with us, a transfer won't be problem."

I was elated by the news. I tried to play it cool but failed miserably. "Thank you, Mr. Tolliver. You don't know how much this means to me." I stood, shook his hand, and started toward the door.

I'd only gotten few steps when Mr. Tolliver stopped me. "Kyla?" I turned back to him and was shocked to see a smile on his face. "You've done a good job here. Welcome aboard. We're lucky to have you."

I returned his smile. "Thank you for the opportunity. I appreciate it. You know everyone here was wrong about you... you're not so bad," I said with a wink.

And just like that his smile was gone. He put back on his tough-guy exterior. "We'll talk about your transfer next week." He looked back at the papers on his desk, and I was dismissed.

I packed up my desk and headed to the dealership to pick up my new car. I was a little sad to say goodbye to my old car. I'd had her a long time. But, as soon as I jumped into the seat of my Grand Cherokee, I forgot about that old piece of shit. I laughed at myself, because I had never wanted to admit how bad my old car was, but it really was awful.

I drove home and packed my things. Since Tyler and I were going home to look at condos, I was going to stay the weekend at his place. MSU was closer to home than Western, so it only made sense. I let Tori and Chris know I was leaving. They'd been insistent since they found out what had happened to me that we all stay in close communication. I knew that Chris felt partially responsible for what Jake did to me. Chris had promised Ty that he would watch out for me and he hadn't been there. It didn't matter how many times I tried to explain that it was my decision to come home at Christmas. Guilt was a bitch, but Chris didn't deserve any. He'd been nothing but wonderful to me.

As I was loading my stuff in the car, I wondered how it was that Ty always had one small duffle bag, and I looked like I was moving out.

I started on my drive and was happy that for once I wouldn't have to worry about Jake. My run in with him earlier in the week had shaken me more than I wanted to admit. How in the world could he possibly think I would ever go back to him? He was positively delusional. Delusional, unpredictable, possessive, and a mean drunk made for a scary combination.

I pulled up in front of Tyler's apartment and grabbed my stuff from the back. I hadn't even made it to the door yet, when Cody came out and picked me up in one of his signature bear hugs. "Hey, girl! I've missed you!" He spun me around and set me back on my feet.

"Let go of my girl and quit man handling her," I heard Tyler teasingly shout from behind me.

"She's too good for you anyway," Cody teased back.

"Yeah, she is. But she's still mine," Ty answered as he walked over to give me a kiss. He took my bags from me and slipped his arm around my waist to lead me inside.

I turned over my shoulder. "It's good to see you too, Cody."

Chapter 19
Tyler

"I see you got your car today," I said to Kyla.

"Yeah. That thing drives like a dream. I love it! Guess what else I got today?" she asked.

I carried her stuff to my room and put the bags on my bed. "I don't know. What?"

Kyla wrapped her arms around my waist. "I got my transfer approved for my job," she said smiling.

"That's great, baby," I kissed her on her forehead. Everything was coming together. She had a job and tomorrow we would find a place to live.

"I'm starved. Take me out to eat?" She looked up at me with big wide eyes. How could I possibly say no to that?

"Sure." I laughed. "What are you in the mood for?"

"What I really want is a big, greasy bar burger, with bacon and mushrooms. Oh… and fries."

I picked Kyla up and she wrapped her legs around me. "I know the perfect place."

"Should we ask Cody to go? I haven't seen him in ages."

"We can. Let's go ask him." I carried her in a front piggyback out to where Cody was. "Hey, Cody? Do you want to go to the bar with us to grab something to eat?"

Cody flicked off the TV and downed what was left of his beer. "Yeah, I'm starving. You sure you don't mind if I tag along?"

I set Kyla down on her feet. "No, come on. I haven't seen you in forever," she said.

We hopped in my car and headed towards a local sports bar. The three of us found a high-top table and ordered our drinks. They arrived a few minutes later and Cody was in the middle of telling us a ridiculous story about some girl he went out with, when he stopped mid-sentence. "Oh shit! Here comes trouble."

I looked over Kyla's shoulder and I couldn't believe it. *Why did this always have to happen when I was out with Kyla?*

She walked right over to me and hung on my arm. "Hi, Tyler," she said with a big fake smile.

This was not going to end well. "Madison," I said curtly. She was so oblivious, that I don't even think that she realized Kyla was sitting at the table. With Ky's dark hair, she did look different.

Kyla cleared her throat and Madison turned to face her. She stuck out her hand. "I don't think we've ever been properly introduced. I'm Kyla." Madison didn't reach for her hand, so Kyla dropped hers. Madison had on her classic bitch face. "Oh, come on, now. Don't be such a poor sport. As you can see, *I* haven't been replaced. *You* have. Did Ty tell you were moving in together?" Kyla shrugged her shoulders. "I guess I just fuck better than you."

The look on Madison's face was priceless. Then she pulled it together and narrowed her eyes at Kyla. "You're a bitch!" Madison turned to walk away.

Kyla called after her. "Back at ya, honey. Thanks for stopping by."

Cody burst out laughing. "Ouch! That was fucking awesome!"

I was just stunned. That didn't turn out at all the way I had anticipated. "Wow!" It was all I could manage.

Kyla took a sip of her drink with a satisfied smile on her face. "I'm so over her skanky ass. Every time I've seen her, she's been a bitch."

Cody turned to me. "This one's a keeper. You better not fuck it up again."

I grabbed Kyla's hand over the table. "Yeah, she is. I'm not fucking up again." I looked around the bar. Madison wasn't the only one here I'd had sex with. Suddenly, I felt disgusted with myself, that I'd brought Kyla to this bar. Luckily, she didn't know just how many of these women I'd had my dick in. I was glad we'd be moving back home soon and could leave all of this behind us.

When we got back, I pulled in next to my Harley. While we were walking up to the apartment, I saw Kyla looking at it in appreciation. She had no idea it was mine. "It's nice, isn't it? Want to go for a ride?"

She looked at me in surprise. "It's yours? How come I didn't know about this?"

"I bought it last year when I got my trust fund. It was the first thing I bought. I didn't tell you about it yet because I wasn't sure how you would feel about it."

Kyla walked to the bike and ran her hand over the chrome handle bars and then over the sleek black frame. She swung one leg up and sat on the back part of the seat. "I think it's hot and I bet you look sexy driving it. No wonder the girls are falling all over you. You're cute as can be, have a great body, you're smart, a football star, you drive a cool car *and* this fine piece of machinery. You've made yourself the ultimate chick magnet." She beckoned me toward her. I sat backward on the seat in front of her, so we were facing each other. She put her hands on my shoulders. "I'm a lucky girl, but none of those are the reason I love you."

"Oh, yeah," I said breathlessly. She looked good sitting on the back of my bike. I reached my hands under her ass and put her right on top of my hard-on. "Why do you love me?"

She wrapped her legs around me and placed her hand on my chest, right where her favorite tattoo sat. "I love you for the things that people can't see from the outside. I love your heart. And I love your soul."

God, she made me want to fuck her right here on my bike. She leaned in, captured my lips, and stuck her tongue deep inside. Her hands went to the back of my head and pulled me in closer, if that was even possible. We devoured each other like starving lovers.

She pulled back. "I think we're giving your neighbors a show." She lifted her chin at something over my shoulder.

Sure enough, the old guy that lived next door was staring out the window at us. Kyla gave him a little wave. I shook my head at her. "Your just full of piss and vinegar tonight, aren't you?" She cocked her head to the side with a shrug. "So, do you want to go for a ride?"

"I'd love to, but I don't have a helmet," she said with disappointment.

I unwrapped her legs from around me and set her back on the seat. "That's where you're wrong, my love. Come with me." I held her hand as she got down off the bike. I led her inside and walked to the hall closet. I pulled out my leather and set it on the chair. Then I pulled out another black leather jacket. "I'm pretty sure this is your size." I held it up and she slipped her arms into it.

She turned around and ran her hands down the soft leather. "You bought this for me?"

"I had to make sure my girl was dressed properly for riding on the back of a bike." I reached up to the shelf in the closet and pulled down her helmet. "This is yours too."

She took it from my hands and inspected it. "It's got purple on it." Her eyes lit up.

I winked at her. "Purple and black. It matches your hair."

"Let me go change my shoes." She ran back to my room excitedly as I followed. She was sitting on the bed replacing her wedges with black boots. Then she went to the mirror and braided her long hair.

She looked like a wet dream in black boots, jeans, a black T-shirt, and the leather jacket. I reached over to my desk and grabbed my extra pair of aviators. "You'll need these." I handed them to her. She put them on, and she looked fucking sexy as hell. "You look so good, I'm second guessing going for that ride. I think I want to fuck you right now."

"You'll get your chance," she teased. "But not until you take me for a ride."

I palmed her ass and pulled her close. "Oh, you're going for a ride either way." She had it so wrong. I was the one who was lucky.

"Bike first," she said.

I'd been looking forward to this day for so long. The day I bought that Harley, I fantasized about what Kyla would look like on the back of it. I took her hand. "Come on." We grabbed our helmets and went outside. I helped her put her helmet on and adjusted the chin strap. "Oh my God, you look so damn adorable."

She climbed on the back of the bike like she'd done it a hundred times. I put on my helmet and aviators. "Put your feet right here on these pegs," I instructed her. She did, and I got on in front of her. "Remember when we went jet skiing? Same concept. Just let your body go with mine."

"Don't worry," she said. "I'll be fine. I'm just gonna hold onto you." She wrapped her arms around my waist, and I kick started the bike. It rumbled to life, and I eased us out onto the road. I drove toward Crego Park, taking the scenic route since it wasn't that far away. I felt Kyla's hands up underneath my leather and her thighs gripping mine. Then she ran her hand up and down the bulge in my jeans and I groaned.

I pulled up next to Fidelity Lake and parked the bike. I got off and took my helmet off. Kyla was having a difficult time with the strap on hers, so I unhooked it, and she climbed off. We walked hand and hand down towards the lake. Kyla sat on a big rock, and I climbed up behind her and wrapped my arms around her waist. "I love you, baby," I whispered in her ear. She leaned her head back and her lips met mine.

"I love my life with you," she said. "I can't wait until we live together. I want to spend every day wrapped in your arms."

"I was proud of you today. The way you handled shit at the bar."

"I've come to the realization that if you didn't want to be with me, you wouldn't. I don't need to worry about bitches like her," she said.

"I know it's in the past, but I made good on my promise to you. There was never anything between her and me. Not for her lack of trying, but nothing ever happened."

Kyla placed a finger to my lips. "Like you said, it's in the past. I have you now. That's all that matters."

I knew she wasn't going to be too keen on what I said next, but she seemed to be in a good mood, so now was as good of time as any. "Since we're going to look at condos tomorrow, my parents want us to come for dinner. They miss you," I said.

"I don't know if that's a good idea," she said. "I mean, do they know about the baby and everything?"

"Yeah, they know."

"Great! They probably think I'm a sleaze bag. It's so cliché. Poor college girl who gets knocked up."

I turned her to face me. "Kyla, they don't think that at all. I told them everything. To be honest, I think they were more disappointed in how I reacted to it. They love you. It's not like they didn't know we were having sex. My dad said he always thought we would get married. My mom was really sympathetic toward the situation. She had her own miscarriage, so she understands what you went through."

"Really? I just feel like it's going to be awkward."

"It's not going to be awkward. Besides if we're going to be together, you're going to have to face them sooner or later," I reasoned.

Ky took a deep breath. "Okay. We'll have dinner with them. To be honest, I miss them too, especially since my own parents are gone."

"You know, my family is your family. Do you want to go to the cemetery tomorrow? We'll be so close."

"Maybe. Let me think about it." She turned again so that her back was to my front. She leaned back and just let me hold her. I saw a tear run down her face and I wiped it away. Even though I didn't see my parents often, I couldn't imagine what it would feel like to lose them. Especially, both at the same time. I wished I'd been there for her at the time, but I was busy being selfish.

We sat there by the lake until the sun started to go down. "Should we head back?"

"Yeah," she said. "Take the long way home."

I did. I drove totally out of the way, just to give us more time.

We were getting ready for bed and Kyla was searching through both of her bags frantically. She pulled everything out and threw it on the floor around her. "Shit, shit, shit, shit," she murmured.

"What's wrong, Ky?"

She looked at me with panic in her eyes and started hyperventilating. "I can't stay here tonight," she said as she started throwing everything back in her bag.

"What? Why?" I asked, genuinely confused. She was packing all her things to leave.

"I forgot my pills. I can't sleep without them. I need to go home," she zipped up her bag and started to change back into her jeans.

"What pills?" I asked,

"My Xanax. I can't sleep without it. I have to go."

She was panicking, so I got off the bed and held her. "Baby, I want you to stay. You'll be okay for a couple of nights."

"You don't understand," she said. "The nightmares... they're bad. Call Tori or Chris. They know. They've heard it before."

"It's okay." I rubbed her back. "I won't let anything happen to you. I don't want you driving back there this late at night. I'll hold you all night long. And if the nightmares come, I'll be right here."

"What about Cody? It's going to scare the shit out of him, and I'll be embarrassed. I don't want it to happen in front of you or him."

"I think we can handle it. Neither one of us would ever let anything happen to you."

"I think it's better if I go," she said.

"You're staying." Even if she did have a nightmare, it was better for me to know what I was dealing with. We were going to be living together soon and her problems were mine.

"Alcohol," she said definitively. "What do you have? Because I can't go to sleep right now."

I led her out to the kitchen and opened our liquor cabinet. She was manic as she reached in and pulled out the bottle of Southern Comfort. "I'll pay you back," she said. She grabbed the cigarettes out of her purse and opened the slider.

She sat at the patio table and lit a cigarette, then she opened the bottle and poured some in a glass. The way she threw it back, suggested that she had done this before. "Kyla, I'm worried about you. This isn't normal," I said.

"It's my normal." She poured herself another shot and threw it back. "I'm not normal. As much as I want to be, or want you to think that I am, I'm not." She took a long drag off her cigarette. "I'm damaged. I tried to tell you that."

"Kyla, you're not. It's going to be all right."

Just then, Cody opened the slider. "Are you two having a party without me?" Kyla threw back her third shot.

I went inside with him and tried to explain. "She forgot her Xanax and she's freaking out. She thinks that if she gets drunk it will keep her from getting nightmares. If she does have a nightmare, can you just pretend like you didn't hear anything? She's afraid you're going to get weirded out if you hear her."

"Everything seemed fine before. She's still the sweet girl I remember, but a lot sassier."

"Please, dude, do this for me? I don't want her to be embarrassed by having a nightmare."

"That's cool. I don't want her to feel uncomfortable here," he said. We both went outside and sat at the table with her. Cody and I each threw back a couple of shots to make her feel like she wasn't alone. She smoked like a chain smoker. I had never seen this side of her before.

After an hour, I led her back to the bedroom. I went to the bathroom and called Chris. "What's up, man?" he asked.

"I need some info. Kyla forgot her Xanax. How bad is it going to be?" I needed to know what I was in for.

Chris let out a sigh. "It's not good, man. Tori's run to her in the middle of the night on several occasions. Sometimes even the Xanax isn't enough to stop her fucked up mind. She's woken us up screaming in the middle of the night."

"Thanks." I hung up. I had no idea what I was in for, but I loved her, and I would help her through this. She wasn't alone.

Kyla was sitting in bed with her tablet out. "I can't sleep. I'm just going to stay up and read."

I took the tablet out of her hands and placed it on the nightstand. "You should be totally wasted right now from all the booze you just drank. I want you to try to sleep with me."

"I'm not wasted. I have a high tolerance." She moved over next to me and snuggled into my side. "I want to sleep. But what if... I don't want you to see me like that."

I held her face in my hands. "Kyla, listen to me. Do you want to be with me?"

"Yes. You know I do."

"Then let me help you. I want you to be my wife. I love every part of you. Even the parts that are a little messed up right now. I'm not going to stop loving you because of a fucking nightmare."

"You want to marry me?" she asked with big doe eyes.

"Yes. My life is so much better with you in it," I admitted.

"Mine, too."

I lay down bringing her with me. "So, curl up next to me and let me hold you. No one can hurt you here. I won't let anything happen to you." She wrapped her arm around my stomach and settled in on top of my chest, then threw her little leg over mine.

"I love you," she whispered.

I kissed the top of her head and turned off the lamp next to the bed. I laid there awake wondering about what the hell had happened to my girl. Before long, I heard soft little snores coming from her. It was probably from all the alcohol she drank. I had to smile because it was the cutest damn sound.

I tried to stay awake, but exhaustion took over and soon I was out too.

I woke up when I heard sounds coming from Kyla. I looked at the clock next to the bed. 3:37. Kyla had moved out of my arms and was on the far side of the bed. She was talking in her sleep, although I couldn't make out what she was saying. I scooted closer to her and ran my hand along her forehead. She was sweating like crazy and was crying. I put my hand on her shoulder and gently shook her. "Baby, wake up."

She rolled to her back but didn't wake up. She was still talking to herself. I heard her murmur, "Please, stop. You don't... no."

I shook her harder. I was afraid of scaring her more but needed to wake her up. "Kyla... Kyla, wake up, baby." Sweat dripped off her forehead and her legs started thrashing. "Kyla!" Her eyes popped open, and her chest rose up off the mattress as she gasped for air. She let out quick short breaths as she oriented herself. I rubbed her arm up and down, "Kyla, I'm right here. You're okay," I said soothingly.

She turned her head to look at me. "Did I? Did I..."

"No, baby. You're okay. You were talking in your sleep." I lifted her into my arms. "I got you. I'll always have you." Her tank was soaked with sweat. "Let's get you in the shower."

Kyla grabbed her hair clip from the dresser and clipped her hair up on top of her head. I led her to the bathroom and turned the shower on. "I'm sorry I woke you up," she said.

"Don't be sorry. We're getting through this together, remember?" I checked the water temperature and kept it on the cool side. I reached for the hem of her soaked tank and pulled it up over her head. She pushed her shorts down over her hips and wiggled out of them. I slipped out of my shorts and pulled out two clean towels.

We stepped into the water and let it wash over us. Kyla took handfuls of water and splashed them on her face, washing the sweat away. I washed her back and down over her breasts. This was the first time we'd taken a shower together that sex was not on my mind. I just wanted to take care of her and make her feel safe.

We finished showering and I wrapped her in a fluffy towel. We went back to my room, and I gave her one of my shirts to sleep in. It hung down and hit her mid-thigh. She used to wear my clothes all the time and I loved seeing her in one of my shirts again. We lay back in bed and I pulled her close. She kissed me deeply, then fell asleep in my arms.

∞♥

I woke in the morning to an empty bed, but the smell of bacon filled the air. I couldn't imagine that Cody was cooking, so it had to be Kyla. I stumbled to the kitchen and saw her standing at the counter wearing just my shirt with her little legs hanging out the bottom.

Walking up behind her, I wrapped my arms around her waist and kissed her neck. "You better have shorts under there. I don't want Cody seeing all your goodies."

She lifted her shirt to show me her shorts. "Don't worry, all my goodies are sufficiently covered. I hope you're hungry."

I nuzzled her neck some more, "Oh, I'm hungry all right."

She squirmed away. "I meant for food. There was nothing but protein in your fridge, so you're getting bacon and eggs." She pointed to the blender on the counter. "I made you one of those gross protein shakes you like too."

"What did I do to deserve you," I asked as I poured my shake into a glass.

She reached up on her tiptoes and placed a kiss on my lips. "Everything."

"Something smells good!" Cody appeared with his hair sticking up all over.

Kyla pointed to the table with the spatula. "Have a seat," she said. "It's almost done."

"You guys should have made up a long time ago. I could get used to this."

"You can visit us anytime and I'll make you breakfast," she said.

"Don't I get a say?" I asked.

"Don't be jealous. I'll make you breakfast too," she teased.

"Damn girl, I don't even know how you're functioning this morning," Cody said as he swiped a piece of bacon from the plate. "You can really throw them back for such a little thing."

Kyla put the eggs on the table. "Yeah, well, I've had some practice." She poured herself a cup of coffee and sat down with us. "What time do we need to leave?" she asked me, changing the subject.

"We've got four places to look at. Hopefully, you'll like one of them. It's hard to tell from the pictures online, so I narrowed it down the best I could. I think we should leave in about an hour. Does that work?"

"I'll be ready."

We were halfway back home, and Kyla was a little quiet on the ride. She slipped off her wedges and pulled her legs up on the seat. I'd seen this before, so I knew what was coming. She always retreated into herself before having a big discussion.

Kyla wrapped her arms around her legs. "So, I was thinking," she started, "I know living together was your idea, but are you a hundred percent sure? I mean... I've still got a lot of shit to work out and being together on the weekends has been great, but this is fulltime. What if you get tired of it? I come with a lot of baggage right now. Maybe in six months, I'll have it more together."

I pulled the car off on the first exit I saw and parked at the McDonald's off the ramp. "Is this about last night?" I asked.

She looked out the side window, not making eye contact with me. It was her attempt at avoidance. "It's about last night, it's about me freaking out on you a couple of weekends ago, it's about not being able to have a normal sex life with you. I've been trying so hard the last few months to fool everyone into thinking I'm all right, but I'm starting to think the only person

I'm fooling is myself. It seems like every time I start pulling it together, something else happens." She turned back to me and with sadness in her eyes. "I can't help but wonder what's next. Don't get me wrong... you've been great. You've been gentle and patient and understanding, but everyone has a breaking point. I'm afraid you're going to reach yours and I can't take that kind of heartbreak again."

I'd had enough. I unbuckled my seatbelt and got out of the car. I walked around to her side and opened her door. She looked at me in confusion, as I pulled her legs around so that they were hanging out the door. I squatted between her legs and put my hands on her knees. "You need to stop. Stop doubting yourself and stop doubting me. We did this for three years. Remember? I know everything important I need to know about you. I know you have a big heart, you're sweet, and no one has ever loved me like you." She tilted her head to the side and a small smile escaped her lips. "Remember when I broke my shoulder?" She nodded. "I realized, right then and there, that the only person I ever wanted by my side was you. But you weren't there, and that broke my heart. I knew why. It was my own fault, but I made it my mission from that point to get you back. To be worthy of your love that I threw away. We're getting our second chance, and baby, I'm in it for the long haul. Are there going to be bumps along the way? Probably. Are we going to fight sometimes or get on each other's nerves? Probably. But that doesn't mean we can't get through it. I can deal with your issues right now. They're temporary. My love, our love, is forever. So, what do you say? Do you want to do this with me or not?"

"Yes."

"Okay. Then you have to stop trying to push me away. I'm not going anywhere. Period."

She leaned forward, practically falling out of the car, and wrapped her arms around me. I lost my balance and we fell backward so she was laying on top of me. In the McDonald's parking lot. I couldn't have cared less that we were attracting attention. This was my girl, and I was never letting her go.

Chapter 20
Kyla

Tyler was right. Maybe I was trying to push him away. Maybe I didn't think I deserved the love he was giving me. Maybe I didn't understand how anyone could love what I'd become. None of it mattered though, because despite everything... that boy still loved me.

I was going to work hard to erase the fear and self-doubt. If I ever wanted to reach my goal, that final butterfly that sat on my rib cage, I was going to have to take a leap of faith. I needed to let go of the pity party I'd been having for myself and move forward. Tyler was the flame that could bring back my fire.

We looked at the first three condos and honestly, I wasn't very impressed. I knew we wouldn't be living there forever, but I just couldn't see us making any of them our home. I so hoped that number four would be better than the first three, because if we didn't find anything today, we would be back at square one.

Condo number four was in a nicer neighborhood, but it was also pricier because it was in Grosse Pointe. I wasn't rich by any stretch of the imagination, but I did have the money my parents left me, and I would be working. We pulled into the tree-lined entrance off Jefferson, and I sat up a little straighter taking everything in. "This is nice," I said. "Do you think we could afford this?"

Tyler rolled his eyes at me. "Yes, we can afford it, but let's see what the actual condo looks like before you go worrying about that." He drove around to the back of the complex, as we tried to find the correct address. We finally located it and pulled into the drive. "That's cool. It has a garage, so you can park in the winter, and I bet my bike would fit in there too."

I was already more excited about this condo, than any of the other three. Tyler and I met around the front of the car and held hands as we walked to the door. I hesitantly reached out and knocked. A middle-aged woman opened the door and greeted us with a smile. "You must be Tyler and Kyla. Come on in."

We thanked her and walked through the door. It was a wide-open floor plan with a big kitchen and sitting room. It had high ceilings that made the space look bigger and more welcoming.

The lady stuck out her hand. "I'm Debbie." We looked around as she explained about the condo. "This place used to belong to my parents and it's just too much for my mom after my dad died. She really needs to be in assisted living but has been fighting me on it."

"This is really nice." I wandered into the kitchen. All the appliances were stainless steel and it had granite countertops. "I love how big this kitchen is. I'm not a great cook, but this kitchen could inspire me."

"It's a two bedroom, well actually three, but we turned one into an office. The master bedroom has its own bathroom and there's another full bath in the hall." She led us down the hallway to the bedrooms.

Tyler spoke up, "Not that it's my business, but why are you renting it out instead of selling it?"

Debbie shook her head. "I'm just not ready to part with it yet. Renting it out makes it feel like it's not really gone." I totally understood that. I felt the same way about my parents' house.

"So, what kind of lease are you looking at?" Ty asked.

"I'd like to start with a year, but I'm flexible. My parents paid off this condo, so really, I just want to make enough to pay the association fees and taxes. You know, that kind of stuff," Debbie answered. "Are you two getting married?" she asked.

"Eventually," I answered. "We dated for over three years and then took some time apart. We're back on the right path again." I walked to the blinds in the bedroom and pulled them open. Behind the blinds was a balcony that looked out over Lake St. Clair. The view was amazing. I unlocked the slider and stepped out. The balcony went all the way across the back of the condo to another slider, which I assumed connected to the sitting room. I stepped forward and held onto the railing. Closing my eyes, I took in the sound of the waves crashing into the shore. The light breeze caught my hair and tickled my face.

Strong arms wrapped around my waist and Tyler leaned down to my ear. "I think we found our new home."

I leaned my head back on his shoulder. "I love it."

After finalizing everything with Debbie, we headed toward Tyler's parents' house, which was about a half hour away. We were so close to the cemetery that I decided I wanted to stop. I mentioned it to Tyler, and he willingly made the detour. I directed him around to where my parents' graves were, and he parked along the side of the road.

"Don't be offended, but I kind of want to talk to them by myself. Do you mind staying in the car?"

"Babe, I'm not offended at all. Take your time. I'm just gonna call my mom real quick."

I leaned over and gave him a peck on his stubbly cheek. "Thank you." I walked over to their graves and sat down cross-legged in front of the headstone.

"I'm back," I said. "Mom, you were so right. That last time I was here, I was a mess and you sent me Tyler. I know that was your doing because you're a hopeless romantic, just like me. He and I have reconnected, and we just signed our first lease together. I know Dad would disapprove of us living together, but I need him. He makes me feel whole, and loved, and I'm healing. So, Dad, keep an open mind, because he's taking care of me, and I know you would approve of that." A butterfly flew in front of me. I reached out my hand and it landed on my palm. I held it up in front of me and looked at its beautiful wings. "This is going to be me," I said definitively. "I'm going to learn how to fly again. Tyler is helping me find myself. I love him and one day I'm going to marry him. If you can help me along the way, I would appreciate it. I don't know where everything is going right now, but it's my journey. I want you to be there for my wedding and I want you to be there for your first grandchild. Because with Tyler, I think all of that is possible. I'm finally starting to be happy again." The butterfly lifted from my hand and flew off into the distance. I watched it until it was no more than a speck in the wind. I was proud of myself. I didn't cry or feel sad. I felt complete, knowing that the man waiting in the car for me was my future. My whole life, in one wonderful package.

We made our way to Tyler's house and I became a bundle of nerves. I tried hard to hide it, but Ty knew all my tells. He could always see through my insecurities. "I think it's been a good day, Ky. We made it through the night without your pills, you made me breakfast," he flashed me that dimpled smile, "we found a place to live, and you visited your parents. This is the last hurdle of the day. It's not going to be bad. My parents are really excited to see you."

"Did you tell them about my hair? What if…"

"They could give two shits about your hair. All they care about is that you make me happy. Besides, your hair is sexy. It's grown on me."

"I'm ready," I said. "I'm just nervous. It's been a long time since I've seen them."

"It's been too long." Ty picked up my hand and kissed the back of it.

"I'm really excited about our new condo. I think it's perfect," I said.

"When I saw you standing there on the balcony, looking out over the lake, I knew it was the one. It reminded me of you looking out over the lake when we were at Tori's family's house. You seemed so calm and centered."

"I think I'll be spending a lot of mornings and evenings on that balcony." I looked over at my beautiful man. "I know I get nervous a lot and sometimes I'm totally irrational, which I'm going to work on, but I do love my life with you. It's more than I ever dreamed of. I'm going to do better and have faith in us."

"I can't ask you for more. This is going to work, Ky."

"Can I ask you just one more question? Without you getting mad I mean?"

"Sure, go ahead. This is going to be ridiculous, isn't it?"

"Why? Why me when it's obvious you could have anybody else?"

Tyler let out a big sigh. "Ky, you are my heart. Nobody else could ever fill that space. From the first day I met you, I knew it. You always loved me for me. You never asked for anything in return. You gave up everything, just to be with me. You never tried out for cheerleading at Western, you were at all my games, you never cared whether I won or lost. You just wanted one thing from me, and that was my love. And I'm going to give it to you until the day I die."

"I love you, Tyler Jackson."

"And I love you, Kyla O'Malley.

"Oh, my goodness, let me look at you!" Tyler's mom held me by the shoulders and then pulled me in for a huge hug. "I've missed you so much!" she exclaimed. She pulled me into the kitchen and sat me down on one of the stools at the counter.

"Hi, Mrs. Jackson. I've missed you too." It wasn't what I was expecting, but it wasn't unwelcomed. I did miss her. She was like my second mom for a lot of years.

"What about me? Am I just chopped liver now?" Ty followed us into the kitchen.

"You know better than that," she said. She gave Ty a kiss on the cheek and hugged him tight. "I always miss my baby boy."

"Mom, I'm twenty-two years old. I'm not a baby anymore."

She reached up and pinched his cheek. "Yeah, but you're my baby."

Mr. Jackson came into the kitchen and gave me a hug. "How's my sweet girl?"

"I'm fine," I said. "How are you?"

"Can't complain," he said. "Although it'd be nice if I got to see you two more."

"Well," Tyler started. "I think that might be able to be arranged. Kyla and I just signed on a lease for a condo in Grosse Pointe."

"You two found something? I'm so excited for you!" his mom exclaimed. "Tell us all about it."

Tyler and I filled them in on the details over dinner and promised to have them over when we were officially moved in. They listened attentively and *oohed* and *aahed* in all the right places. The longer we stayed, the more comfortable I became. It was like riding a bike, I just had to get back in the saddle again.

After dinner, Tyler's dad called him into the den for what I assumed was "man talk". He was probably cautioning Ty about jumping in with two feet after all the shit we'd been through. I stayed in the kitchen with his mom, and I could tell the conversation was about to turn serious.

"Kyla, Tyler told me about everything you went through. I mean, with the baby."

I looked down at my hands as my nerves set in. "Yeah, it was a rough time for me."

She came over and took my hands in hers. "I'm sure it was. I know the pregnancy wasn't planned and I'm sure you were scared to death. Men don't understand these things." She got a little tear in her eye. "But I do. It happened to me too. So, if you ever need to talk, I'm here for you. I know it never really goes away. The sadness. I know you're strong, but I just wanted you to know I'm here."

I was more than a little bit taken aback. "You're not mad?" I asked.

"How could I be mad? You would have given me a beautiful grandchild. And if we're lucky, you still will." She ran her fingers through my hair. "You know, I wanted to reach out to you after your parents died. I just didn't know how. You and Tyler weren't together, and I didn't want things to be weird.

You've been like a daughter to me for a long time. I was never blessed enough to have my own. If you need anything, or need some motherly advice, I'm here for you."

I couldn't stop the waterworks from falling. "Thank you. You don't know how much that means to me," I choked out.

"You two were always meant to be. This is going to be a good thing," she said.

Ty's mom held me like only a mom could. She rocked me in her arms and her touch, one I'd missed so desperately over the last year, soothed me. In this moment, I felt like my own mother's arms were around me. I never got to say goodbye to my mom. I never got that final hug. It broke down my defenses that I had worked so hard to build. I'd put up a wall, brick by brick, to shut all those feelings out. And now that wall was crumbling, and my raw heart was exposed. "I miss them," I managed over the lump in my throat.

"I know, honey," she said softly. She ran her hands down my hair and rubbed my back. "I know it's not the same, and we would never try to take their place, but we're here for you. We've missed you and we love you."

I pulled back. "Thank you." I rubbed under my eyes at the makeup I was sure was running and tried to pull it together. "I'm sorry. I didn't mean to cry like that."

"It's okay. You don't always have to be strong. Sometimes you just have to feel it. Let it out." Now we were both crying and holding each other.

We were a couple of crying fools in the middle of her kitchen. Tyler and his dad came back in the middle of our cry fest. "Thanks a lot, Mom. What'd you say?"

I waved him off. "It's all good. Don't worry."

That night, Tyler and I were lying in bed. "Are you okay, baby?" he asked.

"I'm a little nervous about sleeping, but you've got me, right?"

"Always."

"I'm glad you made me go to your parents' house tonight. Your mom and I had a good talk. And then she hugged me. And it was like a real mom hug. I didn't realize how much I had missed and needed that."

"I told you they loved you," he whispered.

"I know, but tonight I really felt it. I felt like I had a family again."

Ty kissed the top of my head. "You do."

I snuck out from under Tyler's arm and straddled him. "I love you." I reached for the hem of Ty's shirt that I was wearing and pulled it up over my head. "Touch me." It came out breathless and needy. And I was. I needed Tyler to touch me, to kiss me, to run his tongue along my skin, to make love to me. I wanted to lose myself to his touch the way I used to. I wanted him to make me feel everything, like only he could do.

His hands came up and rubbed my breasts. I dropped my head back and basked in the feeling of him touching me. I arched my body and lowered myself, so he could take me in his mouth. "God, I love your tits," he said before taking one hardened nipple into his mouth.

"Suck harder," I encouraged. He did. He sucked and nipped and pulled and the sensation sent heat right to my core. I whispered in his ear, "I want you to make me come and I want you to make love to me. I want to feel you inside me. I want to let go with you. I need you to make me feel the way only you can."

"Are you sure," he answered. "There's no rush."

"I'm sure. I don't want to think. I just wanna feel." I climbed off him and stripped out of my shorts. I lay back on the bed and fanned my dark hair out on the pillow, bending one knee up on the bed. "Please."

Tyler pushed his shorts down his legs and dropped them to the floor. His erection stood long and hard against his defined stomach. His muscles bulged, making his tattoos look even sexier. His body was gorgeous. I was a lucky girl to have this man love me.

He laid down over the top of me. "I've wanted this for so long. I need to make you mine again," he said softly.

"I've always been yours."

Ty pressed his lips to mine and stuck his tongue deep inside. I wrapped my arms around his neck and pulled him closer. We devoured each other with a hunger that could only be satisfied by one another. Ty kissed down my neck to my chest. He kissed the swell of my breasts and sucked each of my nipples into his mouth. It was gentle, yet possessive. I was his. He was my only want. My only need. Only he could satisfy me.

I pushed on his shoulders, urging him to move south. A fire burned within me. I needed his mouth on me. I needed him between my legs. I moved my legs apart and put one foot on each of his shoulders. There could be no mistake about what I wanted. "Lick my pussy, baby."

He let out a growl from deep in his chest. "Say it again, Ky. Tell me what you want."

My voice was filled with lust and desire. "Lick my pussy, Ty. I want you to finger fuck me. I want everything. I need to feel you."

"I love when you talk that way. It's so fucking sexy. It makes me crazy." He lowered his head and disappeared between my legs. He lapped me up over and over again. His tongue was relentless. It slipped in and out of me and had me gasping for air. He replaced his tongue with his long fingers. They slid effortlessly into my wetness. He was gentle and agonizingly slow. He curled them inside of me to hit that special spot that made my hips buck up off the bed. "Is this what you wanted, baby?"

"Yes... God, yes. Lick my clit. I need to come. I need it so bad." My wish was his command. While his fingers were still deep inside me, he flicked his tongue over my clit. I felt like I would burst at any moment. He sucked it deep into his mouth, pulling and sucking and giving me just what I needed. The pressure was almost unbearable. I felt it building, taking me higher and higher. It was like standing on the edge of a cliff waiting for the free fall. I clenched my muscles, and I was gone, falling into the abyss of pleasure. Wave after wave rocked through my body. I fisted the sheets, searching for something to anchor me as Ty's fingers gently pumped in and out of me.

I opened my eyes and Tyler appeared in front of me. His blue eyes locked to my green ones. "You're so beautiful when you come. I love knowing I can do that to you. Make you fall apart from just my touch."

"You're the only one, baby. The only one who's ever touched me like that. You're the only one to make me fall apart like that," I whispered. I laced my fingers with his and he placed them next to my head. He was waiting. Waiting for me to tell him what to do. Making sure I was all right. "Make love to me, Tyler. Slow and deep like the first time. I want to feel all of you."

Our eyes never left each other. I felt his head at my entrance, and I lifted my hips to meet him. He pushed in slow, just a couple of inches, then backed out and pushed a little deeper. By the third push he was all the way in. "You're so wet, baby. Always so ready for me. I love you, Kyla."

Then he started to move. Each stroke purposeful, long and deep. I wrapped my legs around his waist and lifted my hips to meet every push of his. Our rhythm was perfect. Our connection... perfect. Our love... pure perfection. It was slow and sensual. Neither one of us were lost to the meaning of what we were doing. We were breaking through another barrier. We were making up for lost time. We were committing to a lifetime of love for each other.

The slow burn started to rise up in me and I knew I wouldn't last much longer. "I'm almost there, baby."

"Me too," he whispered. He increased his speed, pushing in deeper and harder. Soon I was standing on the edge of that cliff again. With a few more thrusts of his hips, we fell over the edge together. My muscles clamped down on him while he pulsed inside me. And it was perfect. I felt everything.

Chapter 21
Tyler

My sex kitten was back. Her dirty little mouth was such a turn on. When Kyla talked like that, all I want to do was fuck the hell out of her. She wasn't ready for that yet. We weren't there, but we were on our way. She initiated our love making tonight, and that's exactly what it was… making love. It was a huge step for her, to let me be in control without feeling violated. She wanted slow and gentle and that's what I gave her. The rest would come with time.

Looking back at our day, I would say it was a huge success. We made it through the night. I was just glad I woke up and could stop her from getting too deep into her nightmare. We found a new place to live, which Ky was in love with. When I saw her on that balcony looking out over the lake, she looked so content. So calm. I knew it was our new home.

At the cemetery, I wasn't sure what to expect. I thought she was going to break down, but she didn't. It was in these moments that I realized how strong she was. She'd been dealt a shit hand over the last year and yes, she had some issues, but who wouldn't? I watched her sit in that cemetery and I saw a vision of strength. Her holding that butterfly was one of the most beautiful things I'd ever seen. She didn't know I was watching. But I was.

Kyla made it through another night without the nightmares and left early the next morning, because I had finals to study for. I wasn't worried about the exams, but I still had a paper to finish writing. My last final was on Wednesday. She was finishing her last week of her internship. I graduated on

Friday, and she graduated on Saturday. I was glad the graduations weren't on the same night, so that we could attend each other's. My parents were coming in Friday and were going to stay the weekend, so that they could go to Kyla's graduation too. Ky didn't know that yet, but my mom couldn't stand the fact that Kyla's parents were going to miss it. Kyla had worked so hard, she deserved to have someone there to celebrate with. Tori and Chris would be there, because they were graduating too, but Kyla needed family.

Part of me was jealous that she knew exactly what she would be doing when we graduated. She already had a job she loved and was great at. I had planned on being drafted and on my way to a career in the NFL. But that fell apart when I broke my shoulder. Goodbye Heisman Trophy. Goodbye NFL draft.

I was looking forward to starting up this bar with my uncle, but I was a little overwhelmed with the task. I didn't know what the fuck I was doing, but I was smart and with Kyla's help I knew I could do it. My main priority was going to be working with Jerome to make sure I was ready for the free agent tryouts. My dad had secured me an agent, Gary Hoffburn, who would negotiate everything for me. If I was lucky, and continued working hard, a year from now I would be signed to a professional team. I didn't know where in the country it would take me. All I knew was that I was taking Kyla with me.

After my last final on Wednesday, I took the ring I bought Kyla over a year ago back to the jewelry store. I went up to the counter and the same woman who sold it to me was working. I looked at her name tag. "Hi, Miranda. I'd like to trade this ring in." I placed the ring on the counter.

She picked it up and gave me a sad look. "Didn't work out, huh? We won't be able to give you full value for this ring."

I took the ring from her and stuck it back in my pocket. "That's too bad, because actually it did work out. I wanted to upgrade. You work on commission, don't you?"

"Well, yes, but we do have our policies." I knew she was curious. "How much of an upgrade?" she asked.

I shook my head. "I guess it doesn't matter if you can't give me the value of this ring. I'll just take it somewhere else. Thanks for your time." I started to walk away, but I knew she wouldn't let me get far.

"Wait!" she called out. I stopped, turned to look at her, and cocked my eyebrow. "Let me get my manager. Maybe we can help you."

"Miranda, I don't want to put you out. I can take it somewhere else," I said.

"No, no. It's not a problem. Why don't you start looking at rings. I'll go talk to the manager."

I walked back to the counter and played my part. "Well, if you're sure. I really can go somewhere else."

"Nonsense. I'm sure we can work something out." Miranda disappeared into the back room.

I didn't have to look too hard. I knew what I wanted. I wanted to replace the small quarter carat ring with a full two carats. Yeah, it was a major upgrade. I looked through the case and found the perfect ring. It was a princess cut diamond, with a diamond band. She was going to love it. It was perfect.

Miranda returned a few minutes later with the manager. "How can I help you, sir?"

Sir. I loved it. "Well, I bought this ring about a year ago and I wanted to upgrade, but Miranda said you probably wouldn't be able to give me the value of the old ring. I understand, so I'll be happy to go somewhere else."

"Do you have a receipt?" The manager was cocky.

"Actually, I do. I was looking at this ring here," I pointed to the one I wanted. "but I'm sure I can find one just as nice somewhere else." I had just pointed to one of the most expensive rings in the case. I turned to walk away again.

"Wait just a moment, sir. We'll have to see if you qualify for the financing, and then we can talk." Again, with the cocky attitude.

"Oh… I don't need financing. You do take cash, right?" Now I had his attention.

"Of course," he smiled. "Can I see the ring you want to trade?" The cocky attitude was gone.

I handed over the ring, along with the receipt. "This won't be a problem at all. We can give you full credit for the old ring."

"Thank you," I said. I ended up walking out with the ring I wanted and didn't lose a penny on the other ring.

Kyla was going to say it was too much, but in my mind, nothing would ever be enough. I had no doubt she would say yes, but I wanted to make my proposal perfect. That, I still had to figure out. I wanted it to be memorable. If I had my way, we would be married before Christmas and have a baby on the way shortly after that. There wasn't anything holding us back.

I met with Jerome on Thursday. He worked my ass hard, but my shoulder was definitely coming back. By the time Jerome was finished working with me next March, I was sure that I would be in a better place than when I fucked up my shoulder to begin with. I don't know how I got so lucky to get him for a physical therapist, but I wasn't going to question a gift like that.

After our workout, I asked him about Gary. "Hey, Jerome, have you ever heard of Gary Hoffburn?" I asked.

"Actually, I have. Why do you ask?" he questioned.

"Well, my dad seems to think that he would be a good agent for me. What do you know?" I asked.

Jerome rubbed at his chin. "I think he would be a good match. Gary doesn't pull any punches. He's hardcore. You may not like him personally, but he'll work his ass off for you. He'll get you the best deal out there."

"Then it's a good thing to go with him?"

"Yeah. He'll get you every penny you deserve and more."

"Jerome, you know I'm done here in less than a week. Are you sure about the personal training? Are you still up for it?" I asked. I needed to have everything confirmed before I moved back home.

"Yeah, I'm still up for it. Are you changing your mind on me?"

"Oh, hell no!" I exclaimed. "I was just checking. My girl, Kyla, and I have just signed a lease for a condo in Grosse Pointe. How does that work with your plans?"

"It works. My family is about fifteen minutes from there." He gave me that big smile that only Jerome could own. "So, when do I get to meet this girl? You seem pretty smitten with her."

"I know this may sound sappy, but I'm willing to risk it. She's my heart. I love her more than anything. You'll meet her soon enough."

He nodded. "You gonna put a ring on that?"

I looked down at my feet. "I should have put a ring on it a long time ago. We went through a bit of a rough patch, but yeah, I just went and bought a ring yesterday."

Jerome clapped me on the back. "Congrats, man! When are you gonna pop the question?"

"I'm not sure. We've just recently got back on a good track. We started dating in high school and basically took the last year off. She's it though. I've got to find the perfect way to propose. One thing's for sure, I need her to come with me. Wherever I go."

"If she's that great, you've got to introduce us. I want to meet the future Mrs. Jackson."

Mrs. Jackson. I liked the sound of that. I couldn't wait to make her my wife. Things were going fast, but shit... I should have already proposed. When I made it to the pros, Kyla would never have to worry about money again. Although, I could totally see her clipping coupons, even if I made seven figures a year. She was cute like that.

I hoped that Kyla would be able to make a name for herself as a graphic artist. She'd already given up so much for me, I didn't want her to give that up too if I made it to the pros. I was going to put my business management degree to good use. I decided I would help her build her own graphic design business through the internet, so that she could work anywhere we moved. I knew she had the talent, she just needed to believe in herself. We had almost a year to build her business from the bottom up. One thing about Kyla and me, was we were both determined. We could do anything we put our minds to. We were the perfect team.

On Friday, Kyla drove up for my graduation. My parents were staying in a hotel nearby. We all met at my apartment and drove to the ceremony together. Kyla sat with my parents, as I sat with the other graduates.

I couldn't believe this part of my life was done. Now I would have to be a real adult and figure shit out on my own. I sat there waiting for my turn and thought about that. Kyla had already been living her life without a safety net. I couldn't imagine my life without my parents, and yet Kyla had been doing it for almost a year. As much as most kids my age were trying to break free of their parents, it was nice to know that they had your back. Kyla didn't have that. She'd been doing it on her own. Now it was time for someone to have her back, and that someone was me.

When it was my turn to walk across the stage, I could hear her cheering above anyone else. It was just like when she came to my football games. Kyla was always my biggest cheerleader. God, I loved that woman! I collected my degree from the dean and blew her a kiss from the stage.

After the ceremony, my parents took us to dinner at some fancy place. She sat next to my mom, and they chatted the entire night. I was so glad that she and my mom were getting along. Not that it had ever been a problem, but it was more important to me now than ever before.

When my mom and Kyla both excused themselves to use the ladies' room, my dad put his arm around my shoulder. "I'm not trying to push you son, but I remember you talking about marrying that girl. Is that still part of the plan?"

Not so subtle on my dad's part, but I guess he knew me well. "You don't think it's too soon? I mean we just got back together a month ago," I questioned. I knew what I wanted, but getting my dad's approval was important too.

"When you know, you know," he said. "You two are perfect together. Don't let her get away from you again. You know I love her. Nothing would make me happier."

I reached one hand behind my head and grabbed my neck. "I actually bought her a new ring," I said. "I just need to decide when to pop the question. I want it to be perfect."

My dad hugged me. "I'm so happy for you. I don't care what happens with your pro-football career. I just want you to be happy, and you're never happier than when you're with Kyla."

"I know," I said. "I'm thinking I should wait until after Chris and Tori's wedding. I don't want to draw attention away from their big day."

My dad pressed his lips together and nodded. "I think you should not worry about everyone else. Do what makes you happy."

As always, my dad had a point. Why wait? I got a great idea for a proposal while we were sitting at dinner. I would just have to check with Tori to make sure it would work.

Chapter 22
Kyla

Tyler thought he would already have a guaranteed football deal by now, but he handled his graduation with dignity and grace. It couldn't be easy to let that go. He was still planning on trying out as a free agent, but he had to be disappointed.

I enjoyed dinner with his parents. His mom and I were really hitting it off lately. I don't know what it was, maybe the miscarriage we had in common, but we seemed to have a strong connection. I was thankful for that. I was so afraid to face his parents after our breakup, but it only seemed to make our bond better.

Tomorrow was my graduation, and Tyler would be there. It was more than I expected a few months ago, but I was so jealous of him. I wouldn't have any family to cheer me on. It was just me. I knew my parents would be watching, but it made me sad that they wouldn't be in the audience. I had no doubt that Tyler would try to make it special for me, but sometimes there were voids he just couldn't fill.

After dinner, I went back to my own apartment so Ty could spend time alone with his parents. I started packing some of my things. Tyler and I were moving to our new condo this upcoming week and I didn't want to save everything until the last minute. I didn't need my winter clothes anymore, so I got a box and started folding my sweaters and big sweatshirts and putting them into the box, along with my winter coat. I filled the box, labeled it, and shoved it in the corner of my room.

Next, I moved to my desk. I slipped my sketchbook into the bottom of the box with some of my graphic design books. I opened the top drawer of my desk and I felt like a snake had crawled out and bit me. There on top, sat a picture of me. I recognized Tyler's arm over my shoulder, but Ty wasn't in the picture. The picture was torn in half and taped to it was a picture of Jake. He tried to make us look like a couple. It was fucking creepy. What was even creepier was knowing that the picture was not in my drawer this morning. That fucker had been here. In my room. Going through my stuff.

I was fucking done. He wasn't going to stop. The personal protection order meant nothing to him. And it wouldn't stop when we moved back home. He told me he was going to work for the police department in Chesterfield. It was less than a half hour from our new condo. And if he was a cop, he'd have no problem finding out where I moved to.

This had to end before we moved. That gave me literally just a few days to do what needed to be done. I couldn't and wouldn't tell Tyler. I could never tell him what I had planned. If something went wrong, I would be the only one to deal with the consequences.

Packing could wait. I used my printer to make copies of a few important things I had collected and put them in an envelope for Sid. I also wrote the number for an attorney I had researched and slipped it in the envelope as well. I sat at my desk and worked on the last item to go into the envelope. A tear ran down my cheek as I wrote the letter. When I finished it, I put it in the envelope and sealed it. Soon, he would know everything.

I grabbed my purse and headed for the door. Fifteen minutes later I walked into the gun range. Sid was behind the counter like usual.

"Aren't you graduating tomorrow?" Sid asked.

"I am and that means I won't be seeing you for a while. I'm moving back home this coming week. Tyler and I are moving into a condo together."

"So, he's the one, huh?"

"He's always been the one," I answered. "I just wanted to thank you for everything you've done for me. You helped me when no one else could." I gave him a hug and tried to reach my short arms around his big body. Then I stretched up on my toes and kissed him on the cheek, his long gray beard tickling my face.

Sid looked at me with sadness in his eyes. "It was my pleasure. I'm going to miss you," he said. "You still didn't tell him, did you?"

I shook my head. "No. This is my problem. It's better this way." I handed him the envelope. "Just in case," I said.

"I don't want this," he said, trying to give the envelope back to me.

"You're the only one who can do this for me. Please! Just do this last thing for me," I pleaded.

Sid nodded his head. "You practicing tonight?"

"Yeah. I'll need a lane and some extra ammo." Sid put my ammo on the counter. "This is my last night here. It's do or die." Sid cringed at my choice of words.

I went out to the range and fired round after round, burying each one in the center of the target. This was my final rehearsal before the big show.

When I got back to the apartment, Tori and Chris were busy packing. They were leaving on Sunday. They had bought a house together, not far from the condo Tyler and I rented.

I walked in and put my purse on the table in the hallway. "What can I help you guys with?" I asked.

Tori was packing up the kitchen. "You can help me finish up in here," she said. Most of the dishes and things belonged to her and Chris. "Are you sure you don't want me to leave any of this stuff for you?" she asked.

I started pulling the glasses from the cupboard and wrapping them in paper. "No, Ty and I are leaving on Tuesday. I'll be fine." I placed the glasses in a box, careful that everything was cushioned and wouldn't break.

"I feel bad leaving you here alone. Are you sure you're going to be okay?" she asked.

I waved her off. "It's like two days. I think I can handle it."

"But, what if...? I think Ty should stay here with you," she said.

"Tori, look at me," I insisted. She stopped wrapping plates and put her hands on her hips. "It's two days. I'm stronger now than I was before. I think you forget that I can take care of myself now. He's never going to touch me again. And if he tries... I'm ready."

Her eyes started to well up with tears. "I don't want you to be ready. I just want you and Tyler to have a happy life together. Everything has been going so well."

"You're right it has. And I'm thankful every day for him, but you know there are some things he can't help me with. I need to do this on my own. It may or may not happen... but I'm ready."

Tori wrapped her arms around me. "I love you, Kyla. You need to know that. I'm thankful every day that I've had a friend like you. If you go and get yourself killed before my wedding, I'm never going to forgive you." Her attempt at humor fell flat and we both knew it.

"I'm going to be at your wedding. Don't worry about that." I said the words and tried to reassure her, but the truth was I didn't really know. I knew what I had to do, but things didn't always go as planned. If they had, I wouldn't be in this situation at all.

I helped her finish packing the kitchen and then we both went to bed. Tomorrow was our graduation day.

The ceremony started at three, but I had to be there by two. Tyler showed up at one.

When he got to our apartment, he shrugged his shoulders. "I couldn't stop them," he said. Standing behind Tyler were Mr. and Mrs. Jackson.

Tyler's mom pushed her way into our apartment. "I couldn't go home without seeing you graduate," she said, giving me a big hug.

Ty's dad came next. "Congratulations, sweetheart." He pulled me into a tight embrace. It was very dad-like.

My eyes got teary, and I wiped them away before they had a chance to fall. "What are you two doing here?" I asked.

Ty's dad spoke up first. "Did you really think we would let you do this without family? You're like a daughter to us." He hugged me, and the tears rolled down my face.

"Thank you," I choked out.

"Honey, we're proud of you and your parents would be too. We needed to be here for this," Ty's mom said.

We left shortly after they arrived to go to the ceremony. Chris, Tori, and I all had our graduation gowns and caps on. Chris's family was there. Tori's family was there. And my family was there. I sent up a silent thank you to my parents again for everything they were doing to make this day special for me.

When I walked across the stage, I heard Ty cheering me on, just like I had done for him. I barely kept it together as I walked across the stage to receive my diploma. Once I had my turn, I returned to my seat and started crying silent tears. I was so happy that someone was here for me.

After the ceremony, we all went to dinner with Chris's and Tori's parents. Tyler's parents picked up the tab for everyone. I was surrounded by people who cared about me. I had Tyler's mom and dad. I also had Tori's mom and stepdad. They had been my second parents growing up, since Tori and I became friends in third grade. I didn't know Chris's parents very well, but they were nice, especially his mom.

One thing I knew for sure, was that I never wanted these relationships to end. Everyone sitting at the table that night was special to me in one way or another. I hoped that no matter where life took us, Tyler and I would always be friends with Chris and Tori. Since Ty and I didn't have any siblings, this couple had become our surrogate sister and brother. I hoped that one day our children would play with theirs. I didn't ever want life to take us in a direction where Chris and Tori were not a part of our lives.

After dinner, all the parents went home and the four of us went to a local bar to continue our celebration. We were enjoying the music and having a few drinks when "Here's to Us" came on by Halestorm. The four of us had been through so much together. I raised my glass and made a toast to the four of us. "To forever friends," I said. Everyone clinked their glasses and we listened to the words of the song. Yeah, we had messed up a lot, but we'd made it through. In my head, all I could think about was the fact that Tyler thought we had been through the worst, but he didn't have a clue. The worst, I was sure, was yet to come.

That night, before going to bed with Ty, I felt overwhelmingly loved. I needed him more than ever. I needed his strength. I knew what I was fighting for. I was fighting for our future, one that might not happen if I didn't take the next step.

I cherished and worshipped him that night. I pushed him back on the bed. "What's got into you?" he asked with his dimpled smile.

"What? Is it so wrong to want to take care of my man for a change?" I said seductively. I straddled his waist and started unbuttoning his shirt agonizingly slow. Each time I got another button undone, I kissed his chest underneath and moved on to the next. When I finally got to the last button, I spread his shirt open wide and rubbed my hands all along the hard muscles of his chest and abs. He sat up and I helped him push his shirt down over his shoulders and off his arms. I threw it to the floor and started placing kisses along the tattoos on his arms and up over his shoulder, down to his chest. I traced the words over his heart with the tip of my tongue and ran it over his nipples. I kissed the center of his chest down to the happy trail that disappeared into his pants.

I made quick work of the buckle on his belt, then unbuttoned his pants and pulled the zipper down with my teeth. "Are you trying to kill me?" he groaned. He lifted his hips, and I slid his pants and boxer briefs down his legs. I dropped them to the floor with his shirt.

It was unusual for him to be completely naked while I was still dressed. I stood at the bottom of the bed and took in the glorious man laid out before me. Every inch of him was pure perfection. I ran my hands up from his ankles to his thighs. "God, I love you. I am one lucky woman." I kneeled between his legs and took his long hard dick in my hands, gently stroking him up and down. I stuck out my tongue, licked his head, then wrapped my lips around his cock.

I heard Tyler hiss at the contact. "Jesus Christ, baby."

His reaction spurred me on to take him deeper. I used my hands to stroke him from his head all the way down to his balls. I swirled my tongue up and down his length, getting him nice and wet. I sank down with my mouth until I felt him hit the back of my throat. When I felt the pressure, I opened my throat and swallowed him deeper and deeper. I don't know that I had gone down this far before, but I could tell by the way Ty's hips bucked off the bed, that he was enjoying it. I swallowed over and over, my throat clenched down on him in a gentle pulsing rhythm. Tyler's hands went to the back of my head keeping me there and a string of curses escaped him as I continued pleasing him. "Baby… I'm gonna come so hard," he warned me. I kept at it until I felt his body stiffen and his dick harden even more. His warm cum released into my mouth and I swallowed every drop. I sucked him through his orgasm, then slid my mouth up and swirled my tongue around his head one last time. I wiped the sides of my mouth and ran my nails up along his chest. He looked so relaxed and satisfied. It made me happy to know I was the one that put that look on his face.

"Come here," Tyler beckoned me. I still had on my skirt from earlier. I pulled it up to my knees and crawled up the bed. "You're wearing too many clothes."

I leaned down and kissed his lips. "Oh yeah? What are you going to do about that?" I teased.

"I'm going to strip you down. One. Little. Piece. At. A. Time." He ran his hands up my legs under my skirt and tucked his fingers into the sides of my panties. "Starting with these." He slid them down my legs to my knees, then stuck his hand up my skirt and sank his fingers deep into my wet pussy. "I love when you wear skirts. Such easy access." He pumped me slow at first, and when I didn't stop him, he picked up the pace. He slammed his fingers into me harder and harder, finger fucking me until I could barely stay up on my knees. The sounds that escaped me were incomprehensible. "Feel good, baby?"

"God, yes," I moaned.

"Come closer. I want to eat your pussy." I hiked my skirt up and straddled his face. "Lower." I sank down on my knees until I hovered over his mouth.

The first swipe of Ty's tongue had the pleasure ripping through my body. I reached forward and grabbed the headboard for support. His tongue was magic. It swept through my opening and up through my folds to my clit. I leaned forward a little, giving a better angle to please me. I was being selfish. I wanted him to make me come so bad. He used his mouth to nip and suck my clit until I was writhing on his face. "I'm gonna come," I gasped out. Ty grabbed my hips and pulled me in even closer, burying his face in me. He worked me over until I screamed his name. I was panting hard, and my body was weak from the waves that had ripped through my body.

I crawled off him and Ty sat up against the headboard. I sat next to him and rested my head on his chest. He cradled my head and ran his fingers through my hair. "I missed doing that to you," he said.

"I missed having you do it." I smiled up at him, feeling totally content.

Ty reached for the bottom of my blouse and pulled it up over my head. "You look so sexy in this skirt with just a bra on, but this must go too." He reached behind my back and unclasped my bra. He slid the straps down my arms and as my breasts were revealed, he whispered, "So beautiful." He massaged my tits in his hands and captured one of my nipples in his mouth. He sucked and nipped and tugged with his mouth. I grabbed the back of his head and pulled him in closer. When he had given the same attention to both nipples, he whispered in my ear, "I want to make love to you, but first I want to fuck you."

His words sent another flash of wetness between my legs. "Yes," was all I could say. I was filled with lust and desire for the man next to me.

"I want you on your knees. And don't take that skirt off." I complied to his wants and got on all fours. My skirt was covering my ass and my breasts hung down. Ty came up behind me and leaned over my back. I felt his hard chest press into the arch of my back as I pushed my tits out. He reached around me and took them in his hands. "You are so beautiful like this."

Then I felt him pull my skirt up and he placed the material on my back. I knew everything was on full display for him. He ran his fingers through my wetness and slid them in. I could always feel how deep he was in this position. He pumped his fingers in and out a few times and then replaced them with his long length. He pushed in slowly. When he was all the way in, I dropped to my elbows, sticking my ass up higher and making the angle better for both of us.

Ty began to move behind me, pushing in deep then pulling out slowly as he ran his hand up and down my spine. He started slowly like that for my benefit, I was sure. He was testing the waters with me. I pushed back into him, and he understood what I was telling him. He increased the strength and speed of his thrusts, holding my hips for leverage.

I was over my fear of sex. How could I have ever been afraid this man would hurt me? After everything we had explored together, learned together, done together... there was no one in the world I felt safer with.

He reached one arm around me and rubbed my clit as he continued to pound into me from behind. I buried my head in the comforter to muffle my screams. He knew every button to push with me. He knew my body inside and out. My pleasure was always his first priority. He made me come again and again.

Ty pulled out and I immediately felt the emptiness. I let out a whimper of disappointment. "Don't worry. I'm not done with you yet, Ky." Tyler flipped me onto my back and put one of my knees over each of his shoulders. My hips were lifted high off the mattress and Ty was completely in control. He pushed into me slowly, so that I felt every long inch of his dick. I closed my eyes and grabbed for the sheets under me. He thrust into me over and over, using long slow strokes. Then he lowered me to the mattress and lay over the top of me. He twined his fingers with mine and raised them over my head. He held my hands the whole time as he finished making love to me.

Tyler stayed on Sunday to help Chris pack their moving truck. Most of the furniture in this apartment belonged to them, and Chris and Tori were taking it to their new house. When they finished packing everything up, the only things left were my bedroom furniture, the patio set, and a few miscellaneous kitchen items. And of course, all my personal items in the bedroom, which was a lot.

Chris and Ty did the one-armed bro hug before they left. Tori practically had tears in her eyes when she said goodbye to me. She hugged me tight. "Be safe."

"I'll do my best. I'll see you soon. We need to finalize everything for your wedding. We only have a month left." I winked at her. "Don't worry, I'll be fine."

Tyler and I watched them drive away and head back home. It was the end of another phase of my life. Ty put his arm around me and walked us back into the apartment. He looked around, "Jeez, it seems so empty in here. Are you sure you'll be all right?"

I turned and hugged him. "I'll be fine. You'll be back tomorrow night. Go home and finish packing your stuff."

He held me by the shoulders and looked down at me. "I don't like this. Why don't you come with me? The moving truck is coming in the late afternoon, we can be back in the evening."

"Ty, stop. Go home. Finish packing your things. Once you and Cody get everything loaded, you can come back tomorrow. I still have to pack my room up and you know I have a lot of shit. Divide and conquer. Besides, you know if we're together we'll just end up messing around instead of getting things done."

Tyler took a deep breath, "I know you're right. It's just that... I have a weird feeling about this."

"It's going to be fine," I assured him.

"Okay. Once I get my stuff loaded up, I'm coming back here tomorrow. My dad is going to meet the truck from my apartment at the condo. I'm just going to have them unload everything into the garage. Then I'll help you finish up tomorrow night and Tuesday we're out of here."

"I'm so ready to go home," I said. "Call and let me know when you're on your way tomorrow."

"You know I will. I'll talk to you later tonight too."

I wrapped my arms around his neck and gave him a soul searing kiss. "You need to go." I watched Tyler drive off, and then I was alone. I went out to the patio and lit a cigarette and mentally prepared for the night ahead. If Jake was going to make his move, it wouldn't be long now.

Before going to bed, I went to my closet and pulled out the bells I bought. I tied one set around the doorknob on the front door and attached the other to the slider. Then I went out to the patio and brought in one of the chairs. I wedged it under the doorknob. One thing was for sure… if that asshole was coming, he wasn't going to catch me by surprise. I took my gun out of my purse and checked to make sure there was a bullet in the chamber. Before I went to bed, I put the gun under my pillow. I didn't take my Xanax because I didn't want to be totally knocked out. The nightmare in my dreams wouldn't be half as bad as the real-life nightmare that would happen if he showed up.

I woke the next morning and everything was fine. My gun was still safely under my pillow and the bells didn't ring during the night. I made it through. I almost felt like this was the calm before the storm. He wanted me to feel safe, but I had no doubt he knew I was alone. Why didn't he come last night?

I didn't remove the bells or the chair. I left them in place and finished the packing I started a few days earlier. Ty called in the morning, and I assured him I was fine. He promised to call when he was on his way.

By around five, I'd finished all my packing and I still hadn't heard from Tyler. Hunger got the best of me. I hadn't eaten all day and started getting that queasy feeling in my stomach. I decided to run up and get a sub sandwich at the corner store. I attached my holster to the back of my jeans and slipped my gun into it. Having it in my purse wasn't enough. I needed it readily accessible. I removed the chair and walked out to my car.

I made the quick trip to the sub shop and brought my sandwich home. I unlocked the door and walked inside, dropping my purse on the kitchen counter since our hall table was gone. I put the chair back under the doorknob and made my way back to the kitchen to eat my sandwich. I opened the fridge and pulled out one of the two diet Coke's left in the fridge.

I closed the fridge, and I was grabbed from behind. One hand covered my mouth, squeezing hard, and the other around my waist. I heard his voice in my ear, "I told you I'd have you again." I could smell the alcohol on his breath and my fear paralyzed me. I couldn't scream. I could barely move. I couldn't do anything. This was not the plan I prepared for.

Just then, my phone started to ring, and my eyes flitted to my purse sitting on the counter. It was so close, yet so far away. I struggled in his arms to get to my purse, but it was no use. He wasn't going to let me get to it. "Where's your hero now?" Jake questioned. I felt myself being dragged back to my bedroom and flashbacks erupted in my mind. I remembered every moment of what this felt like the first time. I dug my heels into the carpet, but it was no use. He was too strong. I twisted and turned in his arms and the tears started rolling down my face. I thought I was ready for this, but I wasn't. Nothing could have prepared me for the feeling of helplessness I had.

So many thoughts flitted through my mind. I should have gone with Tyler last night. I shouldn't have gone for that damn sandwich. And most importantly... I couldn't let this happen again.

Jake got me to my bedroom and threw me onto the bed. A sense of déjà vu washed over me. I'd been here before and my reaction was the same. I looked for a way to escape. But he was blocking the door, just like the first time. His eyes were black, and his face was more threatening. I felt the fear start to take ahold of me and I took deep breaths to get it under control. *You're not a victim,* I told myself. *Take control. Do what you've been preparing for.*

Jake looked at me like he was the predator, and I was his prey. I was on one side of the bed. He was on the other. "This isn't happening again," I said defiantly.

Jake just shook his head. "You're so cute. You act like you have a choice. Wouldn't it be so much easier just to give in? Remember what happened last time? I really don't want to have to hurt you." He reached into his back pocket and pulled out the one thing that could make my blood run cold. "Look, I even brought your favorite toy." He held the handcuffs up to show me. If he got those on me, it was game over.

I backed up and bumped into the desk behind me. Something hard bit into my back. My gun. I still had my gun. In all the chaos, I had forgotten that I put it in the back of my jeans. This wasn't over. "Please leave. It doesn't have to end this way," I said. "You can leave now, and nobody gets hurt."

"Really? You think I'm going to leave and let you ride off into the sunset with your football star. Come on," he said sarcastically. He reached behind his back and pulled out his own gun and waved it towards the bed. "Get on the bed, Kyla. I just need one more taste. You're making this way harder than it has to be."

No fucking way was that happening. The fact that he had a gun should have scared me and it did. What he didn't know was that I had my own. This was not going to go down the way he planned.

I heard my phone ring in the other room. It had to be Tyler, telling me he was on his way. But I knew he would never make it here in time. My phone rang and rang. And when it stopped, it started again a few seconds later. "Ty's going to be here soon. Trust me, you don't want to be here when that happens," I said.

"I'll be long gone by then," he said. He was cocky and that would be his downfall. I knew Ty would be here in less than an hour. "Will he even want you when he finds out what a whore you are? A little cock tease? You teased me for so long and then pretended like you didn't want it. Come on, Kyla. Those little outfits you wear when you go running. You were practically begging me for it. We had something special. Don't you remember?"

He was delusional. I told myself to just keep him talking. Help would be here soon. *You're not a victim. You're not a victim.* I kept repeating it over and over again in my head.

He waved the gun at me again. "Just get on the bed, Kyla. This will be the last time. I promise."

Not going to happen. I remembered what I looked like after the last time he attacked me. I remembered the shame and the guilt. It all came crashing back to me. I remembered looking at myself in the mirror. I remembered Ty's words to me through the door the next day. *I'm not giving up on you. I'm not giving up on us. I love you, Kyla O'Malley.* I closed my eyes and reached behind my back. *I love you too, Tyler Jackson.*

I grabbed the gun and pointed it at Jake. "Like I said, this isn't happening again."

Jake shook his head at me. "Kyla, seriously? I've seen you with a gun. You're just going to hurt yourself."

"You seem so sure of yourself, Jake. If you think I'm bluffing, go ahead make your move." He took two steps forward. I raised the gun and took aim. "You sure you want to risk it?" I asked.

"Oh, Kyla." He shook his head again and waved his gun at me. "Get on the fucking bed!"

We were at a standoff. "No!"

"You always have to be so difficult!"

He lunged at me, and the gun went off. Two times in rapid succession. I slumped back on the desk behind me and closed my eyes. This was the end. It was finally over.

Chapter 23
Tyler

I pressed send again on my phone. It just kept ringing and ringing. "God damnit, Kyla, answer the fucking phone!" I shouted into the car. Why wasn't she answering? I tried over and over again, and it kept going to voicemail. "What the fuck!" I threw the phone on the seat next to me.

Chapter 24
Kyla

I had aimed at his chest like Sid taught me. Jake's eyes went big, and he looked down at his chest. "You bitch!" He fell to the floor in my room. I stood there holding the gun for what seemed like an eternity. I walked towards him, with the gun still raised and kicked him with the toe of my shoe. The red spot on his shirt continued to get bigger and bigger. He was bleeding out.

He had dropped the gun and it sat next to his motionless body. I kicked it to the side, then stood and looked at him with no regrets as the life drained from his body. His eyes were still fluttering. I crouched down next to his ear. "That was for raping me, you sick fuck."

Then I leaned against the wall and slid down it. I sat there, across the room, staring at Jake. I watched as the blood seeped into carpet beneath his body. "You just couldn't leave me alone, could you? This was your fault, not mine. You left me no choice." I spoke aloud. I sat there until the last signs of life left him.

I slowly stood back up and walked by him with my gun still raised as I hurried to the kitchen. All I could think about was the Michael Meyer's movies, where everyone thought that he was dead and then he disappeared. Where I thought Jake would go, was beyond me. I just didn't want him coming after me.

I reached in my purse and took out my phone. There were several missed calls from Tyler. I dialed 911. When the operator answered, I froze. "911. What's your emergency?"

I answered in a shaky voice. "There was an intruder in my home. I shot him. I think he's dead."

"Okay ma'am. Stay on the line with me. What's the address?"

I quickly gave her the address and hung up the phone. I took the chair out from under the door and unlocked it. Then I cautiously moved back to the bedroom. I never lowered my gun but made one more phone call and waited for the police.

Chapter 25
Tyler

I'd called Ky like a dozen times, and she hadn't answered. *What the hell?* Something was not right. I could feel it. I should have made her come with me.

I broke every traffic law to get to her. When I pulled up in front of her apartment I was blinded by the red and blue lights that were flashing. I ran from my car to her apartment and got stopped by some cocky cop on my way in.

"This is my girlfriend's apartment!" I shouted. I pushed past the cop into Kyla's apartment. I wasn't prepared for what I saw. Kyla stood there with her back to me, and she was being handcuffed. "Kyla!" I cried out as I was being restrained.

She turned her head to me. "Ty, I love you! It's going to be okay, baby! Grab my purse. Sid will meet you at the police station."

So many questions swirled through my head. What the hell was going on? Who the fuck was Sid? I stood there frozen and then saw two guys removing a body, with a blood-stained sheet over it, from Kyla's bedroom on a stretcher. What the fuck happened? Someone tried to grab me from behind. I shirked out of their hold and grabbed Kyla's purse off the counter.

"Who's Sid?" I shouted.

Kyla was being led out the front door in handcuffs. My whole world came crashing down on me. Ky dug in her heels as the police led her past me. "A friend. It's finally over," she said.

What did that even mean? My girl was being taken out in handcuffs. I tried to go after her.

A police officer grabbed my arm. "Sir, you can meet us at the police station."

"What the fuck is going on!" I cried. "What happened?"

The cop wouldn't let go of my arm. "She shot an intruder. Follow us to the station, sir," he said calmly.

I ran out to my car and jumped behind the wheel. No way were they taking my girl away without me. I didn't understand what was going on. *She shot someone?* How could that be true?

I followed the police car and parked in the handicapped parking. When I got inside, I talked to the guy at the desk, "They just brought my girlfriend in here. I need to see her!" I shouted. By this time, all rational thought had left me.

I needed to know what happened and why Kyla was being arrested. Arrested? What the fuck? Never in a million years would I ever have seen that coming. *What had she done? How was I going to marry her if she was in jail? Again…What. The. Fuck?*

The desk clerk looked up at me. "What's her name?"

"Kyla. Kyla O' Malley. I need to see her."

"Have a seat, sir. I'll let you know if, and when you can see her," he said.

Was this guy fucking kidding me right now? "Tyler?" A voice erupted from the chairs in the waiting area.

I turned my head but didn't see anyone familiar. A big, burly biker guy stood up. "Come sit next to me, son." I looked all around me, but I was the only one standing there. "You Tyler?" he asked.

"Yeah," I said defensively. I was not to be fucked with at this point. "Who are you?"

"I'm Sid. I'm a friend of Kyla's."

I walked over to him in total confusion. This was Kyla's friend? I reached out my hand and he grasped it tightly. "She's okay. Trust me." Trust him? I didn't even know who he was. "She said to give you this." He pushed an envelope into my hand, and I looked at him. Who the hell was this guy? "Open it," he insisted.

I slumped down in one of the chairs and opened the envelope. There was the picture from when she'd been attacked, a copy of the PPO and a few other random papers. I already had seen all this. I reached further into the envelope and pulled out a scrap of paper. It read, *Just in Case*, and had the number of an attorney on it. I looked at Sid and he nodded for me to continue. I reached in and pulled out a piece of notebook paper with Kyla's writing. I unfolded it and read.

Dear Tyler~

I love you so much! If you are reading this, then one of two things has happened. Either I am dead, or I've been arrested.

A tear slipped from the corner of my eye. Dead? What the hell? I kept reading.

Hopefully, it is the latter. If I am dead, you need to know that I love you and none of this is your fault. I knew Jake would come for me eventually. It was just a matter of time. I wanted to marry you and have babies with you. You are the love of my life.

If I have been arrested, rest assured I should be out in a few hours. If not, call the number for the attorney. Like I said, I knew he was coming for me. He wouldn't leave me alone, not even after the PPO. He's terrorized me for the last four months. I know I kept things from you, and for that I apologize. I never wanted you to know how bad it was. Jake handcuffed me to my bed on Christmas Eve and raped me. Deep down, I think you already knew that, but neither one of us was ready to say it. The picture you saw was only a small part of what he did to me. I didn't want you to know because I was afraid you would look at me differently. I didn't report it, and I couldn't suffer the humiliation of a trial. It would have been my word against his and he would have gotten off. I shot him, and I hope I killed him. It was the only way I could move on. It was the only way we could move on. I knew he would never let me go and I couldn't live the rest of my life with that hanging over my head.

I didn't tell you about this for so many reasons. One, we weren't together when it happened. It would have destroyed you and you would have blamed yourself. I couldn't hurt you like that. Two, I knew you would try to talk me out of handling Jake. Three, you couldn't know because that would make you an accomplice and I didn't want you to be arrested too. You would have gone after Jake yourself. This was all on me. I take full responsibility.

You're probably wondering about the big biker guy who gave you this envelope. His name is Sid and he's a great guy. He was the first one to know what happened to me. He helped me a lot. The gun I used to shoot Jake with was mine and Sid helped me learn how to use it. He helped me to heal and get stronger. I owe him everything. He was a friend when I really needed one.

If things happened the way I thought they would, Jake came into my apartment. I shot him in self-defense. Yes, he had every intention of raping me again and I couldn't let that happen. I've done my research. The law is on my side.

I hope after you read this, you still want to be with me. I did it for us. I'm not a murderer. I'm not a victim. I'm a survivor. If you choose to walk away, I understand, but I hope you want to continue this journey we started together.

I always have, and I always will love you~ Kyla

I couldn't believe what I read. He raped her. Now it was confirmed. She knew he was coming for her, and she chose to face him on her own. When the fuck did she get a gun? My God! What the fuck had she been thinking?

I looked at the guy sitting next to me. "Tell me everything."

Sid looked at me and then around the lobby we were sitting in. "Let's go outside," he said. I followed him out to the parking lot. "There are too many cameras in there. It's safer out here."

"I don't understand. Did she plan this? Where in the hell did she get a gun?" I asked.

"I own a gun range," Sid said. "She came in the day after Christmas to buy a gun. She was waiting in the parking lot before I even opened the store. She had her face covered and I knew something was up. When she took off her sunglasses and hood…" Sid shook his head. "It was bad. Her face looked like someone had used her as a punching bag and she had welts all over her wrists. I knew what had happened to her. I've seen a lot of bad shit in my days. That was the first time I met Kyla."

"She was scared, but she also had a fire inside of her. Over the next few weeks, I taught her everything she needed to know to defend herself. She had a really hard time at the beginning. She spent a lot of time blaming herself for what happened to her. But she got stronger and more confident. You should know, she's a fighter. That girl's smart too. She planned everything out. It's why she got the PPO to begin with. She left a paper trail to justify her actions in case it ever came to this."

I ran my hands over my face and rubbed at my eyes. "I can't believe this. She's five foot nothing. Why didn't she tell me? I could have done something for her."

"Because you would be sitting in that jail cell instead of her right now, only you wouldn't be getting out. She'd never let that happen. She loves you too much," he said.

"She's my whole life."

"Let's go back in. The law is on her side. She didn't do anything wrong. It was a justified shooting. He attacked her, and she defended herself. She'll be out soon."

"I owe you a thank you. You helped her when I couldn't," I said.

"I love that little girl as if she were my own. Helping her was easy."

I sat with Sid for another hour while we waited. I called my dad and explained what happened. My dad was shocked and wanted to come out, but I told him to hold off until I knew what was going on. Sid said everything was going to be fine, but until I saw Kyla I couldn't relax. This whole situation was like a nightmare. I couldn't believe I was sitting in a police station waiting for my girl to be released.

Finally, Kyla walked out from the back. She wasn't in handcuffs, and she was talking to a guy in a suit. She shook his hand and looked relatively calm. He handed her a plastic evidence bag. She took the gun out of the bag, inspected it, and slipped it into the back of her jeans. I know it was a weird thought but seeing her handle the gun like it was nothing was kind of hot. My girl was badass.

She approached me nervously. I opened my arms for her, and she walked right into them. I crushed her to my chest. "That was so stupid, baby. Did he hurt you?"

"Not this time. He can't ever hurt me again. It's finally over. We can move on now… if you'll still have me."

I looked into her perfect green eyes. "I told you… I'm never leaving you again. You're stuck with me."

She shrugged her shoulders. "That's good, because my lease is up at the end of the week and I'm already packed," she smiled.

Kyla turned out of my arms and walked over to Sid. She hugged him tightly and he hugged her back. I could tell this guy really cared about Ky. "Thank you for everything. I wouldn't have made it through this without you."

"You're stronger than you give yourself credit for. You did good, sweet girl." Sid leaned down and gave Ky a kiss on the forehead. "Now go start your life with your man."

Kyla and I left the police station hand in hand. I opened the door for her, and she slid into the seat. I quickly called my dad to let him know that Kyla was out, and we would see them tomorrow. I slid into the car next to Ky. "I'm so thankful you're all right. I fucking panicked when I pulled up and saw the police. When we get home, I want you to explain all of this to me from the beginning. No more hiding shit."

"There's nothing left to hide. This was the last of it and I'll tell you everything," she assured me.

"I love you, Kyla. Seeing you dragged out in handcuffs... I didn't know what to think." I shook my head. "That guy, Sid, you like him a lot, don't you?"

"Yeah, he taught me a lot. He helped me in ways I don't think anyone else could have. He's the one who told me to forgive myself. He helped me heal. And he taught me how to shoot." She raised her eyebrow at me and got a little smirk on her face. "I'm actually really good at it too."

I couldn't help but smile back at her. I pinched her cheek. "I bet you are. I gotta tell you, when I saw you at the station with that gun... it kind of turned me on."

"Really?" she questioned.

"Really," I said.

We pulled up to her apartment and walked to the door. Kyla pulled the yellow crime scene tape off and crumpled it up. I handed her purse over and she unlocked the door. Bells jingled, and I looked behind the door. "Alarm system," Kyla said. "I didn't want him to surprise me in the middle of the night."

I let out a sigh. "I think we'll get something a little more sophisticated for the condo."

Kyla dropped her purse on the counter and held up a sandwich. "Think this is still good?" She unwrapped it and took a bite. I looked at her like she was crazy. "What? I'm hungry!"

"You're really not fazed by this at all, are you?"

She took her sandwich and led me out to the patio. She plopped down in a chair and I sat next to her. "I know this is a lot for you to take in, but that fucker got exactly what he deserved. When all this shit happened, I looked in the mirror at what he'd done to me, and I swore to myself that I was going to kill him. He threatened that he was going to come back, and I wasn't going to let anything like that happen to me again. I should have never gotten involved with him in the first place. That was on me, but never again." She shook her head and took a bite of her sandwich. "He was here on Friday when I was at your graduation. That fucker was in my room. He left a picture for me with you torn out of it. It was never going to end. He was moving to Chesterfield. That's a half hour from our new place. No way was I going to let him destroy our new life together."

I was still so confused. "How did you know he would come for you?"

"He's been watching me for months. I knew he would see Tori and Chris moving out. It made me the perfect target."

"So why didn't you come with me? It would have been safer. Why would you purposely put yourself in danger?"

"Ty, it was never going to end. I had to do it. I knew he wouldn't be able to resist. I was just surprised he didn't do it last night. I went out to get this stupid sandwich and he got in while I was gone. This…" Kyla took the gun out of her jeans and placed it on the table, "…saved my life." She got out of her chair and came to sit on my lap. "I did it for us. So we could start our life together. I feel so much freer now that this is over. I'm not afraid anymore."

I ran my hand through her hair, "You could have told me. I would have helped you."

"You have helped me. I'm happy again and that's because of you." She pulled me close and kissed me.

"No more secrets," I said. "From either of us. We tell each other everything from this point forward. Deal?"

"Deal," she said. "Now let's go bring my mattress out to the front room. I don't want to sleep in my bedroom."

We went back to her room, and I looked around. There was blood splatter on the wall and comforter and a big blood stain on the carpet. I took a deep breath. "This kind of makes it real."

"Yeah, I don't think I'll be getting my security deposit back," she joked.

"Probably not," I agreed. I couldn't believe how well she was handling all of this. "Weren't you scared?"

"Terrified, but then I thought about what I was fighting for, and I pulled the trigger. It was me or him. It wasn't going to be me." Kyla pulled the comforter off the bed, folded it and placed it over the blood stain on the floor. "I don't want to look at that," she said.

We carried the mattress out to the front room and dropped it in the middle of the floor. We stayed up late into the night and talked about everything. I didn't think I could love her any more than I already did, but as she explained to me about what she had done and why she had done it… my heart swelled. We made slow, passionate love, as I thanked God that she was safe and here with me.

Chapter 26
Kyla

Ty and I finished packing up all my stuff in the morning. We took apart my bed and he took the bloody comforter to the dumpster. We followed the moving truck back home in our separate cars. I called Tori on the way and explained everything that had happened the day before. We made a date to go over her wedding plans and do our final fittings for our dresses.

When we got to the condo, we unloaded and paid the guys a little extra to carry all of Ty's furniture into the house from the garage. After everything was done, we collapsed onto the couch together and looked around. "We have some stuff to buy," I said. "I have a bunch of things at my parents' house in the basement. What do you think I should do with all of that anyway? I mean the house is rented until the end of August, should I sell it?"

"What do you want to do?" Ty asked.

"I want to start fresh. I think I want to sell it. Will you help me? It's going to be a lot of work and I'm dreading it."

Tyler wrapped his arm around my shoulders and kissed the side of my head. "Is that even a question? Of course, I'll help you."

"We really are a team now, aren't we?"

"Yep. And don't make any plans for Thursday through Sunday."

"Why?" I questioned.

"Because after everything you've been through, I want to take you away. Tori and Chris are going to meet us at the lake house. We need some time for ourselves, and it will be good to spend it with our best friends."

I was totally excited. "You know I love that place, but what about everything that needs to be done here? I have to start work on Monday."

"It will all be here when we get back. We deserve this, because when we get back, life's going to get real. You're going to start your job and I have to start on the club. Plus, I need to keep training for football."

"You're right. I want to go." I sighed. "I love our life. You've made me so happy. Six months ago, I never thought this would be possible and look at us now."

"I'm happy, too. This is the way it was always supposed to be." He pulled me by the hand and led me back to our new bedroom. "Let's christen it. I want to make love to my girl."

We did. And it felt so good to be free of everything else. Ty was right. This was the way it was supposed to be.

The next day Ty went to meet his uncle to discuss the club. I went to see Zack.

I walked through the door and Zack embraced me. "You're back," he said. He held me by the shoulders. "You look good. Happy."

"I am. Schools over, I've got a great job, a new place to live, and a great man."

Zack cocked his head to the side. "Dragon tattoo guy?"

"Yeah, dragon tattoo guy. I should be mad at you, you little liar." I laughed.

"What? I didn't lie to you. The guy came in and offered a thousand bucks for you and a hell of a lot more for me to do the work. Nobody would pass up that kind of money." He smirked.

"Yeah, well, Tyler and I are back together. That little stunt with his tattoo helped sealed the deal. How much did he pay you?"

Zack cringed. "I'm almost embarrassed to say."

"How much?" I asked again.

"Five grand. But, Kyla, honestly, I didn't know the whole story when I called you. I didn't know who he was until I was actually inking him."

My mouth dropped open. "He paid six grand for that dragon? I'm going to kill him." Ty and I were going to have a talk about spending money when I got home.

Zack laughed at my reaction. "I have to tell you. The guy was head over heels about you. He took a big risk, but I guess it paid off."

"I would have taken him back without the tattoo. Hell, I've got our story inked all over my body. We were always meant to be together. We just took a little detour."

Zack crossed his arms over his chest. "So… are you going to work for me or what?"

"Yes. Let's figure out the details." I followed Zack back to his office and we worked out a system that worked for both of us.

Life was good.

When I left Forever Inked, I followed the directions Ty gave me to the building for the club. The place was in a great location, right off the water. People were going to love that in the summer, but the building itself looked like a rundown piece of shit. I knew it was the right place because Tyler's motorcycle was out front. I parked next to it and made my way inside. Compared to the inside, the outside looked pretty good.

Ty had his hands on his hips, looking around at everything. "Hey, baby. How'd it go with Zack?"

I walked toward him and kept looking around at the disaster in front of me. "Really good. Umm, Ty... this place is a shithole."

He started laughing. "Yeah, it is. But I've been checking it out and I have some ideas. Come look at this." We walked over to the wall that faced the water. He led me to a small door and out to a big grassy area. "I was thinking about taking this wall out and replacing it with those big roll-up doors. We could cement this area and put a patio out here with its own separate bar."

I looked out over the lake. "It's a great view. I'd sit out here to have a drink. With the doors open it would give the inside an airier feeling too. What about the inside?"

We walked back in and looked around. Ty pointed around. "Horseshoe shaped bar over there, black tile floor, DJ booth there with a dance floor. I know it needs a ton of work, but it has possibilities."

"It's going to need a pop of color. I'm thinking like an electric blue or bright purple. You know it's my favorite," I waggled my eyebrows at him. "What's it going to be called?"

"I don't know yet. But you're right about the color thing."

"I think you should mix the blue and the purple, maybe add a little pink. It'll give it night club feel. You could run colored lights around the top and bottom of the bar. The waitresses could wear purple and the bartenders could wear blue. I could come up with all kinds of ways to integrate the colors." I looked around the space again and my mind was spinning. A bunch of ideas were popping into my head. This place was a blank slate, but I needed to remember this was Tyler's project, not mine. I already had a job. "I'm kind of overstepping, aren't I?"

Ty stepped up behind me and wrapped his arms around my waist. "You're not overstepping, Ky. You're the one with the creative mind. I want to hear your ideas. We're a team, remember?"

I turned in his arms and gave him a kiss. "I know, but this is your project. So, unless you ask me, I'll keep my mouth shut. When are you planning to open?"

"My Uncle Lou was here this morning. He'd like it up and running by mid-summer. He wants to take advantage of the summer season before the weather turns cold."

I took a step back. "That's like less than three months. Do you think it can be done?"

"There's a lot of work to do, but I'm meeting with the contractor on Monday. It can be done."

"Okay, I'm gonna get going. I'm stopping at the grocery store and then I'm going to try out our new kitchen." I pointed at him as I backed away toward the door. "Oh yeah, and we're going to have a very serious conversation tonight. You're in big trouble, mister." My tone was lighthearted, but I was serious. I wanted to talk to him about spending money. I know we had more than most people, but that didn't mean we needed to spend it frivolously either.

"God, something smells good in here!" Tyler walked in just as I was taking dinner out of the oven. He set his helmet on the counter and came over to give me a kiss.

"I hope it tastes as good as it smells, because you know I haven't done a ton of cooking. It's a chicken, broccoli, and rice casserole. My mom used to make it. I should have paid closer attention when she was cooking. I just always assumed she'd be there for me to call when I had questions."

"I'm sure it'll be great. And even if it isn't, I'll choke it down anyway." Tyler laughed.

"Now that's love," I said sarcastically. I served us each up a plate and set them on the table.

He took a bite of the casserole, and I watched him carefully. "Ky, this is really good." He seemed genuine and I chalked one up for me. "So, you didn't really say, how did everything go with Zack?"

"Good. I'm going to work commission based. He's going to call me when he thinks he has I job I can do, and then I'll get a cut. It's going to be very on-demand, but I'll try it and see how it works." I wiped my mouth with my napkin. "Which leads me to our next discussion. How much did you pay for that dragon tattoo I designed?"

Ty hung his head. "Did I tell you how good this is?" he asked, shoveling another forkful in his mouth.

"You don't have to tell me. I already know," I said. "I asked Zack."

"Tattletale," I heard him mumble under his breath.

"Ty, I know it was before we were together, but seriously, five grand?" I cocked my head at him.

He put his fork down. "I know it was a lot. I just really wanted it, and I knew it sounded shady when I asked specifically for you to design it. I had to make it worth Zack's time, otherwise I was afraid he wouldn't call you."

"I understand," I said softly. "But with buying my new car, and the rent on this condo, and all the things we need to buy, I'm starting to get anxiety about money. I'm not used to spending like this."

"Kyla, I don't know how to get this through to you, but we're in a really good place financially. I don't want you to worry about money. We've got this, but I promise I'll be more conscious about what I'm spending and if it's something big, we'll discuss it first."

"Thank you. That's all I'm asking." I didn't want to make a big deal out of it. I didn't grow up with a lot of money. I never wanted for anything, but my parents were frugal.

"That's it? That was the big discussion?" he asked.

"That's it," I confirmed.

"Wow. That was easy. Do we still get to have make-up sex?"

The next morning, we left early for the lake house. We took my car, but Tyler drove. The sunroof was open, and the wind blew through my hair. I slumped down in the seat and put my feet up on the dashboard. Tyler looked at my black painted toes. "Some things never change," he said.

"I'll try not to fall asleep this time," I promised.

He laughed. "You're already in sleeping position."

"My legs don't reach if I sit up straight," I defended. I closed my eyes and the next thing I knew, Tyler was kissing me awake. "Damn it! I did it again, didn't I?"

"Yeah. You always do." He ran the back of his fingers down the side of my face. "Come on, let's go. Our friends are waiting."

The air was chilly, and I pulled my zip-up around me. We carried our bags around to the back deck and I looked out over the lake. "It's so beautiful," I said softly.

"Just like you," Tyler whispered in my ear. He placed gentle kisses along my neck and up the side of my face.

"Are you two coming in or are you just going to make out on the deck?" Chris yelled at us. "Get your asses in here!"

The spell was broken. "We're coming!" Tyler shouted back.

"Not yet, I hope. You haven't even made it to the bedroom." Chris answered.

Tyler shook his head. "Asshole." We went inside, and he took our bags up to our room.

"Hey, girl!" Tori shouted and gave me a hug. "I'm so glad you're here and safe," she said, just loud enough for me to hear.

"I told you I'd be fine. I've got a big wedding to attend."

Tori giggled. "I know. Can you believe I'm getting married in a month?"

"You two have been solid from day one. I'm not surprised at all. I just wish it was me." I shrugged.

"Your day is coming soon. I can't believe how you and Tyler fell right back together. I mean, I knew you would eventually, but damn that was fast. So, how's the living arrangement?"

"It's only been two days, but so far so good. I love knowing that every morning I'm waking up to my best friend."

Tori gave my shoulder a little shove. "I thought I was your best friend."

"You know what I mean," I said. "You'll always be my best girlfriend. But Tyler, he's my whole world. And I already love the life were building together."

We spent the rest of the day just hanging out with Chris and Tori. The weather wasn't warm enough yet to enjoy the water, but we still spent time on the beach. That night, Tyler and I took a long walk along the shoreline, our feet getting wet from the waves crashing onto the beach. We held hands and just talked. Everything was so easy between us again. It was almost as if our time apart never happened. I wished I could go back in time and change things. I would have told Tyler about the baby from the start. I would have fought harder for him. But then again, maybe we needed to go through all the ugliness to get us to where we were today. Maybe it made us appreciate each other more.

After my parents died, I felt so alone. I felt like I was drifting without direction. I was doing the best I could, but everything seemed so overwhelming. With Tyler by my side, I didn't feel lost anymore. He was my anchor.

I turned to Tyler as we returned from our walk. "Thank you for bringing me here."

"You're welcome, Ky. I know you love this place. After graduating and all that stuff with Jake, I thought you might appreciate the time away. Plus, it gives me time alone with you. No distractions. Just you and me." He pulled me into his arms and kissed me passionately. He lifted me up and I wrapped my legs around him.

"Take me to bed," I whispered.

"You don't have to ask twice." Tyler carried me up the steps and into the bedroom.

After a lazy day of hanging out on Friday, the four of us decided to go out for dinner. Tori decided for us, that we should dress up a little bit and go somewhere nice. "Come on, girl. I'm gonna do your hair and makeup for you. It'll be just like when we used to get ready for dances in high school." Tori grabbed my hand and started to drag me up the stairs.

"Help," I mouthed to Tyler over my shoulder. He just laughed and waved me off.

Tori pulled me into our room and locked the door. "What are you going to wear?" she asked.

I looked in my bag at what I had. I had mostly brought jeans and T-shirts. "I don't really have anything nice to wear."

"Hold on." Tori held up a finger. "I bought this new peasant skirt and top. It's a little small on me, but I think it would fit you perfect." She rushed out of the room and came back with a white flowy skirt and blousy top. "Here try this on."

I held it out in front of me. "This is really cute. What would make you buy something like this? You're definitely not a skirt person."

"Impulse buy. Obviously, it wasn't meant to be since it didn't fit."

"Why don't you just take it back? I can find something else," I said.

"No, it'll look great on you. Keep it," she insisted.

Tori curled my hair in soft waves and did my makeup. She did have a talent for this stuff. When she finished, I slipped on the skirt and blouse. I looked in the mirror at myself. This outfit was really cute on me, and it fit perfectly. "I love it," I said.

"Why don't you go find Tyler while I get ready. I'll be down in a few."

"Okay, we'll meet you guys on the back deck." I went down the stairs and looked around. "Ty?" He didn't answer. Maybe he went outside. I opened the slider and stepped out onto the deck. "Ty?"

"Down here," I heard his voice. I looked out to the beach, and he was standing there surrounded by candles. He looked scrumptious in his khaki shorts and long-sleeved shirt with the sleeves rolled up. I walked down to the beach toward him, and he pulled me into the circle of electric candles.

"What's all this?" I asked.

"I just wanted to show you how much I love you." He was holding both of my hands in his. "This lake house was where I gave you this ring." He ran his fingers over my hand. "And I gave you my heart four years ago. I never want you to forget how much I love you. I want to spend the rest of my days with you and have babies with you." He reached into his pocket, got down on one knee and pulled out a ring. My hands flew up to my mouth. "Kyla O'Malley, will you do me the honor of being my wife and spending the rest of your life with me? Will you marry me?"

"Yes! Yes!" I fell into him and wrapped my arms around his neck. He picked me up and spun me around.

"Thank you for making my life whole. I promise to cherish you and take care of you forever and always." He put me down and slipped the ring on my finger. "I love you, baby!" Then he looked up to the deck. "She said yes!"

I turned and looked. Chris and Tori were standing watching us. Chris had his arm around Tori and Tori was jumping up and down clapping.

I was speechless. I knew we were going to get married one day, but I didn't expect it to happen this soon. "They knew about this, didn't they?"

Ty kissed my forehead. "I had some help." He shrugged.

I looked down at the huge rock with a diamond band on my hand. "It's gorgeous, Tyler." I took his hands and stared into those blue eyes that always captivated my heart and soul. "I'm going to be Mrs. Kyla Jackson. We're really going to do this. I'm holding onto you." A tear slipped from my eye. "I can't wait to be your wife."

Tyler leaned his forehead against mine. "Yeah, we're really going to do this. I'm never letting go again." He wrapped me in his arms, and we stood there just holding each other. "I planned on taking you out for a nice dinner tonight, but I just kind of want to take you to bed." As if on cue, my stomach rumbled, and he started to laugh. "Dinner first and then bed," he said definitively.

Chapter 27
Tyler

I was nervous as hell, but Chris and Tori helped make sure everything went smoothly. I knew Kyla wouldn't be expecting me to propose this soon. Sure, we had talked about getting married, but it was some distant dream. When Kyla walked out to me, with her hair and skirt blowing in the breeze, I knew I was making the right decision. I never wanted that woman to doubt my intentions.

Her reaction was just what I had hoped for. When she fell into my arms, I knew the deal was sealed. I wanted to marry her sooner than later. I didn't know what she would think about how long we should wait or how big of a wedding she wanted. None of it mattered to me, all I needed was the two of us.

I took her to this cute little restaurant in town. Thankfully, I'd made reservations because the place was crazy busy. We were seated at a corner table. The lights were low and soft music played in the background. It was super romantic. She looked beautiful in the candlelight and her eyes sparkled.

"I can't even tell you how happy I am." She glowed as she admired the ring on her finger. "This is absolutely gorgeous, but you could have tied a string around my finger, and I'd have been happy."

"You deserve more than that. I wanted a gorgeous ring for my gorgeous girl." The thing was, I knew she was being honest with me. She would have been happy with a piece of string. She never cared about material things or what I could give her. She only cared about having me. "Should we call my parents and tell them the news?"

"Do you think they're going to be upset that you proposed so soon? We've only been back together a month," she worried.

I gave a little chuckle. "No. My dad was the one who encouraged me not to wait. They're excited for you to be their daughter-in-law."

"Okay. Call them."

I dialed my dad's number and put it on speaker. "Hey, Dad. I have news to tell you. I proposed, and she said yes."

I heard my dad yell to my mom in the background. "She said yes!" I laughed out loud. "So, when are you getting married?" my dad asked.

"I don't know. We haven't discussed it yet."

"Well keep us in the loop. Is Kyla there?"

"Yeah. You're on speaker phone."

"Congratulations, sweet girl. I'm so happy that you're going to officially be part of our family. Not that you weren't before, but you know what I mean. Thank you for making my son so happy."

"Thank you, Mr. Jackson," she said. "Your son makes me very happy too."

"I love you both. Congratulations! I'll talk to you soon."

"Okay, Dad. Love you too. Bye." I pressed end and looked at Ky. Her eyes were all watery. "What's wrong?"

She swallowed down the lump in her throat. "He said he loved me."

I took her hand across the table. "They both do. You're easy to love." She nodded her head and wiped at her eyes. "So, the question is, when and where do you want to get married?"

She bit her lip. "I've thought about this since my parents died. Not the when, but the how. I'll do whatever you want, I don't want to take anything away from your family." She lowered her head and looked up at me from under her lashes. "I really want a small wedding. But I can do big if you'd prefer."

I'd always assumed she'd want a big wedding. I was kind of surprised. "I'm fine with small, but why don't you want a big wedding?"

She shrugged her shoulders. "I don't know. It just won't be the same without my mom and dad." She got a sad look on her face. "My mom won't be there to help me get ready. My dad won't walk me down the aisle. There won't be any daddy-daughter dance. I can count on one hand the people I care about being there."

I hadn't thought about it from her perspective. She really had no family left. All the things she probably dreamed about as a little girl, wouldn't happen. "Tell me what you'd want our wedding to look like, if you didn't have to worry about anyone else but you."

"I can't. It's selfish," she said.

"It's okay to be selfish sometimes. If you could have anything, what would you want?"

She sighed. "We would get married on the beach by the ocean at sunset. I'd wear a white sundress with flowers in my hair. And I'd be barefoot." She smiled. "I'd want your parents there and of course, Tori and Chris. I don't really care about anyone else. I just want you to be my husband. And after we said our vows, I'd want to release butterflies because with you I've finally learned how to fly again."

She was making me get teary. It was such a simple wish. No frills. No fancy dress. No invitations or any of the other bullshit everyone else worried about. "That actually sounds really nice. What about a reception?"

"I'd be happy with a nice dinner, as long as I got to have at least one dance with my new husband." She looked down at her lap nervously and then back at me. "I know. It's ridiculous, isn't it? Your parents are probably already making a guest list."

"I don't think it's ridiculous. I think it's romantic and perfect."

"Don't you want a big wedding?" she asked.

"You know what I want? I want you to be my wife. I don't care about the rest of it. Let me talk to my parents. I don't think it's going to be a problem."

"Really? I don't want to rain on their parade."

I shook my head at her. "You always worry about everyone else. It's our wedding. Our day. It should be the way we want it."

We were just finishing our dinner when I decided to ask her another important question. I knew we had just had the talk about money earlier in the week, but this was something I wanted to do. "I have to ask you a question and it has to do with money."

She looked at me suspiciously. "What's that?"

"I was talking to Chris about their wedding. He's totally stressing out because it's so expensive at the Grosse Pointe War Memorial. He's taking out a loan to pay for it."

Kyla took her napkin off her lap and set it on her plate. "I'm gonna kill Tori. I knew that place was totally out of their price range. But she was insistent. I love her, but she's stubborn."

I laughed. "Look who's talking about being stubborn. Anyways, I was thinking…"

She interrupted me, "You want to help them pay for it."

"They're our best friends and they've always been there for us. I don't want to see them struggle if we can help them."

"They've done more for me then you'll ever know," she said. "How much? How much were you thinking?"

I cringed because I knew she wasn't going to like the number I had in mind. "Ten thousand?"

She crinkled her eyebrows at me. "I was thinking more like twenty. I have money from my parents, and I don't have a problem sharing with the two people who helped me get through the hardest times in my life. I owe them more than that. We could each put in ten."

I looked at the amazing woman sitting across from me. "You never want to spend anything on yourself, but you're okay with this? I thought you were going to fight me on it."

"They're not taking out a loan to pay for their wedding. Not when we have the means to help them. I love those two."

"You're amazing, you know that?" Every day she made me fall more and more in love with her.

That night, we were lying in bed and Kyla was snuggled into my chest. "You never answered my other question. When do you want to get married?" I asked her.

"Tomorrow?" She giggled.

I kissed the top of her head. "I'd gladly marry you tomorrow, but I think we're going to need more time than that to pull together a wedding by the ocean."

She turned and rested her chin on my chest. "Sooner than later. I don't see a reason to wait. Do you?"

"No. I'm not changing my mind. What about August?" I suggested.

"August sounds perfect. It'll give us time to get through Tori and Chris's wedding and plan ours. What about the club? How will that work?"

"I'm going to have to hire another manager anyway. They'll just have to get along without me for a week."

"I'm still worried about your parents. What if they hate the idea of a small wedding?"

"They won't," I assured her. "They just want us to be happy."

"I am happy," she said. "Want me to show you how happy I am?" She laced her hands with mine and held them next to my head while she kissed the ever-loving shit out of me. Our tongues twisted together as we devoured each other. Kyla straddled me and slipped my dick into her heat. She rode me up and down, closing her eyes as she shamelessly rubbed her clit on me.

I flipped her over and took control, pushing into her deep and long. I was so happy she was on birth control, so that we didn't have to use condoms anymore. The feel of her, skin on skin, was ecstasy. I pushed into her a few more times and then pulled out to hold off my own orgasm. Running my fingers through her folds and down to her pussy, I thrust my fingers in and out of her as she whimpered for more. She needed to come, so I ran my thumb along her clit in small quick circles and she shattered beneath me. I loved watching her like this.

I moved back into her and felt her clenching around me. Pushing her legs to her chest, I thrust in and out fast and hard. I loved her so much and I couldn't believe this was my life. This was my future. Our bodies glistened with sweat. "I'm gonna come again," she cried.

"I'm right there with you, baby." With just a few more thrusts we fell over the edge together. The waves of pleasure took over and we basked in it. We'd always had amazing chemistry. Our sex life had never lacked, and it just seemed to be getting better and better since Jake was out of our life. I collapsed on top of her. "God, I love you."

"I love you, too," she said breathlessly. "You're officially my fiancé now and I couldn't be happier."

"I can't wait to make you my wife." I'd thought about it for so long and now it was finally going to happen.

Chapter 28
Kyla

The next morning, while we were lying in bed, I asked Ty, "Did you bring your checkbook?"

"Yeah. Why?"

"Because I think we should transfer the money to our checking accounts and give them the money today. I brought my checkbook too. We can each write them a check. We'll give them the checks and then go running so they can't argue with us."

Tyler quirked his eyebrow at me. "You want to literally run away from them?"

"Yes. They'll be more willing to accept it if were not standing in front of them. It'll give them time to talk without an audience."

"That's actually a good idea. You're pretty smart, you know that?"

I grabbed his cheeks in my hands. "So I've been told. Come on let's get dressed."

Tyler and I got dressed in our running clothes and made the bed. We used his laptop to transfer the money and wrote our individual checks. Mine was written out to Tori and his to Chris. We made our way out to the back deck where they were having their coffee. They were already like an old married couple.

We stood in front of them, and I started, "I just want to say thank you for everything you two have done for me over the last year. I don't know how I would have made it through without you both."

Then Ty took over. "We don't know if we would have found our way back to each other without you guys. You've helped us both in so many ways and now we want to help you. We want you to take these, as a gift, to help pay for your wedding."

Ty and I handed over our checks and their eyes popped out. Tori's eyes started watering and Chris wrapped his arm around her. "We can't accept these. It's too much," he said.

"Yes, you can," Ty said.

"We want to. We love you guys," I added.

Tori had tears running down here face. "Thank you. You don't know how much this helps."

Chris stood up and hugged Tyler. "Thanks, man." He was so filled with emotion, that it was a real hug, not a bro-hug.

I leaned down and just held Tori. I whispered in her ear, "Thank you for everything. You've been the best friend I could ever ask for." I wiped a tear from my own face. "We're going to get out of here for a while. We'll see you in a little bit."

Tyler and I walked down to the beach. I wrapped my arm around him. "That felt really good."

"Yeah, it did," he agreed. "Seeing their reaction was worth every penny."

"Will you dance with me at their wedding?" I smiled up at him.

"You know I will. You're my girl." He leaned down and kissed me.

We did some stretches and plugged in our phones. "You wanna switch today?" Tyler asked. "I see you singing the words while you're running. I always wonder what you're listening to."

"Okay," I said. "I don't really think it's up your alley though."

"That's fine. I'm just curious." He handed me his phone and I handed him mine. "We'll stop at that big rock down the beach?" he suggested.

"Sounds good. I'll race you there."

"Is that a challenge?"

I smirked at him. "Maybe." And with that we took off running. I knew I couldn't beat him, but I enjoyed the playful banter. I wasn't surprised at what was on his playlist. He always liked hard rock and metal. I did too, but I was more selective. His music pushed me harder and at one point, I actually passed him. But running on this sand, always wreaked havoc on my muscles.

We made it to the rock, and I was exhausted. My heart raced, and my lungs burned. I crawled up and sat on the rock furthest out in the water, like I always did. Tyler crawled up behind me, so I was sitting between his legs. We looked out at Lake Michigan, and I relaxed back into him. There was water as far as I could see. I knew Wisconsin sat somewhere on the other side, but I couldn't see it from here. We sat in silence for a long time just listening to the waves and the seagulls.

I broke the silence. "So, what'd you think?"

"About your playlist?"

I nodded.

"I didn't realize that it would be such man-hating music," he joked.

I playfully smacked his shoulder. "It's not man hating. It's woman empowering. I like listening to a woman who takes control of her life. I found it inspirational when I was having a hard time. It made me feel like I could take back control of my life."

"I'm just giving you a hard time. If it helped you, then I like it." He kissed the top of my head. "I've been thinking about your idea for our wedding. I really love it and I think my parents will love it too. Your grandparents should be there. You should have family there and I'm sure they would love seeing you get married."

I hadn't thought about that, but Tyler was always thinking about me. "You're right. Gramps would love to walk me down the aisle."

"Where do you want to get married?" he asked. "I know on the beach, but have you given it anymore thought?"

"I was thinking about Key West. It's not that far of a flight and I'm sure they have some beautiful beaches where we could have the ceremony. It wouldn't be too expensive either."

"Kyla… you and this money thing. You just gave Tori ten-thousand dollars, but when it comes to your own wedding you want to save money. I was thinking Hawaii, but Key West would be beautiful too."

"Hawaii is so far away. Let's think about it for a few days."

"Sounds like a deal. At least we have it narrowed down to two places."

"Either way, we'll be married in less than four months. And that's the most important part to me." I leaned back into Tyler, and he wrapped his arms around me. Sitting like this with my future husband was the best feeling in the world.

Tyler was right. When we got back, real-life started. We were two working adults that spent most of our day apart. My favorite time of the day was coming home to each other. I started cooking dinner more and trying new recipes. Most of them were pretty good, but even when they weren't, Tyler would eat it anyways. Unless it was godawful, then he would go get us take out. Sometimes, in the evening, when we both brought work home, we'd work quietly at the kitchen table together, stealing kisses every now and then. I loved falling asleep in his arms and waking up to him too. I guess any time we were together was my favorite part of the day.

My new job was going great. My co-workers were cool, and I had the flexibility to work from home on several occasions. Zack started sending me tattoo design requests. I would draw them up, scan them, and send them back to him. The system was working out well and the extra money was nice. Ty wanted to help me start my own graphic design company. I didn't know the business side of that, but he did, and we started working on a business plan.

Tyler was working his ass off. He left early in the morning to go to the gym and then headed to the club. He had met the contractor the Monday we got back from the lake house, and it had been non-stop since. The outside of the building already had a new look, and the inside was cleaned up. The wall facing the water had been torn out, the roll-up doors were installed, and the cement for the patio was poured. Tyler was constantly on-line researching products for the inside, like lighting, tables, chairs, and a million other things. He decided on the name "Xtreme" for the club, and I got started on designing the signage and logo that would be used.

Tyler and I were the perfect team. We each had a different set of skills to bring to our projects. We were both smart and determined. We worked well together, and I was sure that we could accomplish anything we put our minds to.

It was the week before Tori and Chris's wedding. I went with Tori for our final dress fittings and the boys were going to do the same for their tuxes. She tried on her dress and stepped out of the fitting room. She looked like a princess in her strapless, sequined gown. She stepped up on the pedestal in front of the mirror, and I took her veil and placed it on her head. "You look beautiful. You're going to take Chris's breath away when he sees you."

"You think so?" she asked.

"I know so. Are you getting nervous at all?"

"I'm nervous that everything will run smoothly. I'm not nervous about being married to Chris. He's my best friend."

I bumped her hip and threw the words she had said to me, back at her. "I thought I was your best friend." I laughed.

She realized the irony of her own words. "You know what I mean." She smiled at me.

"Yeah, I do. We're two lucky girls. Not everyone gets to marry their best friend and the man of their dreams all in one package." I looked at her standing there in her wedding gown and thought about how both of our lives were about to change. "Promise me something?"

"Anything," she said.

"Promise me that no matter where our lives take us, we'll still stay friends. You know Ty's still trying to go pro and I don't know where we're going to end up, but I want our kids to play together and grow up together. It would kill me if we drifted apart."

Tori stepped down off the pedestal with tears in her eyes. "I promise. Friends forever."

"I love you, girlfriend," I said over the lump in my throat.

"I love you, too."

I wiped the tears from my eyes. "So, when we're finished trying on the dresses for your wedding, we should look for something for mine." I hadn't told Tori much about our wedding plan since I wanted to focus on her wedding right now.

"Did you guys set a date?"

I nodded. "August."

"This August?" she asked in surprise. I nodded again. "Where?"

"Pack your bags. We're taking you guys to Key West. I want to get married on the beach."

"Oh my, God! We have so much to do!" She clapped her hands excitedly.

"Not really. I'm planning everything with the wedding coordinator down there. She's taking care of everything. All I need to do is find a dress. It's going to be simple and small, like really small. Ty's parents, my grandparents, and you two. You will be my matron of honor, won't you?"

"Yes! Of course! I'm so excited for you!" She cocked her head to the side. "Tyler's parents were okay with this?"

"They were. I almost think they were relieved. We took a lot of the stress out of the planning."

"Are you ready for this? It's so quick. You guys haven't been back together that long."

"I've loved him forever. He's been my whole world since I was seventeen. I'm ready."

"Try on your maid of honor dress to make sure it fits, and then we'll look for your wedding dress."

"We can wait until after your wedding," I said.

"No, we can't. We only have a little over two months." Tori said as she stepped back into the fitting room to take off her wedding dress. "Come in here and try your dress on."

I stepped into the fitting room and took my dress off the hanger. It was a black strapless dress that came just above the knee. I stepped into it and Tori zipped me up. "This fits you perfectly. You look hot," she said.

The top part almost covered the heart-shaped tattoo on my chest, but not quite. I ran my fingers over it and felt the bumps underneath. "I'm sorry about this," I said. "I was hoping this dress would cover it."

"Don't you dare be sorry," Tori said. "You should wear it as a badge of honor. You made it through and you're stronger for it. I can't even imagine. If it bothers you, we'll cover it with makeup. Does Ty know everything that happened to you?"

"He does. I know he suspected, but I did tell him. I thought it was going to freak him out, but he did everything to help me overcome my fear of sex. I could barely let him touch me in the beginning. He was so patient with me. For the most part, we're back to being us."

"You know what you did with Jake was crazy, right?"

"I told you a reckoning was coming. I knew he would come after me. I had to do it. And you know what? I don't feel bad one bit. He got what he deserved. If I wasn't prepared, I would have had to live that nightmare all over again."

"I know. And I'm glad things worked out the way they did." Tori took a deep breath. "Now let's find a dress for you!"

I wanted something summery. I didn't want a bunch of fluff and sparkles. I honestly would have been happy with a regular sundress, but Tori said that would be unacceptable for my wedding. After looking at what seemed like a hundred dresses, I found one that was perfect. It was a V cut in the front and fastened around my neck. It fit me snugly through the hips but flared out at the bottom. It wasn't exactly a sundress, but it was very summery, and I could go barefoot with it, which was a requirement. The dress was covered in brocade and was beautiful. I let Tori pick out her own dress. Since she was the only attendant, I just wanted her to find something she liked and would wear again. She chose a lilac-colored dress, and I was secretly happy with her choice. I put the payment for both dresses on my credit card and we called it a day.

In one week, my best friend was going to get married and soon I would too.

Chapter 29
Tyler

Kyla and I worked our asses off. We both went to work every day and brought work home each night. She was trying so hard to be the perfect wife already. She cooked dinner almost every night. I didn't expect it, but she was insistent. Sometimes it was good, sometimes not so much. I ate it anyway because she was trying. I loved her for the effort she was putting behind everything.

I was meeting with Jerome twice a week. He coached me on my weak spots, and I was improving every day. Kyla finally insisted on meeting Jerome and had me invite him for dinner. I suggested carry out, but she wanted to cook dinner. I just prayed that whatever she cooked was going to be good.

When Jerome came over, Kyla was busy in the kitchen scurrying around. It smelled wonderful. She decided to make lasagna, with garlic bread and salad.

I introduced Jerome to Kyla. "Jerome, this is my future wife, Kyla. Kyla, meet Jerome."

Kyla hurried over and gave Jerome a big hug. Her arms barely reached around him. "I'm so glad to finally meet you," she said. "I've heard great things about you. I think Ty actually loves you." I rolled my eyes.

"It's good to meet you too. You're a tiny thing, aren't you?" he said.

"Don't let her size fool you. She's a spitfire, for sure," I joked.

She smacked me with the towel in her hand. "And you wouldn't have it any other way."

I wrapped my arms around her and kissed her forehead. "That's for sure." I opened the fridge. "Jerome, you want a beer?"

"Sure. I'll take one. So, how did you two meet?" he questioned.

"We started dating in high school," she said. "I was smitten from the start. He was the QB, and I was the captain of the cheerleading squad. Everything else is history."

I loved how she glazed over our time apart. It was nobody's business. We were us. Destined from the start. Kyla served us dinner and it was damn good. She had outdone herself. After dinner, Jerome and I went out to sit on the balcony.

"You got yourself a keeper there," he said.

"Yeah. I know. She never cared about anything else but me. If I don't make it to the pros, it won't bother her a bit. She's not in it for the money or the fame. She was always with me for me."

"Oh, you're going pro. Don't doubt it. The agent you've got will make sure of it." He took a sip of his beer.

"I can only hope. We're getting married in August. I want to be able to provide for her the way she deserves."

"You just said she didn't care one way or the other."

"She doesn't," I explained. "That's on me. She's got her own successful job. I don't want her to ever have to worry about anything. She lost both of her parents last year and I just want her to be happy."

"She looked pretty happy just being with you. It doesn't matter what happens. Don't lose sight of what's important. A good woman can make all the difference in your life."

Kyla popped her head out of the slider. "Can I get you guys anything?"

"We're all good, Ms. Kyla. Thank you!" Jerome said. Kyla nodded, closed the slider, and went back inside. "See. She's a good woman."

"I know. I'm a lucky guy." And I was.

"Jerome seemed nice," Kyla said, sitting on my lap on the couch.

"Don't let him charm you. He's been kicking my ass for months," I admitted.

"But he's helping you, right?"

"He is. He pushed me, even when I didn't want to be pushed."

"That's a good thing."

"It is. Dinner was delicious tonight, baby. Thank you."

"I tried my best," she said. "It's not always great, but you've been a trooper."

"Ky, I could care less if you ever cook. That's not why I want to be with you.

"Oh yeah, why do you want to be with me?" She laughed.

I flipped her off my lap and laid her down on the couch. I straddled her legs. "Lots of reasons." I stuck my fingers up the leg of her shorts and slipped one of them inside her.

She closed her eyes and moaned. "Tell me more."

"I'll tell you everything you want to know," I whispered in her ear as I slipped another finger inside and pumped them in and out of her.

"I can't hear you. Louder!" she cried.

I slipped a third finger in, stretching her. What started as something playful, became hot and heavy. "Do you like that, baby?"

"Yes," she said breathlessly, as she lifted her hips into my hand.

I started rubbing my thumb over her sensitive clit and it didn't take long before she came around my fingers. "What was that for?" she gasped.

"That was just because I love you."

The night before Chris and Tori's wedding, Chris came to stay with me, and Kyla went to Tori's house. Tori had insisted they keep the tradition of the bride and groom not seeing each other before the wedding. It was kind of silly since they already lived together, but Chris would do anything to make Tori happy.

We sat out on the balcony having a few beers. "No wonder Kyla likes it here. It's pretty chill sitting and looking out at the water." He took a sip of his beer, staring out over the lake. "How's she doing anyways? After the Jake thing?"

"I think she's okay. It's hard to tell with her." I decided to ask Chris the question that had been weighing on my mind but been too chicken shit to ask. "Did you know?"

"Know what?" He wasn't going to make this easy on me.

"What happened to her? All of it?" I picked at the label on my beer bottle.

He sighed. "Not at first. She told us the morning she came home from the cemetery. She showed us the picture. She didn't come out and say it, but I asked her, and she broke down crying. We couldn't tell you, man. It would have destroyed you. I'm sorry."

I just shook my head. "I'm not mad. It's just... I still can't believe she went through that shit. I knew something must have happened, but... fuck! I still can't say it."

"He raped her. You not saying it, isn't going to make it go away. How are you dealing with it? I'd be out of my fucking mind if something like that happened to Tori." He finished his beer, and I finished mine. I could tell we would be a having quite a few of them tonight. I grabbed another beer from the cooler next to my chair for each of us.

I looked out over the water and said the words aloud for the first time. "I know he raped her, but I try not to think about it. I can't because then I get this awful picture in my head. I don't want to see it. She's my girl and I love her."

"What about sex? You two used to be pretty untamed."

Chris and I rarely talked about our sex lives. A few times here and there, but we kept most of our shit private. I hadn't talked to anyone about what Kyla and I had gone through. I needed to get this shit off my mind, and I knew Chris wouldn't judge. "She had a really hard time at first. She wanted to, but she just couldn't. I grabbed her wrists one night and she freaked out. I didn't know that fucker had handcuffed her." I swallowed the bile in my throat. "She wouldn't let me put my fingers or dick in her for a long time. It's been a process. She's still learning how to trust again, but we're getting there."

"You're a good guy. Kyla's lucky she has you. Not everyone could have dealt with it the way you have."

"Did you know about the gun? What she planned to do?"

Chris nodded. "Yeah, she pulled it out of her purse and shocked the shit out of Tori and me. She knew how to work it though. She'd been going to the range for like two months before we knew anything. We tried to talk sense into her, but she was determined. She wouldn't give us any details. She said it was plausible deniability."

"She fed me the same line of crap afterward. It was dangerous and brave and stupid. It could have gone wrong in so many ways." I took another sip of my beer and shook my head. "But you wanna know something crazy? When I saw her with that gun and how she handled it… it turned me on. I got so fucking hard."

Chris's eyes popped out and he nearly spit his beer out. "You're kidding me, right?"

"I'm not! It was fucking sexy as hell." I laughed. "My girl's kind of a badass."

When we finished laughing, Chris got serious again. "I owe you an apology, man. I told you I'd watch out for her, and I didn't. I just never thought something like that would happen. I should have been there."

I smacked him on the shoulder. "It wasn't your fault. You always had her back. If I hadn't been such a jackass, she would have never dated that fucker. If anyone is to blame, it's me. I'm the one that let her down. I think that's why it was so hard on me. I'm the one who should have been there." I didn't know if my guilt would ever go away. All I could do was move forward and promise to take care of her from now on.

Chapter 30
Kyla

Tori and I planned on spending the day getting beautiful for her wedding. She hired a stylist to come to her house to do our hair and makeup. Besides me, Tori's cousin, Sadie, was standing up in the wedding with Chris's brother. The stylist started with Sadie's hair first, while we drank mimosas in our sweats. We turned on some music and danced around the family room.

"I'm getting married today!" Tori sang out. I grabbed her hands and spun her around the room. We were jumping around and singing at the top of our lungs. The mimosas were going down quickly and honestly both Tori and I drank too many for this early in the day. It had been forever since the two of us just let loose together.

Suddenly the music turned off. "What the hell is going on in here?" Tori and I froze and turned to see Tyler standing in front of the stereo with his arms crossed over his chest. He had on a Mötley Crüe T-shirt with the sleeves cut off and he was wearing his hat backward. He looked hot! I couldn't help but eye fuck him. He looked between the two of us. "Are you two drunk?"

Tori hiccupped and covered her mouth with her hand. "No," she giggled. We both broke out into a fit of laughter.

"Oh my God, you are!" He couldn't keep a straight face and broke out into huge smile, then shook his head. "As much I love seeing you two having fun together, there's a wedding in five hours and you need to be sober." He took our glasses to the kitchen and dumped them in the sink.

"Party pooper," Tori mumbled.

"What are you doing here, anyway? We're not supposed to see you until the wedding. It's the rules," I slurred.

"I'm allowed to be here. I'm not getting married today." Tyler started making coffee for us. "Besides, Chris wanted me to deliver this to Tori." He pulled a box from his back pocket and handed it to her.

There was a note tied to the top of the box. Tori opened it and I hung over her shoulder to read the note. *I'm so excited to finally make you my wife. Today all my dreams are coming true. I Love You~ Chris.* Tori started bawling and she opened the box. A pair of diamond earrings sat nestled inside. "They're beautiful," she cried. She took them out of the box and attached them to her ears. "Is that coffee done yet, I've got to pull it together."

Ty made us each a cup of coffee and placed them on the kitchen table. "You two are bad together. Are you girls going to be okay for the wedding?"

"We'll be fine," Tori assured him. "How's Chris holding up?"

"He's good. Really happy."

Sadie came into the kitchen with her hair all done. "Were you two partying without me?" She frowned. Tori and I both got guilty looks on our faces. "You're next, Kyla."

I got up from the table and went over to Tyler. "Just so you know, you look fucking hot right now," I whispered in his ear. "I can't wait to see you in your tux tonight. I haven't seen you in a tux since prom night. Maybe we can relive it after the wedding." I pressed my lips to his and walked away with a smirk on my face. Yeah, I was a little drunk, but it felt good. I was already thinking about the afterparty that would take place in our bedroom. And I'm sure he was too.

We were sitting in a room set aside for the bride. The wedding was starting in ten minutes. I tucked a curl up under Tori's veil and looked at her. "You look beautiful. It's almost show time." Tori's mom and Sadie had already gone out into the hallway, so it was just the two of us. "Are you ready?"

Tori took a deep breath. "Yes. My nerves are kicking in though."

"You've got nothing to worry about. Everything is going to be perfect. Let's go." I took Tori's hand and led her out in the hallway to the French doors we would be walking through that would take us out to the patio by the lake. Tyler, looking handsome in his tux, was there talking to Chris's brother, Jim. They turned to look at us as we walked out.

"You look beautiful, sis," Jim said. "You're going to take my brother's breath away. He's already out there waiting for you." Jim leaned in and kissed Tori's cheek.

"Thanks," she said.

I saw her nerves kicking up another notch. "Just breathe," I told her.

The music started to play, so Ty clapped his hands together and shouted, "Let's do this!" We all lined up for the procession. Chris's parents walked out first, followed by Tori's parents, and then Sadie and Jim. When it was our turn, Tyler and I hooked arms and started down the aisle. He leaned over and whispered in my ear, "You look beautiful, Ky. This is going to be us in a couple of months."

"I know. I can hardly wait." We didn't have to fake the smiles that were on our faces. They were genuine. When we got

238

to Chris, we split to take our places. Tyler and Chris knuckle bumped and then the Wedding March started.

All eyes were on Tori as she walked down the aisle with her stepdad. He'd been with Tori's mom since Tori was three, and always treated Tori as if she were his daughter. He kissed her on the cheek and turned her over to Chris. I took Tori's bouquet, and they began their vows. Ty and I kept sneaking looks at each other during the ceremony and I'm sure he was thinking the same thing I was. We couldn't wait for this to be us. My eyes got watery as they proclaimed their love for each other and were officially pronounced husband and wife.

After dinner, it was time for Tyler and me to make our toasts to the newlyweds. Neither one of us had shared our speeches with each other, so I had no idea what to expect when Tyler stood up to do his first.

"When I moved here from Bay City, at the beginning of my senior year of high school, I was agonizing over the fact that I had left all my friends behind. And then football season started, and I met this guy." He pointed to Chris. "Chris and I quickly became friends, and he helped me fit in and find my way. When we graduated, he went to Western, and I went to Michigan State. I was afraid our friendship wouldn't last, but it did. He was there for some of the greatest parts of my life and some of the worst. He always stood by my side, trusted me, and believed in me. I don't think he knows how much he's done for me over the years, including introducing me to my future wife. We've had our ups and downs, but through all of it, our friendship has remained. He's the best friend a guy could ask for. So, raise your glasses and join me in wishing Tori and Chris a long and happy life together. You two deserve it!" Everyone raised their glasses and toasted the new couple.

Next it was my turn. I stood and faced Tori. "Tori has been my best friend since I was eight years old. Since neither of us had any siblings, we quickly became like sisters. We were attached at the hip for most of our time growing up. She has been there through all the good times and the bad. She gave me advice when I didn't want to hear it and has held me up more times than I can remember. When I felt like my life was falling apart, Tori was always there to help me pick up the pieces and put them back together. And though our lives may move in different directions, we've promised to never let that separate us. Chris and Tori have been an important part of my life and I can never truly thank them for all that they have done for me... for us." I pointed to Tyler. "You two are the best friends a girl could ever ask for. And when we all have families, I want our children to play together and grow up knowing the kind of friendship we have had. I love you both and wish you happiness in this journey you have started together. Everyone, please join me in wishing Chris and Tori a life full of happiness and love." Everyone raised their glasses and wished them the best. I hugged them both with tears in my eyes.

  Shortly after the toasts, the dancing started. We all stood as Chris and Tori shared their first dance as husband and wife. They looked so happy together as they swayed to the music and held each other close. After their dance, Chris took the microphone and invited the rest of the wedding party to join them. "This song was picked especially for our Maid of Honor and Best Man, who will be tying the knot in August. We love you two." Tyler and I made our way to the dance floor along with Sadie, Jim, and the parents.

  Nickelback's "Never Gonna Be Alone" started playing and I nearly broke down. Tyler held me close and whispered in my ear, "I love you, baby. Just hold onto me and I'll never let you go. You've made me the happiest man alive, and I can't wait to share the rest of my life with you." I locked eyes with him and the look we shared told everything that was in our hearts and souls. He held me close, and we listened to the words as we danced. This song was perfect for us and what we had been through. With Tyler, I would never be alone again.

We danced and chatted throughout the night. Ty's parents were invited to the wedding and his dad approached me. "Can I have this dance?" he asked.

"Of course." I smiled at him as I took his hand and he led me to the dance floor.

"You look beautiful tonight, sweet girl. Love looks good on you."

"Thank you," I said. "I'm very happy." Now that I had him alone, I asked the question that had been weighing on my mind. "Are you and Ty's mom really okay with us getting married so soon? I know it's really quick and probably not what you envisioned for your son's wedding. I just want to make sure you're not upset."

Ty's dad smiled down at me with eyes that matched his son's. "Jackie and I are ecstatic. We were heartbroken when you and Tyler separated. We've always wanted you as our daughter. After everything you two went through, you deserve this. I've never seen Ty as happy as when he's with you. And the wedding, although not traditional, is going to be beautiful. We're more than okay with everything."

"Thank you for accepting me as part of your family. I'll do my best to always make Tyler as happy as he makes me."

The song ended, and Ty's dad kissed me on the forehead. "I know you will."

At the end of the night, we'd both had a little too much to drink, so Tyler called an Uber to take us back to our condo. We walked through the door and headed back to the bedroom. I stripped Tyler out of his tuxedo jacket and started unbuttoning his shirt. "I've been thinking about this since your comment this morning," he said. "Which kept me hard all day imagining you naked in our bed."

"I want you so bad," I gasped as I continued to work on his buttons. I finished quickly and pushed his shirt off his shoulders. Tyler unzipped the back of my dress and it fell to the floor. The fire we once had was back. We became animalistic and primal as we finished stripping each other and clothes flew in every direction. Tyler picked me up and I wrapped my legs around his waist. I held his head and stared down at him. "I don't think I'll ever be able to tell you how much I love you. I'm holding on to you forever."

"And I'm never letting you go." It had become our new phrase for each other, and it was perfect.

We made love through the night and into the early morning hours. It was just like prom, only this time, we knew exactly what we were doing.

The next morning, Tyler and I were lounging around in bed. I was running my nails up and down his muscular chest when I got a great idea. "I have to go see Zack today to drop off some designs. Do you want to go with me? I thought maybe we could take your bike."

Tyler ran his fingers up and down my back. "I'll never pass up a chance to have you on the back of my bike with your arms wrapped around me. So yeah, I'll go."

"I was thinking about getting a couple's tattoo. Interested?"

He looked down at me. "Hell, yeah. What'd you have in mind?"

"I have an idea. I just have to draw it up. Let me call Zack and see if he can squeeze us in." A few minutes later I had talked to Zack, and he assured me it wouldn't be problem. I drew up the design and showed Ty. He was on onboard.

I put on my riding gear—jeans, boots, and leather jacket—and met Tyler in the garage. He helped me fasten my helmet and I climbed on the back of his bike. "God. You're sexy like that."

I looked at him in his leather jacket and boots. "You look pretty sexy yourself."

Ty got on in front of me and started the Harley. I wrapped my arms around his waist, resting my head on his back. Twenty minutes later we pulled up in front of Forever Inked.

I walked in first. Zack came around the counter and pulled me into a hug. "Hey, girl!"

"Hey yourself. I brought someone with me today."

Tyler held out his hand. "Hey, Zack."

Zack took it. "Dragon tattoo guy."

I laughed. "Also known as Tyler."

"I know, but it's a great story," Zack said. "You have those drawings for me?"

I handed him the envelope and he opened it. "Kyla, your shit keeps getting better and better. Do you know how many tats I've sold off your other designs?" He walked behind the counter and pulled out another envelope. "As promised, here's your check." I took the envelope, folded it, and put it into my purse. "So, you two really worked out, huh?"

Ty wrapped his arms around me in a possessive gesture. I wondered if he thought there might have been something between Zack and me at one time, because he was definitely staking his claim on me. "We're getting married in August," he said. "I would say the dragon was a success."

"That's awesome! Let's see the bling." I held out my hand for him to see. "Wow! Go big or go home, right?"

"Nothing's too good for my girl." Ty kissed me on the side of the head.

"Do you have time to do our tats?" I questioned.

"Yeah. Come on back." We followed him back to his tattoo station.

"I'll go first," I volunteered. I handed my part of the tattoo to Zack. "I want it right here." I pointed to the back of my right shoulder. I jumped up on the table and pulled down the spaghetti strap of my tank.

Zack got to work on my tattoo. Then Ty and I switched places and Zack placed Ty's tattoo on the back of his upper left shoulder. "Were you two always this cute together? I gotta admit, when Tyler came in here the first time, I didn't see it. But seeing the two of you together, you're pretty perfect for each other."

Ty and I looked at each other. "We've been like this since day one," I said.

"I knew from the first day I saw Kyla, that I'd marry her someday."

Zack wiped down Tyler's tattoo. "You're done. Check it out."

Ty and I walked to the mirror and stood shoulder to shoulder backwards. Mine said, *I will always hold onto you...* Ty's said, *...And I will never let you go.* Under each set of words was the infinity symbol. It was perfectly us.

The Fourth of July fell on a Wednesday, and we were going to Chris and Tori's for a barbeque later in the day. Tyler wanted to hit the gym before we went. I kissed him goodbye and then grabbed my keys. I started driving and turned the radio up loud. Tyler hadn't said a word about it. Why would he? This day was important to me and me alone. Christ, he wasn't even around when it happened. I couldn't be upset with him. But I couldn't help feeling alone.

I pulled into the cemetery and drove around to the grave site. I pulled the blanket out of my back seat and walked over to their tombstone. I placed the blanket down and sat cross-legged.

"It' been a year, since you left me," I started. "So much has happened in that time. You've missed so much. Where should I start? I got a few tattoos. I know you wouldn't like them, but I do. Tyler broke his shoulder in November and didn't make the draft. It was heartbreaking really, but he's still working on playing pro football. I really hope he makes it. A pro football career is all he's ever wanted." I paused to collect my thoughts. "I survived my first Christmas without you. Just so you know, that sucked, but I made it." I laid back on the blanket and stared at the clouds. "I got through a lot of tough times. I met a new friend. His name is Sid and he's a great guy. He helped me a lot. Let's see... what else? Oh yeah, I got arrested. I killed Jake and I don't feel bad about it. I should have some guilt, but I don't. They released me after a few hours, so no biggie, right?" I laughed out loud. "Tyler and I are back together and we're getting married in August. He's been the best. You'd be proud of the man he's become." I closed my eyes and sighed. "You missed Chris and Tori's wedding, by the way. She was a beautiful bride. I was jealous at her wedding. All I could think about was how my mom and dad were going to miss mine."

I spent the next fifteen minutes telling them about all the plans Tyler and I had made for our wedding. I didn't skip any little detail. I told them about the hotel, the beach, the flowers, my dress. Everything.

"Please make me a promise," I pleaded. "I know that you will be there in your own way, but can you send me a sign, so I know you're watching. I just need to know you're there." I kissed my hand and touched the top of their tombstone. "I love you both."

Chapter 31
Tyler

The last few weeks had been crazy. I felt like I'd hardly seen Kyla at all. We'd been like two ships passing in the night. She'd been kicking ass at her new job, doing work for Zack, and planning our wedding. I'd spent too many late nights getting things ready for the opening of the club. Sometimes Kyla would bring me dinner, but most nights I was so busy that I forgot to eat. I'd hired a staff for the club, and we were ready to open the doors. Kyla had done all the promotional stuff and worked with me on the advertising.

It was Friday and Xtreme was ready to open the doors. I met with my staff, and everyone was psyched. The DJ was ready, and music was quietly thumping. We dimmed the lights. The pink, purple, and blue lighting Kyla had suggested, set the mood. My bouncers assured me there was a line of people waiting to get in. Kyla, Chris, and Tori were there mainly as a support team, but they were also my eyes and ears to let me know of any problems that arose throughout the night. I called my staff together, "Huddle up, everyone! We're ready for this! I'm sure some problems might come up during the night, but we're all here to support one another. Let me or Kyla know, and we'll handle it. You ready to get the place rocking?" Everyone cheered. "Turn up the music!" The DJ turned up the bass and we were ready to go. I turned to the bouncers. "Check every ID. Open the doors!"

Kyla hugged me. "This is amazing, baby. I'm so proud of you."

"I couldn't have done it without your help and support." I pulled her in and kissed her hard. I turned to Chris and Tori. "Drinks are on me. Go get your buzz on."

"Hell yeah," Chris answered as he and Tori stepped up to the bar.

People started coming in and finding tables. Our waitresses were quick to take their orders, and so the night began. The tables out on the patio filled quickly, confirming that the addition to the bar was worth every penny. Everything seemed to be running smoothly.

Around nine I saw my Uncle Lou meandering through the crowd. I approached him, and he patted me on the back "You've done good, kiddo."

"Thanks. It was a big job, but Kyla was a huge help. Everything seems to be going well."

"Yeah, I'd say so. People are still coming in," he said.

Kyla stayed with me until close since she didn't have to work the next day. Chris and Tori stayed too, which is more than I expected. By the time the bar cleared out, around 2:15, we were all exhausted. "Thank you for staying. I didn't expect you to stay all night."

"Dude, we were here to support you. You did an excellent job. I'd say it was a successful night," Chris said.

"I enjoyed myself, but my feet are killing me. Do you mind if we take off?" Tori said, shuffling side to side in her three-inch heels.

I gave them each a hug. "Go on and take off. Thanks for coming tonight." They hugged Kyla and left.

My staff was finishing wiping down tables and cleaning up the bar. I let them work another twenty minutes and then sent everyone home. Finally, it was just Kyla and me. "Well, what did you think?" I asked her. She was standing in front of me in a tight little black dress and her curves were kicking.

"I think all your hard work paid off. It was amazing, baby," she said as she wrapped her arms around my neck.

"You know what I was thinking about all night?" I asked her.

She shook her head but got a mischievous smile on her face.

"I was thinking how much I wanted you. I was thinking about how bad I wanted to take you back to my office and fuck you."

"So, what's stopping you?"

I picked her up and carried her back to my office. I swiped everything off my desk and sat her on top of it. "God, I want you!"

"So, take me! I want you to fuck me," she said breathlessly.

I reached under her dress and slid her panties down her legs. She wrapped her legs around me and I pushed into her. I would never tire of how she felt around me. I took her there in my office, on my desk, with no inhibitions. It was the perfect ending to a perfect night.

Because of our late night, we slept in the next morning. Tonight, would be a replay of last night. The thing about running a club, was that Kyla and I would be on different schedules. I knew this was temporary, but it would suck in the meantime.

I was brushing my teeth with a towel wrapped around my waist and she was putting on her makeup. She held up her birth control pills. "I need to get these refilled today."

I took them out of her hand and looked at the case. "I was thinking… do you really want to get them refilled? I mean… we're getting married in a month. Do you want to start trying?"

She looked at me with a shocked expression on her face. "Do you?"

I wrapped my arms around her. "Yeah, I do. I wanna have a baby with you."

"You don't think it's too soon?" she questioned.

"No. I want this with you. I want everything. I want to see you big and round carrying my baby."

She got a little nervous. "What if I can't get pregnant? What if the miscarriage messed me up?" It wasn't anything I had ever thought about, but obviously she had.

I kissed the top of her head. "I was there. Your doctor said you should be fine. I wanna try. Let's see what happens."

"Okay." She tossed the case in the trash. "Let's see what happens. We'll know the week before the wedding." I could tell she was rethinking it. Then, she leaned down and pulled them back out of the trash can. "Are you sure? You've got the tryouts coming up in March. Do you want to wait until after then? There's no rush."

"I don't want to wait," I assured her. "I've wanted this ever since you showed me those ultrasound pictures. We missed our first chance. I want a baby with you."

She tossed them back in the trash can. "So do I. You know it's going to change our lives."

"I know and I'm ready. As a matter of fact, I think we should go practice right now." I scooped her up and led her to our bedroom.

The week before the wedding, I got home after another long night at the bar. I peeked in our bedroom and Kyla was already sleeping. She had quit taking her Xanax. She didn't want anything interfering with her chances of getting pregnant. Now that Jake was out of our lives, her nightmares had subsided. Occasionally she would wake in a cold sweat, but most nights she slept peacefully.

After working in the bar all night, I needed a shower. I stripped off my clothes and stepped into the bathroom. All I could think about was waking my girl for a midnight love session. I couldn't get enough of her.

As I was drying off, I happened to look over to where the trashcan sat. I saw the wrappers from her tampons in the trash. My heart sank. I guessed this month was a no go as far as the baby was concerned. It had only been one month. She'd been taking those pills for over a year. I knew it probably wouldn't happen on the first try, but I was still a little disappointed. I wondered how she'd reacted and how she'd felt when she realized she wasn't pregnant.

The next day when we saw each other, she didn't say a word about it. She acted totally normal. She never acted crazy during her time of the month like I'd heard some guys say about their girls. She didn't have mood swings or yell at me for ridiculous reasons. If it weren't for the fact that we weren't having sex, I wouldn't have even known she was on her period. Since she didn't say anything, neither did I. I was just happy it would be over before our wedding night.

The week went by quickly. Kyla worked from home so that she could finalize all the details of our wedding with the coordinator in Key West, but I had a few surprises for her that she didn't know about. Kyla and I were flying down on Thursday, so that we could get our marriage license and have some time alone before everyone else showed up on Friday. We sent her grandparents airline tickets and arranged to have a limo pick them up from the airport to bring them to the hotel. They were so excited to be included in our small ceremony and Kyla's Gramps was tickled about walking her down the aisle. My parents volunteered to pay for all the airline tickets and hotel rooms for the wedding. I let them pay for everyone else, but I wanted to pay for Kyla's and mine. I booked us the Honeymoon Suite and from the pictures online, it was going to be super romantic. I couldn't believe that in a few short days, we would be married.

Kyla and I headed for the airport early Thursday morning. Kyla had her dress in a black garment bag, so I couldn't see it. She hadn't given me a clue as to what her dress looked like. She and I had discussed what I would wear to keep in line with our beach theme. I was wearing a tux with a vest. No jacket, thank God, because I expected it to be hot. She agreed that the vest with a tie would be fine and even said I should roll up the sleeves.

I got us first class tickets for the flight. "I've never flown first class before," she said as we took our seats. We had plenty of leg room and we put up the arm rest between us, so she could get closer to me.

"Nothing but the best for my wife." I smirked.

"I'm not your wife yet," she pointed out.

"But you will be in two days." I threaded my fingers with hers and kissed the back of her hand. "I think we should check in and go right to the courthouse so we can get our license. Then, we'll have the rest of the day to do whatever we want."

"You know what I want to do? I want to lay by the beach with a drink and soak up the sun. With working so many hours I haven't gotten much of a tan this summer. We both deserve a break."

"I couldn't agree more. Are you going to make us spend the night apart tomorrow? I know Tori was insistent upon it for their wedding."

"No way. I'm not giving you up for even one night. Screw tradition. We make our own traditions. However, once we get up and moving Saturday morning, I'll need the day away from you until the wedding," she said sheepishly.

"I can agree with that. I'll just hang out with the guys. I'm sure your grandpa will be a blast," I joked. "We can do body shots and all that fun stuff."

"Ewww! That's just a gross visual." She laughed and snuggled into me. "I can't wait until we get there."

Three hours later we were about to touch down and I kissed Kyla's head. "Time to wake up, baby."

She stretched out next to me. "I can't believe I fell asleep again. I think I have some sort of sleeping disorder."

"You're kind of cute, you know that? Anytime we go somewhere together, you fall asleep."

"Just storing up for a long weekend." She winked at me.

We finally landed and went to collect our luggage. When we walked out of the airport, standing at the curb was a limo driver with a sign that said *Mr. and Mrs. Jackson*. Kyla pointed to it. "Is that us?"

"I think it is," I said nonchalantly.

She jumped up and down. "You got us a limo?"

"Like I said, nothing is too good for my wife." We approached the limo, and the driver took our bags and put them in the trunk. We climbed into the back, and I put up the privacy screen. I pulled out the champagne that had been chilling and poured us each a glass.

"To my new husband," Kyla toasted.

"To my beautiful wife," I responded. We clinked glasses and drank down our champagne. By the time we reached the hotel we were both giddy from the alcohol and the fooling around we had done in the back of the limo. I checked us in, and we headed up to our room. I swiped the key card and let Kyla go in first.

"Holy shit!" she exclaimed. "This is awesome!" We walked into the main sitting room. The whole wall on the outside was windows that looked out over the ocean. We ventured further into our suite, and she headed toward the bedroom. We had a king size bed and another amazing view of the ocean. "Oh my God!" Kyla hopped up on the bed and began to jump around. "I can't believe this is my life!" It was fucking adorable.

I walked to the edge of the bed and grabbed her around the legs. "Do you like it?"

"I love it! Thank you!" She plopped down on her ass and wrapped her legs around me.

"I want to spoil you. It's our wedding, you deserve the best." We were later than we planned on getting to the courthouse, because I had to make love to my girl first.

When we got back, we did exactly what Kyla wanted. We laid on the beach and had too many tropical drinks to count. We were both buzzed by the time we got back to our room. Shower sex, dinner, and more sex. So far, this trip was everything I could have ever hoped for and more.

Chapter 32
Kyla

Friday, everyone else flew into the Keys. Tyler's parents, Tori, and Chris all came on the same flight. They arrived shortly after noon. My grandparents wouldn't be arriving until later. Even though I was glad Tyler and I had the day before to ourselves, I was excited to see our friends and Ty's parents. While we were all having lunch together, I looked around the table and a little pang of sadness hit. I should have been thrilled, but I was getting married tomorrow and two very important people were missing.

Tyler sensed that something was wrong and excused us from the table. He took me out of the restaurant and sat us down on a bench. He wrapped his arm around me, and I rested my head on his shoulder. My eyes welled up with the tears I was trying to hold back. Ty had done so much to make everything perfect, and I felt like I was ruining the day.

"Do you want to talk about it?" he asked.

I was trying so hard to hold it together and keep the waterworks at bay. I just shook my head.

"Are you changing your mind? Do you not want to get married?"

My head popped up. "God, no! I can't wait to marry you." A single tear escaped, and I blew out a breath to try and get my emotions under control. "I love you, Tyler. You're my best friend, my anchor, my everything. You're the only thing that holds me together."

"Is it about not getting pregnant?" he asked. "Because it was only our first try, it'll happen." He kissed the side of my head.

"I'd be lying if I said I wasn't disappointed, but no." I wiped my face. "You know what? I'm fine." I straightened up and took a deep breath. "Let's go back in. Everyone's probably wondering what we're doing."

"You always do this. You say you're fine, when clearly, you're not. Stop worrying about everyone else and start taking care of yourself." He took my face in his hands. "Talk to me, Ky." He stood up and took control of the situation. "I'm going to tell everyone that we'll meet them back at the hotel. I think we should take a walk."

I didn't stop him. I watched him disappear into the restaurant and he was back a few minutes later. He reached for my hand and pulled me to my feet. We started walking towards the beach that led back to our hotel. When we got to the water, we let the warm waves wash over our feet. He took both my hands in his. "What's going on?"

My eyes welled up and then the dam broke, "I miss them. They should be here for this. It's so fucking unfair," I choked out.

Tyler pulled me to his chest and held me tight, "Oh, baby. I'm sorry. You're right. It isn't fucking fair." I just kept crying, soaking his shirt with my tears. "They'll be there in their own way. I promise."

I pulled back. How could he possibly promise me something like that? He was trying, and I couldn't fault him for that. The sentiment was sweet, but he couldn't understand how hard this was for me. "I just... I try to put up this wall," I gestured with my hand, running it up and down in front of me. "But sometimes the wall isn't tall enough or thick enough. As much as I try to compartmentalize and contain it, shit keeps seeping through. And when it does, it's like a goddamn flood. I have every reason to be the happiest girl alive right now. What the fuck is wrong with me?"

"Nothing is wrong with you, Ky. You're human. I'm not a very good fiancé. I should have seen this coming."

"You don't have anything to apologize for. You've done everything possible to make this wedding… our life… perfect. I know I have your parents and our friends, but sometimes I feel so fucking alone. Nobody really gets it, and I don't expect them to. It's my issue. I thank God every day that I have you, because honestly, if I didn't, I'd just be existing. You fill that empty space inside me. I'm so lucky to have you."

"We're lucky to have each other. And you're right I don't always think about it because you're so strong and you make it look easy." He brushed my hair out of my face and tucked it behind my ear. "You're fearless and I love that about you."

"I feel guilty even talking about this. I have a pretty damn good life. I'm standing on a beautiful beach with a man who couldn't love me more. I shouldn't be complaining."

"You're not complaining. You shouldn't ever feel guilty about feeling sad. Sometimes it's going to hit you and when it does, you gotta let it out. You can't hold it all in."

"I know, but sometimes it's easier to not think about my mom and dad. If I just stay busy, I can push it out of my mind. Does that make me a bad person?" I questioned.

He shook his head. "No. I think they'd understand." He hugged me tight and rubbed my back. "Feel better?"

"Actually, I do. You always know what I need."

"Come on. I'll text everyone to meet us at the bar by the pool. You need a drink," he suggested.

We walked back along the water hand in hand. I did feel better. Lighter. I was glad I got it all out because, I didn't want to think about it tomorrow. I wanted to be the happy bride I should be.

We changed into our bathing suits and met everyone by the bar. I took my Mai Tai and found a lounge chair by the pool. Tori sidled up next to me with her own fruity concoction. "You okay?"

I tried to play it off. "Just an emotional moment. I miss my mom and dad, but I'm fine."

"You know I'm here, right?"

I got teary and wiped at my eyes. "I know you are. You've seen me at my worst." I laid back in my lounger. "I don't want to think about it. We're here in paradise. Let's enjoy it."

Ty's mom grabbed the chair on the other side of me. "This place is just awful," she joked. "Remind me again why you would want to get married here."

I smiled at her. "It's pretty awesome, isn't it?"

"Yeah, it is," she said, taking a sip of her drink. "I feel like I haven't done anything. What can I do to help you for tomorrow?"

"You've done plenty," I assured her. "You gave me your son. I couldn't ask for more than that."

She leaned over and kissed me on the cheek. "That part was easy."

"I'm meeting the wedding coordinator at four. Would you like to come with me to finalize all the details?"

Ty's mom clapped her hands together. "I'd love too!"

Tori piped up, "What about me?"

"Of course, you're coming too!"

The three of us laid by the pool soaking in the sun and sipping on tropical drinks. The support of these women was just what I needed. And in that moment, I knew I wasn't alone.

After meeting with the wedding coordinator, Ty and I went to the lobby to meet Grams and Gramps who were just arriving. I saw them walk in through the front doors and turned into Tyler's chest to let out a little giggle I couldn't contain.

"Looks like someone got the memo that this was a tropical beach wedding," he said, letting out his own laugh.

My Gramps had on a brightly flowered shirt, sunglasses, and a big floppy hat. Grams wasn't much better. She had on a pink floppy hat and a flower lei. "I think they got confused and thought the wedding was in Hawaii," I said.

They saw the two of us and started waving frantically. They had met Ty on several occasions over the years and they loved him. I rushed over and wrapped them in huge hugs. "I'm so glad you're here!" I exclaimed.

"Oh, sweet girl, we're so happy to be here!" Grams gave Tyler a hug.

Gramps shook Ty's hand. "We were surprised about the wedding, but we we're happy it was you. I always liked you. How's that football career coming?"

"I'm still working on it, but things look promising." Tyler and I took their suitcases. "We've already checked you in. Let's take your things to your room."

Grams and Gramps chatted the whole way to their room. They *oohed* and *aahed* at the hotel and their room. We gave them some time to get acclimated and planned to meet them for dinner at the hotel restaurant.

After making love again and showering, which led to more sex, Tyler and I made our way down to the hotel restaurant. Ty's dad reserved a small private room for the eight of us. We were the last to arrive and everyone clapped when we walked in.

"It's about time! You know the honeymoon doesn't start until tomorrow night, right?" Chris joked.

I felt the color creeping up my neck. "We know," I said shyly. Leave it to Chris to embarrass me in front of my Grams and Gramps.

"You don't think we forgot what it's like to be young and in love, do you? We were wild and crazy once too," Grams said, hugging Gramps.

I held up my hand. "Okay, that's more than I want to know right now." I laughed.

Everyone ordered their drinks and when they arrived, I stood to say what was in my heart. "First, I'd like to say how happy I am that all of you could be here to share our wedding day with us. Everyone at this table has a special place in my heart. I am fortunate to be surrounded by the love of all of you. My heart is overflowing. Thank you for loving me and being my support system."

Tyler's mom, who might have had one too many drinks, shouted out, "So when am I getting my grandbabies?"

Ty took it in stride. He wrapped his arm around my shoulder. "We're working on it."

Chris couldn't resist. "Why do you think they were late for dinner?"

Everyone laughed, and I blushed. Later that night Ty and I went back to our room and worked on making those grandbabies his mom wanted so bad.

The next morning, I woke wrapped in Tyler's arm. The sun was shining, and a light breeze fluttered in from the door to the balcony we'd left cracked during the night. The gentle sound of waves crashing onto the shore soothed me. This was my last day being Kyla O'Malley. After tonight, I would officially be Kyla Jackson. I'd been writing it my notebook since back in high school and tonight it would finally be true. I laid there and thought about the journey we'd taken from Homecoming senior year until now. For the most part it'd been a pretty great ride. Our breakup was bad. Devastating, actually. It nearly destroyed me, but since we'd gotten back together, I didn't dwell on the bad times. I soaked up all the good ones and held onto them tightly.

I kissed up Tyler's chest. He opened one eye and smiled down at me. His stubbly face was so damn cute. "You're not kicking me out yet, are you?"

"Nope. We have until two o'clock together, and then you'll have to spend some time with the guys."

Tyler groaned, "Think your Gramps will wear his big floppy hat?"

I giggled, "Maybe. Come on, it's kind of cute."

"I guess," he said. Ty ran his fingers up and down my back. "I don't want to get out of this bed. I could lay here all day and ravage you." He flipped me over onto my back and pinned me to the mattress. His strong arms caged me in, as he hovered above me. "I have to say it one more time, before you become my wife. I love you, Kyla O'Malley." He peppered me with soft kisses along my face and neck. "I can't wait for you to have my name. Tonight, you'll be Mrs. Tyler Jackson. I've waited so long to make you mine."

I ran my fingers along his stubble. "I've always been yours. We're just making it official."

"I can't wait to see you in your dress. You're going to be a beautiful bride."

I touched the tattoo over his heart that held the words that were so true. "Have you written your vows yet?" I questioned.

"I don't need to write any. Everything I need to say is already in my heart." He pressed his lips to mine and pushed them apart with his tongue. They tangled together in a slow dance that wasn't fueled by lust or fevered passion. It was true love. Our hearts and souls twined together to form an unbreakable bond. "I love you, baby," he whispered in my ear.

"I love you too."

After spending some time in the sun, I headed back to the room to shower. Tyler moved his things to Chris and Tori's room, where he would get ready. I unzipped the garment bag hanging in the closet and pulled out my dress. It was beautiful. He was going to love it.

I took a long relaxing shower and then headed down to the hotel salon for my mani-pedi and hair appointment. I knew it would take them a long time to do my hair, so I got there before everyone else. My hair was being blow dried, when Tori, Grams, and Ty's mom came in for their appointments.

Tori held her hands up to her mouth when she saw my hair. "He's going to be so surprised. It's going to be beautiful, Kyla."

"I think it was time." I smiled at her.

Each of us took a seat in one of the salon chairs as the stylists curled and pinned our hair. I opted for a half updo. The front was pulled back from my face, but the back hung down in long, soft curls.

After getting our hair done, we headed back to my room to meet the woman who was going to do our makeup. We drank champagne and chatted while we took turns getting all made up.

As we were finishing, there was a knock on the door. Tori opened it and Chris walked in. "You're just in time," she said to him.

I looked at the two of them in confusion, "In time for what?"

Tyler's mom stepped forward. "We all know you wanted an untraditional wedding, and we understand why." My eyes started to tear up. "But some traditions are not meant to be broken."

Tori turned to the makeup artist who was trying to quietly slink out of the room. "I think you better stay. We may need some touch-ups."

Grams spoke up next. "We got together and decided we couldn't let this tradition go. You need something old, something new, something borrowed, and something blue."

Ty's mom went first. "I knew you wanted to be barefoot for the wedding. I got you something blue." She reached into her bag and pulled out a turquoise bracelet. She held it up. "This is an ankle bracelet. I thought it would be cute on your bare feet." She kneeled down and attached it around my ankle.

I hugged her tightly "Thank you. It's perfect."

She kissed me on the cheek. "You're welcome, sweetheart."

"My turn," Tori said. She pulled another box out of her bag. "I have your something borrowed. I want you to wear these today." She opened the box and inside sat the diamond earrings Chris had bought her for their wedding. She pulled them out of the box and placed them in my hand.

I took them from her and fastened them in my ears. "Thank you. You're the best friend a girl could have. I love you." I wrapped my arms around her and squeezed. The tears hadn't fallen yet, but I was damn close.

"Well, because I'm the old lady here, I brought you something old." I smiled at my Grams who was even shorter than me. She was the only person who actually made me feel tall. "I wore this on my wedding day. Your mother wore it on her wedding day. And now I'm giving it to you. I wanted you to have a little piece of your mother on your wedding day, because I know they're watching." My Grams held up a crystal hair comb, shaped into a butterfly.

I leaned down and she placed it in my hair. The tears were falling freely now. I held onto my Grams. "Thank you. I wish they were here."

Grams rubbed my back. "They are, honey."

Everyone in the room had tears in their eyes, including Chris. He stepped up next. "You look beautiful, Kyla. He's going to love it." He cleared the lump from his own throat. "This gift is actually from Tyler. He got you something new." He pulled a long box out of his pocket and handed it to me.

I opened the box and inside sat a diamond tennis bracelet. "Oh my, God!" I took the bracelet out and held it out to

Chris. "Will you help me put it on?" Chris took the bracelet from me and fastened it around my wrist. I held it up in the light and watched it sparkle. "It's absolutely gorgeous! Tell Tyler thank you and I can't wait to be his wife." I hugged Chris tightly and whispered in his ear, "Thank you. Thank you for always being there for me. I love you."

He whispered back, "I love you too, baby girl."

Tori snapped her fingers at the makeup artist. "Yeah, we're going to need you. We have some major touch-ups to do."

The poor woman had tears in her eyes too. "Who's first?" she asked.

We let Grams and Tyler's mom go first, so they could go back to their rooms to get dressed. Tori and I were left alone. When our makeup was finished, Tori went to the fridge and pulled out the small purple orchids that would be placed in my hair. She strategically pinned them into my curls. "That's perfect," she said. "You look amazing."

We slipped into our dresses, sans shoes. We were both going barefoot. We stood in front of the full-length mirror and stared at ourselves. "I can't believe were both going to be married," I said. "It's pretty incredible that we both ended up marrying our high school sweethearts."

"Yeah. The four of us have been through a lot together. Some good. Some bad. But all of it led us to this moment. Tyler is going to be swept away when he sees you." She hugged me tightly. "It's time."

Chapter 33
Tyler

I looked at my watch again. Eight o'clock. Time to get this show on the road.

Kyla did a beautiful job planning this wedding. Tiki torches lined the sandy aisle that would make the path down to the beach. A bamboo arch sat at the end of the aisle wrapped in some flowy white fabric. It was decorated with white roses and purple orchids. Orchids were scattered down the aisle and on the sand that surrounded us. The waves of the ocean gently lapped the shore behind us.

The officiant was standing at the arch, waiting for us. My mom and dad were seated on one side of the aisle and Kyla's Gram and Gramps on the other side.

Chris came over and clapped me on the shoulder, "You ready for this, man?"

"I've been ready since the day I met her."

"I saw her when I gave her the bracelet. She's going to take your breath away," he said.

"She takes my breath away every day. Did you see the dress?"

"Nope. Just a few more minutes."

The sun was just starting to set over the ocean. The sky was splashed with pinks and purples. It was just as Kyla had imagined. Chris and I walked over to the arch and waited for her to arrive. My dad came up and hugged me. "I'm so proud of you son. You're going to make a good husband. Cherish and take care of her."

"I will dad. I had a good role model."

Kyla's Gramps came up to us. "It's time." He walked back to where Kyla would appear.

Chris and I took our places and waited. Music started to play, but it wasn't traditional. It was "I'm Yours" by Jason Mraz. I should have known my girl would buck tradition right down to the music. A smile broke out on my face that I couldn't contain if I wanted.

Tori walked down the aisle in a purple sundress. She looked beautiful. She stopped in front of Chris giving him a kiss and then gave me peck on the cheek. "Take care of her," she said.

"Always."

Kyla appeared at the top of the aisle, her arm linked with her Gramps. I was blown away.

Her blond hair blew in the breeze, and she glowed as the fire from the torches lit up her face. This was the girl I fell in love with. I had gotten used to the black hair, but she was exquisite as a blond. Once I got over the shock of her hair, I looked at her dress. It wrapped up around her neck and was cut low in the front, showing just enough of her breasts to make me sigh. It hugged her hips and flared out at the bottom. Sticking out underneath, were her bare toes which were now painted a pink instead of the black she usually wore.

She was stunning. I was a lucky son of a bitch. When she was in front of me, her Gramps gave me her hand and led her to the arch. "You are stunning," I said in a low voice. "You take my breath away."

She fluttered her eyelashes. "You look pretty good yourself," she said quietly.

We had agreed on a simple service. The officiant started, "We are gathered here this evening to join Kyla Marie O'Malley and Tyler Jonathon Jackson, as husband and wife."

I only half listened as he spoke about love; all I could do was think about how beautiful my girl was. I wanted to get to the important part.

"Tyler and Kyla have prepared their own vows. Tyler..."

I took both of her hands in mine. "Kyla, from the first time I laid eyes on you, I fell in love. I knew from the moment you walked across the high school parking lot, that we were destined for each other. You captured my heart, and I willingly gave it to you. You've always supported me and believed in me. You are my every breath. You are what makes my heart beat. You always have been and always will be the light in my life. I know whatever life hands us, we'll be able to get through it together. I promise to support you, cherish you, love you, and keep you safe until my last breath." Chris handed me her ring and I slipped it on her slender finger.

Kyla wiped the tears from her eyes and then started her vows. "Tyler, you have been my whole world since the first day I met you. We've shared so many important moments together, and there is no one else I want to share my future with. You have helped me through the hardest times in my life. You healed me when no one else could. You have been my light in the darkness. My shelter from the storm. You've had my heart from day one. I know that together we can do anything. I promise to support you, cherish you, and love you. I will always hold onto you..."

"...And I will never let you go," I finished. She placed the platinum band on my finger.

As the sun was hitting the horizon, the officiant continued, "By the power invested in me by the state of Florida. I now pronounce you husband and wife. You may now kiss the bride." I wrapped my arms around her waist as she wrapped hers around my neck. I gave her a soul searing kiss and dipped her low.

When we came up for air, Chris moved the white box, that had been sitting to the side, to the space in front of us. We lifted the top together and a kaleidoscope of butterflies flew out in every direction. She giggled, and we watched them take flight into the sky around us. Two stayed behind. One landing on her shoulder and one on my shoulder. They fluttered their wings but stayed with us. We both looked at the two butterflies that had stayed behind. "They're here," I said.

She nodded, and tears welled up in her eyes. "I know."

Finally, they took flight and flew off into the twilight together. I wrapped Kyla in my arms and held her tight. "I love you, Kyla Jackson," I said.

"I love you too, Tyler Jackson."

Our reception consisted of a table for eight set off to the side of the patio by the pool. Tiki torches surrounded us, and candles lit the table. Soft music played in the background from a playlist we had selected. It wasn't traditional, but it was perfect for us. We were married and surrounded by the people we loved the most.

We feasted on steak and lobster. During dinner, we went around the table and each person gave their own short speech, wishing us a life of love and happiness.

After dinner, I went up to the DJ and requested our song. I went back to the table and held out my hand. "I'd like to dance with my wife." She took my hand, and I led her to our makeshift dance floor. "*Far Away*" began. I held one of her hands to my chest and wrapped my other arm around her waist. She wrapped her arm around my neck. "You have made me the happiest man alive, Kyla. I can't believe we're finally married. I've dreamed of this day for so long. Have I told you how beautiful you look?" I ran my fingers through her long, blond hair.

"It was time. With you, I have nothing to be afraid of anymore. Nothing to hide."

When the song ended, our family joined us on the dance floor. We switched partners every song, so that we all got to dance with each other. Dancing with Kyla's Gram was comical with me being six-foot two and her being shorter than Kyla.

Finally, I got to dance with my mom. "Thank you for helping us to make this day perfect," I said to her. "I know it wasn't what you originally envisioned, but you have to admit it was beautiful."

"Oh, Tyler. I couldn't be happier. My baby is all grown up now. I'm so proud of the man you've become."

"It took me a while to get it right, but I'm never letting her go. She is my everything."

"I know," my mom said. "And you're her everything. She just glows when you two are together."

"I love you, Mom."

"I love you too, Tyler. You're everything I could have asked for in a son."

Around midnight, everyone decided to call it a night. We would all have brunch in the morning together, and then everyone was flying home on late afternoon flights. Kyla and I were staying two extra days. It was a shortened honeymoon. I promised we would go somewhere later, but neither one of us could spend too much time away from work right now.

I led Kyla toward our room and swiped our key to let us in. She tried to go in, but I grabbed her hand to stop her. I scooped her up in my arms. "What are you doing?"

"Carrying my new bride over the threshold."

She giggled, and I loved the sound. I carried her right to our bedroom and set her on the floor in front of our bed. She reached up and loosened my tie, slipped it off, then went to work on the buttons of my vest. I loved when she undressed me. It was so sexy. Once my vest was off, she got to work on the buttons of my shirt. She kissed down my chest and then pushed my shirt over my shoulders.

I reached behind her neck and undid the clasp that held the top of her dress up. I let go of the straps and the top fell to her waist. Her tits were bared, and I cupped them in my hands. I ran my thumbs over her hard nipples, and she shivered. "God, I want you," she rasped out.

"I want you too, baby." I found the zipper at the back of her dress and slowly slid it down. Her dress pooled on the floor, and she stepped out of it. She was beautiful standing there in only a white thong. I picked up her dress and laid it over a chair.

Her hands went to my belt. She slowly undid it and then worked on the button and zipper of my pants. I slid them down my hips and slipped them off along with my socks.

I picked her up and placed her in the middle of the bed. Moonlight shown through the slider and cast her in an ethereal glow. Her blond hair was splayed out on the pillow. She looked like an angel laid out before me. She was too good for me, but she was mine, nonetheless.

I crawled on the bed and hovered over her. I closed my eyes and kissed her forehead, down to the tip of her nose and finally her lips. I was going to take my time with her. Explore every inch of her perfect body. Make love to her slow and deep. I wanted to feel her inside and outside. Every soft curve would be under my hands and wrapped around me.

I took her hands in mine and threaded our fingers together. I raised them up to the pillow, stretching her arms above her head. "I've got you. You're safe with me," I whispered in her ear. Then I held both of her wrists in my one hand like I used to do. Her eyes widened for a brief moment, and then she relaxed, trusting me to take control but keep her safe. It was the first time she'd let me do that since we'd gotten back together. I knew, then and there, that she was with me. There was no holding back. All her trust had returned. We were us again. That was the best wedding present she could have ever given me.

I ran my other hand down the valley of her breasts, as I kept her hands captive. She was stretched out before me. Beautiful. I massaged one breast and leaned down to take her nipple in my mouth. I gently sucked as she arched off the bed further into me. I swirled my tongue around her hard peak and ran it over to her other breast. When I'd given her other nipple the same attention, I released her wrists. Her hands ran through my hair and cupped my face. "I love you, Tyler. With all my heart, with all that I am. I trust you completely to take care of me and always keep me safe."

"I promise I will. Forever and always."

I kissed down those beautiful butterflies that curved down her body. My fingers traced them, her skin so soft under my touch. I hooked my fingers into the sides of her thong and slid it down her slender legs. Parting her folds with my fingers, I found her sensitive clit. I ran my tongue over the soft bundle of nerves, and she lifted her hips off the bed. She was so responsive, so utterly perfect. I pressed her back to the bed with my hand on her stomach, then I swiped my tongue over her again. I lapped at her with slow swipes, knowing each one was taking her closer to orgasm. But I didn't want her to come yet. I wanted to make this last. I lowered my tongue down to her sweet pussy and stuck it into her wet heat. She tasted so good on my tongue. It was a taste that made sparks run through my veins and my cock harden even more. I ate her out as she writhed on the bed.

"My God, Tyler. Don't stop. Take me there. Make me feel the way only you can," she rasped out.

I replaced my tongue with my long fingers. I slid them in and out of her, feeling her from the inside, curling my fingers, and pumping harder. She moaned in ecstasy. With my fingers deep inside her, I worked her clit again with my tongue. I licked and licked, then sucked it into my mouth. Tugging and pulling, moving her closer to the edge. "I'm right there, baby. Just a little bit more," she gasped. I buried my face in her. She fell over the edge and shattered into a million pieces. I pumped her through it and pulled back.

I slid my boxer briefs off and her delicate hand wrapped around my dick. She stroked me up and down, with just enough pressure. I closed my eyes and let my head fall back as she rubbed me from root to tip. God, it felt good.

I unwrapped her from my dick and put her hand on my shoulder. I leaned over the top of her and slowly slid my painfully hard dick into her wet, swollen pussy. It gripped me just right and it took all my restraint not to thrust into her fast and hard. I pushed in until I was buried deep inside her. I slowly pulled back and then pushed back in. Slow. Long. Deep. She wrapped her legs around my waist and began meeting me thrust for thrust. She pushed herself into me and I slowly circled my hips. She felt so good. She was my heaven.

"I'm not going to last long," I whispered.

"We have all night," she answered.

I reached under her and squeezed her ass, bringing her up and into me with every thrust. I quickened the pace, pushing deep into her, searching for my release.

"Ty... I'm gonna come again. Keep going." A few thrusts later and her walls clenched my dick and pulsed around me. It was my undoing. I released everything inside her and pleasure shot through my body.

I collapsed on top of her, both our bodies covered in sweat and glistening. Both of us were breathing hard, trying to catch our breath. She kept her legs around my waist and wrapped her arms around my shoulders. She pulled me into her with her heels, pushing me even deeper inside. Pumping out the last of my orgasm. "I'm going to crush you."

"No, you won't. I just want to feel you pressed tight against me." We were so tight together that you couldn't tell where she ended, and I began. We were one. One body. One heart. One soul.

The next day we said goodbye to family and friends, then the honeymoon began. We took long walks on the beach, made out in the waves, drank too much, and had sex not enough. I could stay inside my girl twenty-four seven and it wouldn't be enough. We knew that this was a short break before we needed to return to reality. We enjoyed every minute of it.

On the flight back, Kyla snuggled into my side. "I don't want it to end," she said.

"I know, baby. Neither do I." I kissed the side of her head and pulled her in closer.

When we got back, she would work her regular eight to five. I would be working bar hours and wouldn't get home until three in the morning a lot of days. I made a mental note to hire another manager at the club so I wouldn't have to spend so many nights away from Kyla. The crazy hours I worked wouldn't be helpful to our relationship, especially if we wanted to have a baby.

Chapter 34
Kyla

We'd been home from our wedding for a little over two weeks. It wasn't what I thought it would be. Tyler and I hardly saw each other at all, except for the few hours of sleep that overlapped. I knew we were doing what needed to be done right now, but I missed my husband. The club was closed on Sunday and Monday, but that didn't stop Ty from going in to place orders and do paperwork. We had this beautiful condo, and I felt like I was living here alone.

I got home from work on Friday night, and again Ty wouldn't be home until late. I got the mail and changed out of my work clothes. I went to the bathroom and swore under my breath, "Fucking hell!" I'd started my period again.

No baby.

I tried to keep the disappointment at bay. Why was it that when I didn't want to get pregnant, I did? Now that we were actively trying, I couldn't. I wondered if the miscarriage was going to prevent us from having kids. And if I did get pregnant, would I even be able to carry it to term? All these thoughts swirled around in my head as I went through the mail.

There was a plain white envelope addressed to Kyla O'Malley. I thought that maybe someone had sent us a congratulations card. We'd received a lot of those since Ty and I got married. There was no return address, which was odd. I opened the envelope, and it was not a card. There was a handwritten letter inside the envelope. I unfolded it and began to read.

Kyla,

I don't know you and you don't know me, but you did know my son. My son was Jacob Hening. From what I understand, the two of you dated for a while. None of that it important to me though because my son is no longer here. You shot him and now he is dead.

I don't know what happened, except that my son is gone. You stole him away from me and my family. You destroyed any type of future he may have had and destroyed our family.

I believe in karma, and hope that one day you suffer the same kind of loss. I hope that your child is ripped from your family, and you understand what you have done to us.

Jake was a kind and loving son. He was our only son. The devastation you have brought to our family is immeasurable.

You are a murderer. I hope your guilt kills you and you rot in hell.

The letter was unsigned, but I could only guess that it was from his mother. I collapsed into the chair at the kitchen table and reread the letter. This was too much for me to deal with. They had no idea what kind of son they had raised. They didn't know he raped me or broke into my apartment. Or maybe they did. Was shooting him my only choice? I began to replay the events in my head. He didn't leave me many choices, but I did plan his demise. Was I a murderer? Yes, I'd been let go by the police, but was I guiltless? I had killed him without remorse.

All of it was too much. My breathing became quick and shallow. White dots began to spot my vision and I got lightheaded. I moved to the kitchen floor and put my head between my legs. *This was not happening.* I couldn't get it under control. I lay back on the kitchen floor and the room began to spin around me. My phone rang, but I couldn't find the strength to answer it. I lay on the floor and waited for the spinning to stop. I needed Tyler and he wasn't home.

I don't know how long I laid there. Time was irrelevant, as the words from the letter ran through my head over and over again.

You are a murderer.
You are a murderer.
I was a murderer!

What had I done? I went through every day pretending I was justified. Was I? Did the punishment fit the crime? I was so dead set on revenge. Was that all it was... revenge? If so, did that make me any better than him? He took my trust and choices away from me. In return, I took his life. I was a murderer.

My phone continued to ring as I lay there on the kitchen floor. When I finally regained my senses, the sun had gone down. I raced to the bathroom and threw up. Then, I opened my nightstand drawer and pulled out the bottle I hadn't touched in months. I poured two pills into my hand and swallowed them down. A double dose. The Xanax would take it all away.

I went to the kitchen and pulled out the bottle of Southern Comfort. If the Xanax didn't help, surely the booze would. I didn't need a glass. I grabbed my smokes out of my purse. I hadn't smoked in weeks, but tonight was a special occasion. I was fucked up and I needed to get more fucked up to deal with everything.

Between getting my period and the letter, I was a mess. I opened the slider and made my way out to the balcony. I brought the letter with me, so I could read it again. I sat at the patio table and put my feet up on the railing. I reread the letter several times and searched for something that would give me redemption. I never found it.

I was a murderer!

I drank down several shots, and let the alcohol warm my insides. I let it numb my senses and take me away.

I sat there in the dark, with only the dim glow of the porch light, and listened to the waves crash onto the shore below me. The wind picked up and lightning flashed across the sky. A storm moved out across the lake, and I welcomed it. I prayed that it would take me away. I wanted to be swept away so I wouldn't have to deal with the reality of what I had done. Maybe not getting pregnant was my penance. I didn't deserve shit.

I deserved to rot in hell for what I had done.

I just wanted these feelings to go away as the lightning flashed and the thunder cracked around me. The wind changed directions and the rain pelted me. I didn't care. I welcomed the storm. I let it soak me. I let it take me. I disappeared into a world where everything was okay. Between the Xanax and the booze, I couldn't feel the pain.

Chapter 35
Tyler

I tried to call Kyla several times during the night, but she never answered. It wasn't like her. I was the only manager working tonight, so I couldn't just take off like I wanted to. I had a feeling that something wasn't right. As soon as the bar closed, I sent the staff home. The paperwork would have to wait until tomorrow, I needed to get home.

When I came home, the kitchen light was on, but the rest of the house was dark. I went to our bedroom, and saw that the bed had not been slept in.

No Kyla.

I went to the office. Maybe she was working on a design.

No Kyla.

Where could she be? It was 2:30 in the morning, for God's sake. Her car was in the garage, so I knew she had to be home. *Where the fuck was she?*

"Ky?" I called without an answer.

I was starting to freak out. Going back to the front room, I noticed that she hadn't closed the blinds to the balcony. The slider was unlocked, and my girl was sitting out there.

"Baby, what are you doing out here?" In the dim light, I saw that she was soaked from head to toe. Her wet hair was slicked back from her face, and she was smoking again, something I hadn't seen her do in months.

"Getting fucked up," she said. Kyla stared out over the lake, watching the storm.

Okaaay. "What's going on? Why are you still up?" I noticed the bottle of booze on the table next to her.

"I had a panic attack." She turned and looked at me. "Did you know you're married to a murderer?"

That kind of pissed me off, but she'd been drinking so I let it slide. "What are you talking about? It was self-defense. That asshole attacked you."

She pulled a paper from her back pocket and tossed it at me. "Seems not everyone agrees."

I unfolded the crinkled piece of paper and began to read. I read the letter over. Twice. Now I was fucking pissed. "Who the fuck would send this to you?" No wonder she was out here getting wasted.

"His mother, I assume." She took a hit off her smoke. "She's right though. I had choices. I could have shot him in the shoulder and called the police. But no, no, no. I was so dead set on revenge, I went right for the heart."

I sat down next to her. "Baby, listen to me. That fucker handcuffed and raped you. He beat the shit out of you. He broke into your apartment, and he was going to do it again. You didn't have any choices. And you know what... I would have killed him too."

"You don't need to remind me what he did. After he did that to me, I stood and looked in the mirror. I didn't even recognize myself. And all I could think was that I was going to kill him. I went and bought a gun. I planned it for months. I prepared for it. I'm no better than he was." Self-hate poured from her lips.

"That's not true. You could have gone after him. Sought him out. That fucker wouldn't leave you alone. If he hadn't come after you again, none of it would have happened. You're not a murderer!"

"What about that letter? It says I am."

"You know what I think about this letter?" I went in the house and grabbed the metal garbage can from our office and brought it back outside with me. I held the letter over the can. "Light it."

"What?"

"Kyla, people only believe what they want to believe. Whoever sent you this, doesn't know the truth. They don't know the monster their son was. We know the truth and this letter doesn't mean shit. Light it."

She grabbed her lighter off the table and lit the end of the paper. Together we watched it burn until it was too hot for me to hold, and I dropped it into the can. It continued to burn until there was nothing left but ashes.

I took her by the hand and pulled her to me "Come on. I want to take my wife to bed."

She breathed out a frustrated breath. "That was the cherry on top of my day. I started my period again. We're not pregnant." She started to cry. "And I miss you! I feel like I hardly see you at all. I know this is your job and getting home late is part of it, but I'm so fucking lonely.

I held her close to me and rubbed her back up and down. She was right. We'd been spending way too much time apart. This was not the way a marriage was supposed work. I had been putting off hiring a night manager, partially because I had a hard time letting go of the control. But if my wife wasn't happy at home and we never saw each other, I needed to fix that pronto. Nothing was more important than her. I couldn't let this become like football had… all consuming. "I'm going to hire a night manager tomorrow," I said. "That doesn't mean I'll never have to work nights, but it'll be better. I promise."

She sniffed. "I'm sorry. I don't mean to be so needy. I just miss my husband."

"No, you're right. I would be worried if you didn't miss me. Cuz you know what? I miss you too." I kissed her on the forehead. "Let's go in and shower. I want to have sex with my wife."

She raised her eyebrow at me, "Did you miss the first part of what I said?"

"I don't care, if you don't. We've been together forever. What's a little blood? We'll be in the shower, it'll be fine."

"This ought to be interesting," she said as she walked inside.

It was a first for us and honestly it wasn't as bad as she thought it would be. She was my wife, and this was part of life.

I promoted one my best employees to be a night manager so that I could spend more time with Kyla. It was the best thing I could have done for our relationship. I had been so busy that I didn't realize how much I missed doing all the day-to-day things with her. We started taking evening runs and having dinner together again.

We put a lot of effort into getting her business up and running. Within the first week she'd already gotten a couple of hits on the site. One was for a fiftieth birthday party and the other a small business. It was a start. If this took off, she would be able to quit her job and run her own business full time. That was what I was hoping for. If I made it to the NFL, I didn't want her to have to quit her job, and there was no telling where we would end up. Also, when we did finally get pregnant it would give her the flexibility to work from home. She could take as little or as much work as she wanted. I would be fine with her not working at all, but Kyla would never be happy with that.

As the season turned to fall, Kyla still wasn't pregnant. I knew every time she started her period because she would smoke again. This was killing her. She started buying ovulation tests and keeping track of everything on a calendar. Things were becoming scheduled and the spontaneity we had always loved, disappeared. It was becoming a job and was sucking the enjoyment out of our sex life.

She suggested we see a fertility specialist, but I was holding off. The last thing I wanted to do was jack off into a bottle to have my shit examined under a microscope. I never thought we would have this problem. I was starting to feel like a failure as a husband and I knew she felt like a failure as a wife. I kept assuring her that it would happen. But whenever we were out, and she saw a pregnant woman, I could see the disappointment on her face. I understood her feelings, because I wanted it to be my wife with a big, round belly.

It didn't help when Tori and Chris told us they were pregnant. Kyla smiled and acted happy for them. She did a damn good job pulling it off too, but I knew the truth. They didn't know how hard we'd been trying and how devastating this would be for us.

We got home from dinner with our friends and Kyla grabbed her smokes and walked outside. I grabbed a beer and followed her out.

"I'm a shitty friend," she said as she lit her cigarette.

"You're not," I assured her, taking a large gulp from my bottle.

"I am. Instead of being truly happy for them, all I felt was jealousy."

"I felt it too. I don't understand why I can't get you pregnant. I mean we fuck like rabbits and still nothing," I said. "I swear if one more person asks me when we're going to start having kids, I'm going to choke them." This was the first time I had expressed my frustration to her.

She came and sat on my lap, and I wrapped my arms around her. She gently ran her fingers through my hair. "I didn't realize you were getting that question too," she said. "I get it all the time. I just want to throat punch people sometimes." She laughed.

I had to laugh too at the visual she had just put in my head. I could picture my five-foot nothing wife throat punching someone up on her tiptoes. "You're feisty, you know that?"

"Yeah, well, people suck." She continued to run her fingers through my hair. "You know, I don't think this has anything to do with you. You got me pregnant before. I think it's me. I think the miscarriage messed me up. I'm going to make an appointment with that specialist. I want to be able to give you babies. I don't want you to ever regret marrying me."

Kyla's words hit me like a ton of bricks. I hated that she would even think that. I took her face in my hands. "Baby, if it doesn't happen, it doesn't happen. I'll never regret marrying you."

Her eyes got teary. "Even if I can't give you what you want? Your mom will be devastated."

"Ky, I married you because I love you. No other reason than I want to spend the rest of my life with you. We haven't even explored fertility treatments yet. If we can't get pregnant and we still want kids, there are other options."

She laid her head on my shoulder. "I know, but it won't be the same. I really want to be able to give you this."

"I'm not ready to give up yet. Let's try for a few more months and if we still can't get pregnant, then you can make the appointment," I suggested.

"Okay," she agreed. "We need a distraction. Take me for a ride on your bike? We won't be able to ride pretty soon, with the snow coming."

"That sounds like an excellent idea. You'll need to dress warm." Kyla stood up off my lap and I gave her ass a little swat. "God, I love that ass. Go get ready." She hurried inside to change her clothes and get her jacket.

I finished the last of my beer and thought about what she'd said. How could she possibly think I would ever regret marrying her? She was the light of my life. My whole fucking world. Even if we never had kids… I didn't want to go down that road yet. We were young and had plenty of time. It would happen.

A ride on my Harley was just what we needed. We cruised down Jefferson and up towards Anchor Bay. Night riding was so relaxing. Kyla's arms were wrapped around me, and she rested her head on my back. There wasn't much traffic, and we just enjoyed the cool air and the wind whipping by. Every now and then Ky would run her hand down the front on my jeans and I groaned. She knew how to turn me on with just the lightest touch. I was more in love with her now than ever.

I wondered if we were ever going to get to just live and be happy. It seemed like there was a complication around every corner. We'd been through so much already, it was a miracle we had survived it. I was jealous of Chris and Tori. Their relationship always seemed so easy. I'm sure they had their problems too, but not like us. Loving Kyla was easy, but the shit we'd dealt with hadn't been. I just wanted to get my wife pregnant. Was that too much to ask?

When we pulled back up to our condo, I opened the garage door and drove my bike in. I got off the bike and pressed the button to close the garage door. I was about to go in the house when I realized Kyla hadn't gotten off the bike yet. "What are you doing?" I asked her.

She leaned her hands forward and rubbed the spot I was just sitting in. "You know what I thought about when I found out you bought this bike?"

"That I was ridiculous and spent too much money?" I answered lightheartedly.

"Nope," she shook her head. "Guess again."

I walked back toward her. "I don't know." She gave me a seductive look and I liked where this was going.

"First, I thought about how much I wanted to ride on the back of it with you. Then I thought about how much I wanted to fuck you on it."

I sat on the bike backward, so I was facing her. "Yeah?"

She nodded her head. "Yeah," she rasped out. "You want to? I don't want to think about making a baby. I want to do this just for us. Just for the thrill and enjoyment of it."

"You know what's funny?" I asked. "One of the first things I thought about doing when I bought this bike was fucking you on it. You laid out on the seat or bent over it." I groaned. "I've fantasized about it."

She smiled big. "So... you wanna?" She waggled her eyebrows at me.

I pulled her one leg up on my lap and started untying her boot. "Definitely." I got her other boot off and undid the button on her jeans. She lifted her hips and slid her jeans down her legs. I grabbed the bottoms and pulled them off her legs. She left her leather jacket on and that was sexy as hell.

She slid her ass down further on the seat, laid back, and put her feet up on the handlebars. I could barely control myself at the sight of her. I quickly pushed my jeans down my hips and stuck my fingers in her pussy. She was soaked. No foreplay tonight. This was down and dirty fucking. I stuck my dick in her and pushed in hard. My God, she felt good.

"Don't be gentle with me. I want you to fuck me hard!" We were so on the same page. I thrust into her hard and fast. She screamed out my name and I fucked her harder. We needed this so bad. No pressure, no objective… except to get off. She put her hands on the seat and raised herself up, making the angle so fucking perfect. Kyla threw her head back as she came around me and I was right behind her. I pushed into her, burying myself to the hilt and released everything I had.

Chapter 36
Kyla

I was so glad Ty had hired a night manager. We could spend so much more time together. I loved crawling into bed with him and wrapping myself around his warm body. It sure as hell beat going to bed alone. Everything was getting better, except that one thing... we still weren't pregnant.

Thanksgiving came and went. We spent it with Tyler's parents. It was nice to be surrounded by people that loved me, even if my parents weren't around. We went the day after Thanksgiving and bought a grave blanket for them. I let Tyler come with me to the grave site. While he was securing it into the ground, I talked to my parents. He pretended not to listen as I begged them to help me. I wanted to give Tyler a baby so bad, and I was frustrated. He snuggled me into him as we left the cemetery, and I knew he had heard me. Even if he pretended not to.

We went and bought a Christmas tree. I spent hours putting the lights on, so they looked just right. We had sold my parent's house to the couple who was renting it, and now all the boxes that sat in the basement were in our garage. I searched through the boxes while Ty was at work and found the box marked "Christmas". I brought it into the house and opened it. I was overwhelmed by nostalgia as I went through the box. My mom had saved everything. There were ornaments from the first year I was born through my twenty-first birthday. I carefully unwrapped each one and hung it on the tree. When I was finished, something was missing.

What was missing was Tyler and me. I jumped in my car and headed towards the closest store. I found the perfect ornament for us and took it back home. I hung it in the very front of the tree and felt satisfied. We needed to fill this tree with memories of us, not the past. We had a lot of years in front of us and I had no doubt that pretty soon this tree would be filled with our lives and hopefully… the lives of our children.

Christmas was here before we knew it and I still wasn't pregnant. We spent time with Tyler's parents again and they were more than generous with me. I don't know if Ty talked to his parents, but the subject of grandbabies didn't come up. I was thankful for that. I didn't need his mom adding extra pressure to what I was already feeling.

After Christmas dinner, we headed home and cuddled up on the couch together. We watched the replay of *The Christmas Story* on television. I remembered watching this the year before by myself. What a difference a year could make. Last year I had been miserable and alone. Now I was in the arms of the man I loved. I was a lucky girl. Not everyone got the chance to be married to the man who was their soulmate.

That night we went to bed and made love until the sun was peeking through the blinds. We slept late into the next day, and I didn't feel guilty about it one bit. We ate leftovers his mom sent home with us and ice cream for dessert. My life with Tyler was everything I could have asked for and more.

By the end of January, when Ty's birthday was coming around, I was ecstatic. I didn't know what to get him, but an idea hit me, and I hoped it would be enough. We went out to dinner for his birthday, and as usual, he tried to make this special for me, not him. Halfway through dinner I couldn't contain myself any longer. I reached into my purse and pulled out his birthday present.

"I don't know if this is going to be good or bad, but I hope you like it," I said to him as I passed it across the table.

"You didn't have to get me anything," he said. "Having you as my wife is enough."

"Just open it," I encouraged. He carefully removed the silver wrapping paper and the look on his face was priceless.

"Are you serious?" he asked.

"I'm a week late," I said. "I don't know. But I thought we should do the test together." I had given him a pregnancy test for his birthday. "This could be a total bust, but you said you wanted to be there when I peed on the stick. So... we'll find out tonight."

"This is the most perfect gift you could have given me," he said.

We quickly finished dinner and headed home. "Are you ready?" I asked. "It might be negative, but this is the closest we've been so far."

"I'm ready," he said. "Good or bad we're in this together." We headed to the bathroom and Tyler opened the test. He handed it to me. "Here goes nothing."

"I need you to turn around. I can't pee with you watching me," I said.

"Really? After everything we've been through."

"Just turn around," I demanded. He did, and I pulled my pants down and peed on the stick. I placed the cap on the test and pulled my pants back up. I handed the test to Tyler. "It says we have to wait at least three minutes."

Ty placed the test on the counter. "This is going to be the longest three minutes of my life." I stood in front of him as he wrapped his arms around my waist. He rested his head on my shoulder. "How much longer?" he asked.

"Just another minute." That minute seemed like an eternity as we waited for the test to show the results. I closed my eyes. "What does it say?" I asked.

Ty picked up the test and scrunched his eyebrows. "What does two lines mean?" he asked.

I smiled. "It means we're going to have a baby."

He picked me up and spun me around the bathroom. "We did it, Ky! We're pregnant!"

We were so happy. It took us over six months, but finally we were going to have a baby.

Chapter 37
Tyler

Thank God, we got pregnant. Gone were the calendars and planned sex. Kyla had called her doctor and we didn't have to go for our first appointment for another month. We didn't care if it was a boy or a girl, as long as he or she was healthy. After suffering her miscarriage last year, Kyla worried about being able to carry our baby full term. I was convinced that life couldn't be that cruel to us twice. I tried to be optimistic, but inside I was scared to death.

Now that February had hit, it was time to step up my training for the Free Agent Combine. The tryouts were held in March, and although I'd been training hard, I needed to put even more effort into getting ready.

I hired another manager for Xtreme, so I could devote more time to football and not take away too much time from my wife. I convinced Jerome to work with me three times a week. It cost a pretty penny, but this was go big or go home. I was in contact with my agent more, and Gary had secured me a place in the combine. He was already trying to work deals behind the scenes.

The Free Agent Combine would not secure me a place in the Draft, however, it gave me a chance to showcase my skills. There were several drills each competitor would be scored on, as well as rating me on my overall quarterback skills.

Football was second nature for me. I'd lived it my whole life. However, I'd been out of the game for over a year. New talent showed up every season and those guys were going to the Draft. That left very little room for me. Last year I would have been a first-round draft pick. Now, all I could hope was that someone would take a chance on a guy who got injured but had worked like hell to make a comeback.

Kyla never complained about the time I spent training. She knew how important this was to me. To us. She'd been there right beside me since senior year of high school. She'd always cheered me on and now wasn't any different. Every morning before I left, she made me one of those protein shakes she hated. We both knew this was a big chance I was taking. If I didn't make it onto a team roster, I didn't know what the backup plan was. I didn't want to run the club forever, but right now I didn't know what the future would hold.

Since the day we found out Kyla was pregnant, she'd had morning sickness. Every morning, like clockwork, she untangled herself from me and ran to the bathroom. I felt bad for her, and I felt even worse that I wasn't there for her the first time around. All I could do was hold her hair and rub her back as she threw up into the toilet. She was miserable. She said it would get better after the first trimester and I hoped, for her sake, she was right.

Ky and I went to her first doctor appointment together. I was more than a little nervous. This was all so new for me.

My knee bounced up and down while we sat in the waiting room. Kyla squeezed my hand and pointed at my restless knee. "That's just what I did when Tori came with me to my first appointment last time. She practically had to chain me to the chair to keep me from running out," she admitted. "It'll be okay. Trust me."

I wished I'd been holding her hand the last time, but that was the past. "I don't know why I'm so nervous. It's not like I'm the one who's pregnant."

"Because this is a big deal. We're entering a new phase in our life together. This is what we wanted. This part isn't as scary as it seems. It's the pushing this baby out that has me worried."

"I'll be right there holding your hand," I kissed the side of her head. "And you can yell at me all you want when the time comes."

"When do you think we should tell everyone we're having a baby?" she asked.

We hadn't told anyone yet. It was our secret. We were both a little afraid of telling anyone just in case something went wrong. We didn't want to face our loved ones with a second miscarriage. "I don't know. Let's wait to see what the doctor says," I said.

Just then, the nurse called us back. She led us to a room and instructed Kyla to get undressed from the waist down. Kyla did as requested and sat up on the table with a sheet covering her. She didn't seem that nervous, but I didn't know what to expect.

She must have sensed my discomfort. "Scoot your chair over next to me so you can hold my hand," she said. "This is all part of it."

I moved my chair right next to the table she sat on and grabbed her hand. She squeezed it in reassurance. "I'm glad I'm here for this," I confided.

"So am I," she said.

There was a quiet knock at the door and a woman in a lab coat walked in. "Hi Kyla. Good to see you again." She turned to me. "I'm Dr. Chang." She reached out her hand and I took it.

"I'm Tyler. Husband," I said proudly.

She seemed nice enough. Her attention turned back to Kyla. "I guess congratulations are in order. I know you two have been trying for a while."

"We have," Kyla confirmed. She turned to me with a nervous look. "We're concerned that I'm going to miscarry again. What are the chances?"

"Well, complications can always arise, but let's try not to worry about that," Dr. Chang said. "Let's see what we've got going on. I want to do a pelvic exam and then we'll do an ultrasound."

She pulled up the stirrups and Kyla laid back. She put her feet up and the sheet covered her. It was all very private. I didn't know what to expect. It wasn't like I'd ever been to a gynecologist's office before. Kyla squeezed my hand as Dr. Chang did her exam and I kept my focus on Ky's face.

"Everything feels all right. You can put your legs down now." Kyla did, but stayed laying on the table. "Now let's see what's going on in there."

Dr. Chang pulled the sheet down to expose Kyla's stomach. "This will be a little bit cold." She squeezed some type of gel on Kyla's stomach and turned on the machine next to the table.

Dr. Chang got up to dim the lights and Kyla looked at me. "We're going to get to see our baby," she said. Ky couldn't keep the excitement out of her voice, and it was contagious. I squeezed her hand tighter.

Dr. Chang ran the wand over Kyla's stomach. "There it is," she said.

I looked at the screen, but I couldn't see anything. All I saw was a bunch of nothing. "I don't know what I'm looking at," I admitted.

Dr. Chang pointed at the screen. "Right here is baby number one." She moved her finger a little bit. "And right here is baby number two."

Kyla and I looked at each other. "We're having twins?" I questioned.

Dr. Chang let out a little laugh. "It looks that way," she said.

I couldn't contain myself. I stood and hugged Kyla. Tears started to run down her face.

"I can't believe it," Kyla said, wiping her eyes.

"Do you want to hear the heartbeats?" Dr. Chang asked.

"Fuck yeah," I answered without thinking. "I'm sorry. I'm just really excited."

"That's okay," Dr. Chang laughed. "It's not the worst I've heard." She flipped a switch on the machine, and you could hear a soft swishing in the background. "Sounds like their heartbeats are in sync."

I pulled out my phone and recorded it. I couldn't believe we were having twins. This whole experience was so amazing.

Dr. Chang finally turned off the machine. "Congratulations Mr. and Mrs. Jackson. I want to see you in a month. But as we get closer to your due date… which looks like October 7th, I'll want to see you more frequently. With twins, you may not carry full term, but we'll monitor it," she assured us.

"Thank you, Dr. Chang," Kyla said. The doctor left the room and then it was just the two of us. "We're having twins."

"I heard." I hugged her tight. "This was one of the best moments of my life."

"How in the world are we going to take care of two babies?" Kyla asked. "This is so overwhelming!"

"We can do anything we set our minds to," I answered. "We'll do it together, just like everything else."

Chapter 38
Kyla

Twins? That was insane. Thank God we had almost seven months to prepare for it. But I was afraid that time was going to fly by. I still worried that something would go wrong, but I couldn't be happier in the moment. If this was the only chance we got, at least we would get two children out of it. Hopefully, we would end up with two healthy babies.

We decided to wait until after our next appointment to tell anyone that I was pregnant. Miscarrying again would be traumatic for us, but we didn't need everyone else to know too. Keeping the secret was extremely hard when all I wanted to do was shout from the top of the nearest building that we were having twins.

Tyler's practice and work schedule were crazy. And through it all, he still made time for us. Now that the time was getting closer to the Combine, I would never complain. This is what he had worked for. If he made it, all his dreams would finally come true.

I wanted it too, but I wanted it for him. I could care less if Tyler was some superstar pro athlete. I always loved him for what he gave me emotionally, not what he could give me financially. I didn't care what Ty ended up doing, as long as he was happy.

He and I worked on my website, tweaking it here and there. Business was picking up and while Ty was gone for work or practice, I kicked out designs right and left. I was thankful for the distraction. This had the possibility of turning into something

I could do fulltime. If we had twins, I would definitely need the flexibility that a home business could provide.

By the time March rolled around, I was sporting a little baby bump. Tyler found it sexy, and he couldn't resist kissing my tummy every day. He would talk to our babies and tell them what an amazing mom they were going to have. It was super cute! I sometimes got sad that I hadn't shared this with him the first time around, but we were more than making up for it now. He was going to make such a wonderful daddy.

When it was time for the Free Agent Combine, I wanted to go to Minnesota with him. Tyler didn't want me traveling. His dad, his agent, and Jerome were going with him, so he had more than enough support. Ty and I had hardly spent a day apart since we moved into this condo, so being away from each other was going to be tough. The tryouts lasted Friday through Monday. Four days was a long time to spend away from my husband, but I would survive.

I went to Tori and Chris's Friday night for dinner. The distraction was welcome. I knew that Ty was probably stressing out at the Combine, but he had a good support system.

Tori was sporting an evident baby bump. I let her expel all her excitement onto me, as I kept quiet about our secret. It was cold outside, so I wore a heavy shirt that covered my own bump.

Tori was making tilapia for dinner and the smell was making me nauseous. I couldn't take it anymore and ran to the bathroom to throw up. After rinsing my mouth, I returned to the kitchen where she and Chris were sitting.

Tori pointed at me. "Your pregnant, aren't you?"

I couldn't keep it a secret any longer and broke out into a huge grin. I nodded. "Yes!"

She ran and grabbed me, jumping up and down. "I knew it! I knew it! Didn't I tell you, Chris?"

"Yeah. You called that one. Congratulations, baby girl!"

"Why didn't you tell me?" she questioned.

I shrugged my shoulders. "With our history, we thought we should wait a little longer."

"How far along are you?"

I pulled up my shirt exposing my stomach, "A little over two months."

Tori scrunched her eyebrows. "Are you sure? You looked farther along than that. You're already showing."

I laughed. "I'm sure. We're having twins!"

"Are you serious?" Chris exclaimed. "Damn Tyler. He always has to be the overachiever."

I couldn't help the smile that spread across my face. "I'm serious. Please don't say anything to anyone yet. We haven't even told his parents. You guys are the first to know. We're just worried that something might go wrong," I admitted.

Tori wrapped me in her arms. "Nothing is going to go wrong. I can feel it." She turned her attention back to the food she was cooking. "You know what's so cool? Our kids are going to be really close in age. I'm so excited for them to grow up together."

I sat down at the table, feeling a little frustrated. "I don't want this to sound like I'm unsupportive, but Ty doing this tryout has me a little worried. I mean, if he makes it, we could end up across the country. I want him to make it, but I don't want to move too far away. We'll never get to see you guys."

Chris took my hand across the table. "If I know one thing about Tyler, it's that he takes you into consideration with every decision he makes. If he has any choice at all, you won't go too far."

"I know, but he may not have any choices. What if we end up in San Francisco or something?"

"Then I guess we'll have a great place to vacation," Tori piped up. "We're not going to let distance kill this friendship," she assured me.

"I love you guys. I know you're right, but I really don't want to move. I wouldn't tell Tyler that because I don't want to kill his dreams, but I would miss you guys if we had to move far away."

"Let's just see what happens," Chris said. "I know you're worried but try not to until we see how the Combine goes."

"I'll try," I promised.

Later that night, I talked to Tyler on the phone. "Don't be mad," I prefaced, "but Chris and Tori know about the babies. She guessed, and I couldn't lie."

"What happened?" he asked. I could tell he was a little annoyed, but I didn't care at this point.

"She was cooking dinner and the smell made me nauseous. I threw up!" I started crying. The pregnancy hormones were killing me. "I'm sorry!"

I could hear Tyler sigh on the other end of the phone. "Baby, stop crying. You can't help that you threw up. I wish I was there, but I understand."

"I didn't mean to," I defended. "The smell of the tilapia just made me sick. I'm sorry," I said again through a sob. "And I don't even know why I'm crying. These hormones suck!"

"Calm down, Ky. It's not the end of the world."

I pulled it together and caught my breath. "I'm cancelling dinner with your mom," I stated. "I don't trust myself and I want to tell them together. We'll reschedule when you're home."

Tyler surprised me by laughing. "That's probably a good idea. I love you, Kyla."

"I love you too. I miss you," I admitted. "How did today go?" I asked, taking the focus off me.

"Great, I think. They post the rankings every night, so I just have to wait to find out."

"I wish I was there with you, but I guess you really don't need me."

"I always need you, baby." he said. "I'll be home Monday night."

"I know," I said. "I'm going to work on some designs while you're gone, but when you come home, it's on." I'd been so horny since I'd gotten got pregnant and Ty knew it.

"That gives me something to look forward to." I could almost hear him smile through the phone.

"Good luck tomorrow. Even though I'm not there, doesn't mean that I'm not cheering for you," I encouraged.

"You're my number one cheerleader. I haven't forgotten," he said.

"I love you and miss you."

"I love and miss you, too," he repeated back to me and hung up.

I missed him so much and it had only been one night. I crawled into bed and felt the emptiness beside me. I pulled up the blankets and turned on a *Lifetime* movie. There was no better cure for feeling sad than to watch someone else's misery.

The weekend passed at a snail's pace. I rescheduled with Ty's mom for the next Friday. She was disappointed, but I didn't want to blow it.

I went to work on Monday and couldn't wait to get out of there. Tyler would be coming home.

That night, he didn't get home until nine. He was exhausted, but I jumped on him anyway. I wrapped my legs around his waist. "I missed you so much! How did everything go?"

"Really great! I ranked way ahead of a lot of the new recruits. Now we just have to wait." Tyler kissed me long and hard.

"How long?" I asked.

"Well, because I'm not eligible for the draft, we should hear something soon. Gary is going to field the calls. He knows what I'm looking for, so he'll sort everything out."

"I'm so happy for you! But I'm even happier that you're home." I was still hanging around his waist. He always held me like I weighed nothing, even if that wasn't the truth.

He set me down on the floor. "How are my babies?" he questioned, picking up my shirt to kiss my stomach.

"We're all good. We're going to your parents' house on Friday for dinner. I think we should tell them," I said. Keeping this secret was killing me.

He let out a low laugh. "Okay. You're right, it's time."

Chapter 39
Tyler

Friday night we went to my parents' house for dinner. My mom was thrilled to see us. She acted like she never saw us, although she had seen us more in the last few months than she had in the last year.

My parents sat at the ends of the table, while Kyla and I sat across from each other. She gave me a little kick under the table. She wanted to get this over with and wanted me to do it. I hesitated too long and finally Kyla blurted out, "We're pregnant!"

My mom and dad paused mid-bite and dropped their forks. My mom shouted out, "Congratulations! I had my suspicions, but I wasn't sure!" She got up from the table and hugged both Kyla and me.

"How did you keep this from me all weekend?" my dad joked. "You must have been out of your mind."

"It was really hard," I admitted. "We thought we should wait, with what happened last time." I felt like I had to explain why we kept them in the dark.

"Tell them the best part," Kyla encouraged.

I quirked my eyebrow at her, and she nodded, giving me the okay. My mom and dad looked between the two of us, wondering what the hell was going on. "We're having twins!"

My mom covered her mouth in surprise. "Oh my, God!" She jumped up and down. "Two babies?"

"Yeah, two," Kyla and I said in unison.

The passing days were stressful to say the least. I knew I had done my best at the Free Agent Combine, but I couldn't help but wonder if it had been enough. Jerome said I had done well and to just be patient. My dad said he was proud of me no matter what happened. Gary hadn't said shit yet. What the fuck was I paying him for? Finally, I caved and called him.

"What's up Gary?" I asked. "Anything yet?"

"Hey, Ty. Yeah, I got a few offers. I'm just trying to weed through the bullshit."

I was kind of pissed. He should have been keeping me in the loop. Jerome said to trust him, and so I did. He'd said I wouldn't like Gary personally, but he would get me the best deal. I swallowed down my irritation. "What do you have?"

"I need to know what's more important to you. Money or location?" Gary asked.

That was a good question because it meant that there was interest. I had given this a lot of thought. Kyla would follow me anywhere, no questions asked. But since she was pregnant, she would need family to support her. That included Tori and Chris. I wanted her to have that security, especially if I was on the road.

I answered without hesitation, "Location. My wife is pregnant."

"I figured as much," Gary said. "I've talked with Tampa, San Fran, Denver, and Detroit."

"Detroit?" I questioned. "What are they offering?" This could be perfect.

"Not as much as the other three. But they're excited about the prospect of signing the Hometown Hero. Seems your college record has preceded you. They want you bad but can't offer as much money."

"How much?" I questioned, although it didn't really matter at this point. Being home and having Kyla happy was worth whatever they were willing to pay.

Gary and I went over the numbers. It wasn't as much as the other three, but it was still a shitload of money. Gary said he was going to push for a little more. Since I had other offers, they might be willing to sweeten the pot. I was just thankful that the Lions were willing to take a chance on me. A year ago, I was totally out of the game. This was a win-win. I got to play professional ball and Kyla got to stay at home. I would start as a back-up quarterback, but hell, everyone had to start somewhere.

"Take it," I told Gary. "Just get me the best you can. I want to stay close to home."

"Done," Gary said. "Congratulations, Tyler. Looks like you're going to be a Lion."

I hung up the phone and was pretty damn happy. The money I'd given up couldn't compare to the happiness this would bring my wife.

Kyla and I went to her next doctor appointment. Again, we got to see the ultrasound pictures. We could see a more definitive picture of our babies. Just tiny arms and legs, but it was amazing. Kyla was still worried about miscarrying, and I couldn't blame her, but I didn't want to go there. I couldn't wait to find out what we were having. Boys or girls or one of each. It didn't matter to me, but I knew Kyla would feel better if we could prepare properly.

Between the fact that we were having two babies and I would be on the Lion's roster, I figured we should start looking at bigger homes. Kyla was totally against it because she loved where we were living now. The ride to the stadium from our condo was actually perfect, about twenty minutes. I didn't want to move, except for the fact that I thought Kyla deserved better. But she was happy here. She loved being able to look out over the lake and the twins could stay in the same room for a while. We decided... well, she decided, that we should stay in the condo for a while longer.

Since getting pregnant, Kyla was so damn horny. I was a fucking lucky bastard. When I came home, she practically jumped on top of me. Our sex life had never been better. I was worried about hurting our babies, but she insisted it wasn't a problem. That girl couldn't get enough, and I was more than happy to oblige.

I needed to let my Uncle Lou know that I would be done at Xtreme by the end of June. The managers I hired would be more than capable of handling things and Uncle Lou would have to step up his presence. I never saw the club as a long-term thing, so quitting that job didn't break my heart. Plus, my training would be mostly during the day, so I got to spend more time with Kyla. Again...win-win.

Training camp kicked my ass. Although I kept in shape, it had been a year since I'd had daily practices. I felt like a little fish in a big pond again. The guys were cool, but I still felt out of place. I worked my whole life for this. It didn't help that I was the guy that took MSU to the Rose Bowl. The expectations were high. Being the backup quarterback, I wondered if I would ever get playing time.

I just held on and bided my time. I was getting paid, no matter what.

Once the season started, Kyla wanted to go to all my games. I wouldn't have expected anything less, but she was so big now, carrying our twins, that it made me nervous. She should have been home on bedrest like the doctor said, but my wife was determined to go to the games. She had been working from home, but I couldn't keep her there when it was game time. I insisted that she could stay home, since the chance of me playing was minimal, but she was afraid she going to miss something.

I had my parents come to the games. Then I didn't have to worry about my very pregnant wife. Kyla was waddling around like a penguin. She was so damn cute, but I also knew she was also damn uncomfortable.

"I'm going!" she insisted.

"No, you're not! You need to stay home and rest." It was an argument we'd had since the season started.

"Your mom and dad will be there if I need them. It'll be fine!"

I couldn't argue with her anymore, and honestly, I didn't want to. "Fine. Stay with my parents."

She rolled her eyes. "Honestly, Ty, my due date is October. It's barely the middle of September. All I've done is rest. I'm bored and what good am I if I can't be there for my husband?"

"You don't have to be there to prove you love me. I probably won't even get to play."

"But you might, and I need to be there!"

"I love you, but you're stubborn," I said. "I'm calling my mom to make sure she's going."

Kyla threw her hands up in the air. "Whatever!" She waddled to the couch and plopped down.

I couldn't help but laugh at her. She'd been a trooper through all of this. We had long since passed the point of worrying about a miscarriage and the nursery was ready for not one, but two babies. Two baby boys to be exact. She wasn't thrilled that she would be outnumbered, but she was thrilled that we had made it through this far.

I was ecstatic. Two sons. What more could I ask for? I wondered if they would like football too. It was kind of inevitable in this house. Each day that brought us closer to her due date, brought me closer to the excitement of being a dad. I kissed Kyla's tummy on a daily basis and assured our boys that I couldn't wait for them to make their arrival.

Chapter 40
Kyla

Ty fought me tooth and nail about coming to the game today. But I was here, seeing my husband in his Lion's uniform. That was all that mattered to me. I sat beside his mom and dad and cheered even though Ty hadn't gotten a chance to play yet.

It was fourth quarter and I didn't know if the quarterback just wanted a break, but we were up by 14 and they put Tyler in. If I had stayed home, I would have missed this. Tyler was making his first play in a pro game, and I would have been pissed if I missed it.

I stood up and cheered loudly when he ran out onto the field. The energy at Ford Field was electric and I thought back to the first time Ty played on this field—senior year for the State Championship Game. He had come so far since then.

I got a sharp pain in my back and winced. Well, that hurt like hell. I didn't want to miss Ty's first play, so I muscled through it and stayed standing. I watched him call the play and then he fired the ball through the air to the receiver. It was a perfect pass. The receiver caught the ball and started running down field. He was tackled at about the thirty-yard line. It'd been a good run.

The Bears called for a timeout. After a couple of minutes, they lined up again and Ty called out the next play. As he stepped back to throw, I saw the linebacker from the Bears coming in fast to his left. I held my breath. He could not get tackled and go down. His shoulder was healed but I wasn't sure it could take a blow like that again. Our left tackle slammed into the Bears player and took him down in time for Tyler to release the ball. I let out a sigh of relief and watched the ball fly down the field. We gained another ten yards.

Another pain shot through my back, and I let out a growl. I braced my hands on my back to try to ease the pain.

Ty's mom shot me a concerned look. "Are you all right, sweetie?"

"I don't know," I said honestly. "I'm getting sharp pains in my back. It could just be Braxton Hicks."

"You need to sit down. We don't want to take any chances. How far apart are the pains?" she asked.

"I don't know. I think about ten minutes," I guessed.

"Sit," she ordered me. "We're going to time the next one."

I did as was told and pulled out my phone and found the timer app. I watched the next several plays from my seat. I didn't have another contraction, so I relaxed a bit.

The game was almost over, and I was relieved. I didn't want to have to admit to Tyler that he was right, and I probably shouldn't have come to the game. Ty threw another pass, and the receiver ran it into the end zone as the clock ticked down. We won the game!

I was so excited that I stood up and started cheering again. My big belly prevented me from jumping up and down too much. Suddenly, I felt wetness gush down my legs. Oh Fuck! I looked down. My leggings were soaked and there was a puddle where I was standing.

I tapped on Ty's mom's shoulder and leaned over to her ear, so she could hear me above all the shouting and cheering, "I think my water just broke!"

She looked down at my legs and her eyes went big. "I think you're right!" She leaned over to Ty's dad and whispered in his ear. We were seated a few rows behind the Lion's bench.

His dad jumped up and started pushing across the aisle and down toward the bench. He grabbed one of the coaches and was gesturing wildly with his hands. The coach ran onto the field and grabbed Tyler. All three of them were running back toward where I was sitting.

Then another contraction hit and this time I knew it was for real. I started taking quick, sharp breathes until it passed. Ty ran across the seats to me. He kneeled down with his hands on my knees. "Are you okay, Ky?"

I looked at him in panic. "I think we're having our babies. Soon!"

"Shit!" He looked at his coach. "We've got to get out of here quick! She's gonna have these babies!"

The coach never hesitated. "There's an ambulance waiting out back. Pick her up and let's go!"

Tyler scooped me up while his dad and the coach cleared us a path and led us out to the ambulance. The paramedics helped me inside and Tyler jumped in the back with me. "St. John's Hospital and hurry!" Tyler shouted.

He held my hand as I laid back on the stretcher. "I don't want to have these babies in the back of an ambulance," I cried.

"We'll make it, baby," he promised.

Another contraction ripped through my stomach, and I screamed out from the pain. "I want drugs!" I squeezed Tyler's hand so tightly; I was probably cutting off his circulation.

"Honey, I think you're past that," the paramedic said calmly. "Just try to breathe through the pain."

I gave him a death glare. "Are you fucking kidding me right now?"

Ty brushed my hair back off my forehead. "What can I do to help you?"

Tears were running down my face. "I'm scared," I admitted. "I was counting on an epidural."

The paramedic looked at Tyler, "We need to get her pants off. We might not make it." Tyler slid my leggings down and undressed me. The paramedic grabbed a sheet and put it over my legs. He reached his hand under the sheet and checked me. "She's fully dilated. Try not to push yet, Kyla."

I wasn't trying to do anything. This was just happening. The pain was tremendous, and I squeezed Tyler's hand again as the next contraction hit. I looked at him with pleading eyes and cried, "I changed my mind. I don't want to do this!"

"I'm right here, baby. You're going to be okay!"

The paramedic checked me again. "We can't wait any longer. You're going to have to start pushing, Kyla."

"No!" I screamed.

"Yes," he said. "The baby's crowning. It's coming out whether you're ready or not."

"Babies," Tyler corrected. "She's having twins."

"Hope you're ready for this, man. Because I'm going to need your help."

We arrived at the hospital about fifteen minutes later. Tyler and I each cradled one of our newborn sons in our arms. The labor and delivery had been so quick, there was no time for anything. The ambulance was met at the Emergency Room, and they whisked us inside. They took the babies to check them out and tended to me. Tyler never left my side. He'd been the perfect husband and my hero.

Chapter 41
Tyler

An hour later we were moved to a room on the maternity floor. Kyla and I each held one of the babies. They had come three weeks early and they were so tiny. But they were perfect. "You did it, Kyla. I'm so proud of you," I said to my beautiful wife.

"We did it. You were pretty amazing," she replied. "Should we let your parents come in?"

I set the baby I was holding into Kyla's arms. She had one on each side of her. "I'll go get them."

"Hurry back," she pleaded.

"I'll only be gone a minute." I went out to the waiting room and saw my mom and dad sitting on a couch holding hands. They didn't see me approach. "Want to come meet your grandsons?" I asked.

Their heads popped up and they were on their feet in a split second. My mom practically knocked me over with her hug, "Yes!"

I led them back to the room where Kyla snuggled our sons close to her. She was going to be a great mom. I looked at her in admiration of her strength and beauty.

I took one baby and handed to it my mom. "Meet Xander James, named after Kyla's dad."

I took the other baby and handed him to my dad. "And this is Ryder Thomas, named after you."

Kyla and I decided to use our dads' names as the boys' middle names. We thought it would be a nice tribute to the most important men in our lives. Both of my parents had tears in their eyes. "That was super sweet," my mom choked out. They cuddled our sons tightly. "They look like you Tyler."

Kyla smiled. "Yeah. They're going to be double trouble when they get older. Little chick magnets."

"You two did good," my dad said to Kyla and me. He looked down at Ryder with love in his eyes. "You boys are lucky to have such a great mommy and daddy."

Later that evening, it was just Ky and me and our baby boys, Xander and Ryder, who were sleeping safely in our arms. I looked at our little family and I couldn't be happier. Life changed so much for us in the last year. I never thought we would get here, but we did. We were destined to be together from the start. Our road to happiness was a little bumpy for a while, but it led us to this moment. And nothing was more perfect than this.

"I love you, Kyla Jackson."

"I love you too, Tyler Jackson."

Epilogue
Kyla

I sat on the deck and looked out over Lake Michigan as the wind blew through my hair. We made sure to make this trip with Tori and Chris at least once a summer. I wanted my children to grow up with all the wonderful memories I had as a kid.

"Should we go down and save them?" Tori asked, sitting down next to me.

"Nah. I'm enjoying watching them try to handle all the kids by themselves." I laughed.

Xander and Ryder were six now, and indeed looked like their daddy. Two years after they were born, we welcomed Tristan Jonathon. Our last bundle of joy was Alexis Marie. She was only two and was going to be just as tough as the boys. Tristan and Alexis looked more like me, blond hair and green eyes. We'd made four beautiful children together.

Chris and Tori had three of their own. Savannah was a few months older than the twins. Jayce was five and Katarina was three.

When the seven of them got together, there was no telling what would happen.

Tori smacked me on the shoulder. "You're so mean."

"I'm not mean. This is good for them," I insisted.

The boys were throwing a ball back and forth on the beach, while Tyler and Chris had the girls in the water. I watched as Tyler held Alexis's tiny hands and lifted her in and out of the waves. She was giggling and looking at her daddy with adoration.

"How'd we get so lucky?" I asked.

"I don't know, but it doesn't get much better than this," she said as she wrapped her arm around my shoulder. I leaned into her and tilted my head into hers.

"No, it doesn't," I agreed.

We sat a little longer and watched our beautiful families play on the beach. Finally, I stood up and took Tori's hand. "Come on. They're having too much fun without us." We ran down to the water.

Tyler had put Alexis safely up on the beach and I ran right for him. He picked me up and spun me around. "There you are. I thought you abandoned us."

"Never in a million years," I answered.

Tyler pressed his lips to mine and kissed me deeply. Even after all this time, his kisses still filled me with butterflies and made my knees weak.

"They're kissing again!" Ryder said with disgust.

"They're always kissing!" exclaimed Xander.

Tyler and I broke apart and ran toward the boys. We each scooped one up and started covering them with kisses. "Eww!" "Gross!" they complained.

We fell to our knees, each of us snuggling one of the boys. Tristan ran up and jumped on Tyler's back. Alexis wouldn't be left out, as she tumbled into my lap. We all fell back into the sand in a pile of laughter and happiness.

This was my life, and I wouldn't trade it for anything! I would always hold on and I was never letting go.

Thank you for taking this journey with me. I hope you enjoyed Kyla and Tyler's story.

Look for Chris and Tori's story in the ***Wild Hearts Trilogy.***

Wild Hearts **is the first book in the Wild Hearts Trilogy, a steamy romance about fated lovers, deep secrets, and coming out on the other side of heartbreak.**

When I was eight, I met Tori.
At twelve, I kissed her for the first time.
Fireworks exploded between us, and I was hopelessly in love.

I begged for years to make her mine, but she just wanted to be friends.
Until the night I defended her honor.

It was everything I ever imagined… only better.
I adored her. Would do anything for her. She completed me.
Tori was more enticing than any drug and I was totally addicted.

We were perfectly imperfect together. Wild and untamed.
We challenged each other. I pushed and she pulled.
But this time, I might have pushed too far.

♥♥♥

Chris was one of my best friends.
He was my perfect match and an all-around great guy.
If I let him in, I'd be done for.

I'd built a wall around my heart, and Chris had the power to destroy it.
That's why I stayed away from him.

He knocked down my wall, brick by brick.
Assured me he was worth the risk.
I gave him everything and trusted him with my heart.

Every part of me was laid out, raw and exposed.
Falling for him was easy. The fallout… not so much.
I was such a fool!

Song List on Spotify

I Am the Fire- Halestorm
The Reckoning- Halestorm
Far Away- Nickelback
Just For- Nickelback
Here's to Us- Halestorm
Never Gonna Be Alone- Nickelback
I'm Yours- Jason Mraz

Acknowledgments

To my husband~ I could have never done this without your love and support. Thank you for putting up with my endless hours of writing, all the take-out dinners, and my never-ending questions about football. I know I made you crazy, but you were a trooper through it all! Thank you for believing in me!

To my daughter~ Thank you for enduring the countless hours I spent writing this book. Your constant questions about what was going to happen next, were inspiring, because even I didn't know. I am giving you permission to read this book when you are 30! Ha Ha!

To Ari, Denise, Kristy, and Amy~ You girls are the best beta readers anyone could ask for! You supported my journey and spent endless hours reading and rereading. Your suggestions, critiques, and encouragement helped me in ways you'll never understand. Thank you for listening to my obsession day after day!

To Jill~ You've been a great friend! When I came to you about my cover designs in frustration, you immediately volunteered to help. Your graphic designs alleviated a ton of stress for me and helped to capture the essence of my books. Thank you for saving the day!

To my readers~ Thank you for supporting me in this journey. Please spread the word if you have enjoyed this book. Without you, writing would still be a dream.

About the Author

Sabrina Wagner lives in Sterling Heights, Michigan. She writes sweet, sassy, sexy romance novels featuring alpha males and the strong women who challenge them.

Sabrina believes that true friends should be treasured, a woman's strength is forged by the fire of affliction, and everyone deserves a happy ending. She enjoys spending time with her family, walking on the beach, cuddling her kittens, and great books. Sabrina is a hopeless romantic and knows all too well that life is full of twists and turns, but the bumpy road is what leads to our true destination.

**Want to be the first to learn book news, updates and more?
Sign up for my Newsletter.**

https://www.subscribepage.com/sabrinawagnernewsletter

**Want to know about my new releases and upcoming sales?
Stay connected on:**

Facebook~Instagram~Twitter~TikTok
Goodreads~BookBub~Amazon

**I'd love to hear from you.
Visit my website to connect with me.**

www.sabrinawagnerauthor.com

Printed in Great Britain
by Amazon